FATAL FINALE

A DR PIPPA DURRANT MYSTERY

MIRANDA RIJKS

PROLOGUE

They make it look so easy on the television. *Grab the person from behind, throw some fabric over their head, tie them to a chair and 'bingo'.*

She is waiting at the bus stop, jiggling from one foot to another. Her battered violin case lies on the ground, discarded at her feet. She has earbuds in and is looking at something on her mobile phone. Watching and listening to a video, I suppose. How stupid. Careless. If you're out in a public space, you should be aware of your surroundings, be on high alert. She is the only person at the bus stop, as was the case last week and the week before. Just as well, otherwise I would have to abort my mission.

The bus is never early but even so, I can't risk waiting. So I tug on the disposable gloves and ease the cloth soaked in halothane out of the plastic bag. I tiptoe out from behind the hedgerow, where I've been crouching for the last ten minutes. My legs feel tight, but the adrenaline rush quickly dispels any discomfort.

Three steps and I'm standing right behind her. She doesn't move an inch. The fingers of her right hand are tapping against her upper thigh. Her black yoga pants show every taut muscle. If I wasn't wearing a balaclava, I could exhale and my warm breath would tickle the back of her neck and whisper against those tumbling blonde curls.

I breathe in her delicious Jasmine scent.

Then I count slowly, trying to still my rapidly beating heart.

One.

Two.

Three.

I step forwards, bringing the soaked cloth up to her face with my right hand as I grab her around the neck with my left arm.

She struggles, as I knew she would. Tries to kick out. Her headphones get tugged from her phone and fall to the ground like a tightly coiled snake. But I am stronger, and I am prepared. Even so, I am shocked at how heavy she is as the drug weakens her muscles. Such a slender girl.

And then the elation kicks in.

She is mine!

I drag her a few yards into the woods and then to the car that I have backed up to the gate, tucked neatly out of view from the road. It's a rental car, a silver Vauxhall Corsa. Ordinary and inconspicuous, and all prepared for her. I am careful as I tug her onto the passenger seat. I mustn't scratch or dirty the car. Positioning her correctly, making sure she is sitting upright without toppling over, is harder than I had anticipated. I lean the seat back and put the airline pillow around her neck, then pull the seat belt across her. Standing back, I admire my handiwork. Yes. She looks like she is fast asleep.

She is fast asleep.

I hear the bus then, the low rumble as it slows without stopping. And now it is my turn. I must hurry; get us both away to safety.

It isn't until we are nearly there that I remember the bag. Fuck it. I left her violin case at the bus stop. How damned stupid I am!

I'll have to go back to collect it. Assuming it's still there.

1

'Where the hell is Cat?' The tall, skinny young man tugs at his earlobe, then slaps the palm of his hand on the top of his cello case. 'She's so bloody unreliable.'

He places his cello case up against the brick wall and then paces up and down the platform, his white trainers squeaking. His cheeks are flushed. 'She'll miss the concert!'

A girl with jet-black short-cropped hair sighs melodramatically. 'Calm down, Christophe! She'll just be running late. I've got her concert gear.'

It is quite commonplace to see musicians at the station, coming to and from the leading music school located just fifteen minutes from the centre of Horsham. I smile at the young man, but he ignores me.

The train arrives, a door to a second-class carriage opening straight in front of where I'm standing. I climb on board and slide into a window seat.

'Can I sit here?' the girl with the cropped hair asks.

'Of course,' I say, shifting my handbag onto my lap.

She shoves what looks like a violin case onto the shelf

above us. Her skin is so pale it is almost translucent, shocking against her black hair and heavily kohled eyes. The cellist is sitting in one of the four-person seats on the opposite side of the carriage to us, his cello taking up much of the space. He is peering out of the window, his knee jiggling up and down, still craning to look at the platform even after we have left Horsham Station behind.

'Are you together?' I slide my eyes to the cellist.

'Unfortunately, yes,' she says.

'Is everything all right with him?'

'Nope. Cat should be on the train with us. She's our first violinist.' She waves a hand in the air. Her fingers are long and thin with scrupulously clean, short, unpainted nails. 'I know why Christophe is uptight. Despite what he said, Cat is always on time. Miss Perfect she is, never late for anything. And her phone goes straight to voicemail. She must have missed the bus or something has happened to her.'

'What do you play?' I ask.

She looks at me strangely. 'Viola. Classical, mainly, some crossover.'

'Are you performing tonight?'

'Yup. At The Cadogan Hall.'

'I'll be there,' I say, grinning. 'My partner is treating me.' DS Joe Swain, who has been my lover for the past three months, and my occasional business partner, won two tickets to the recital at a charity dinner. He wasn't that keen, but I persuaded him that we should go. It's a Saturday and I normally have clients, but I've freed up the afternoon to spend a few hours shopping and wandering around London before meeting up with Joe later. That's one of the advantages of being a psychologist with my own practice. So long as I give my clients sufficient advance notice, I can organise my diary to suit myself.

'Do you like classical music?' she asks.

My hesitation says it all. She sighs. 'Most people only know us as The Shostablades.'

I frown. Just because I can read other people's faces doesn't mean I can control my own.

'We were runners-up in last year's Britain's Got Talent.'

I didn't watch the programme, but I must have read about them somewhere, so I nod and smile.

'We're playing Schubert—assuming Cat turns up, of course. They couldn't give a toss about the rest of us. It's Cat they come to hear, to see.'

'What's your name?' I ask, wanting to be polite.

'Sophie Buck, the official viola player in The Shostablades.' She smiles wryly. 'You should come and see us after the performance. You might even get a free drink if you're lucky.' She rummages in her pocket and hands me a business card. 'What's your name, so I can put you on the guest list?'

'Thank you,' I say, surprised by the offer. I have no intention of accepting, but it would be rude not to show some interest, so I dig into my bag and hand her a business card.

'A psychologist.' She runs her fingers over my card. 'What are all those letters after your name?'

'I'm a specialist in lie detection methods. I have my own practice helping people with issues such as depression and anxiety, but I also work with the police.'

'Doing what?'

'I have helped them solve a couple of murders.'

Sophie's eyes widen. 'How do you do that?'

'I study micro expressions—fleeting changes in facial features—body language and linguistics to assess if people are telling the truth. It's really helpful when the police are interviewing suspects.'

'I know who you are!' She almost jumps out of her seat, jabbing a finger towards me. 'I remember seeing you on the news. You helped solve the lottery winner murder and the ones in the garden centre!'

My hands rush to my cheeks. I hate being recognised.

The brakes of the train screech as we pull into Crawley Station.

'We need your help. We're totally screwed up, us musicians.'

I smile wanly. I can sense her looking at me, but I don't know what to say.

After a moment or two, she turns away and clamps a large pair of headphones over her ears. I reach into my bag for a book. But just five minutes later, she pulls the headphones off. 'I think something bad might have happened to Cat.'

'What do you mean?' I say, putting my book on my knee.

'I don't know. I've just got that feeling.'

'If you are really worried, you should talk to the police.'

She quivers melodramatically. 'That would be the end of me! Anyway. I'm glad I've got your card.' She fingers it, turning it over and over. 'Could you help me?'

'With what?'

'You know about psychopaths?'

'Yes, but I'm not a detective.'

'How much do you charge?'

I tell her my hourly rate, wondering where this conversation is going.

Sophie sighs. 'I can't afford you.'

'I have a special rate for people on lower incomes.'

'What about people on no income?' she asks.

I look at her quizzically.

'We're still students, indebted to our professors.' She sighs and turns away, securing the large headphones back over her ears. But now I find it difficult to concentrate on my book. Why did this young woman ask if I know about psychopaths?

2

'How many times do I need to tell you! It's *sautillé*: very fast spiccato on the A-string. From bar 38 again.'

Karl leans back in his chair, crossing his thick arms as he rolls his eyes to the ceiling.

'No!' he yells, jumping up and striding over to the girl. He stands about six inches from her, lifts the toes of a foot up and leans onto the heel of his black boot. The girl quivers. 'Get it right and I won't step on your toes.'

His feet are large, UK size 13s. Like the rest of her, Alice's size-three feet are small for her sixteen years. She forgot to put on her brogues this morning, so she's only wearing thin black pumps. No protection. Karl's foot could easily break the bones in her fragile toes. How can she play correctly when Karl is so close to her, when she's in danger of prodding him with her bow?

'Again!'

His breath is garlicky. Alice tries not to inhale.

Fear and not breathing are incompatible with good, fluid bowing and agile fingering. She makes more mistakes on the fifth attempt of bars 38 to 45 than she did before.

He brings his foot down on Alice's toes. She cradles her violin in her arms, the bow dangling from her index finger. Tears roll slowly down her pale cheeks.

'Go now!' he says, turning his back to her and striding to his desk on the other side of the room. 'If you can't get it right, I'm not wasting my time teaching you. Are you thick or haven't you practiced?'

Experience has taught Alice that this is a rhetorical question. She wriggles her toes. They are sore and bruised but she doesn't think they are broken. She carefully places her violin into the body of the case, covers it with a piece of midnight blue silk cloth, slips the bow into the lid and zips it all up. Sweeping up her music from the metal stand, she shoves it into the front pocket of the case.

As she hurries out of the room, she tries to ignore the pain in her right foot and keeps her eyes down, avoiding Karl's stare. But when she is out in the corridor, she lets the tears fall, hurrying as she normally does towards the toilets, where she can survey the damage and take stock. Again.

'Alice! What's the matter?' Venetia Edstol appears out of nowhere.

Alice stops. With her back to the head teacher, she hurriedly swipes the sleeve of her jumper across her face. 'It's nothing. Just got something in my eye.'

Venetia harrumphs and walks into Karl's room without knocking on the door.

TWENTY MINUTES later and Alice is in a practice room, a narrow, windowless room with a battered upright piano and just enough space for a small violinist such as Alice to play without bashing her right elbow into the wall each time she draws the bow across the strings of her violin.

There's a knock on the door.

'Alice, your mum's here.' The girl is a couple of years younger than Alice but at least three inches taller.

'What! Why?' Alice pales as she places her violin in its case. 'What's happened?'

The girl shrugs her shoulders. 'Dunno. She's talking to Mrs Edstol.' She grimaces and walks away.

With a pounding heart, Alice packs away her violin and music, shrugs the case over her right shoulder and hurries down the corridor towards the front entrance. All the possible scenarios stream through her head. Is Karl booting her from the school because she hasn't practiced hard enough? Has something happened to Gramps or Grandma, or worse still, Dad? What she isn't expecting is the huge grin on her mother's face.

'Go and get in the car, darling. I'll be there in a tick.'

'But—'

Martha Jones turns her back to her daughter. Alice knows better than to question either her mother or Venetia Edstol, so she does as she's told.

Alice is a day pupil. One of only five. The others say how lucky she is, able to sleep in her own bed every night, to have home-cooked food. Alice doesn't think she's lucky. She walks over to the ancient Land Rover Defender parked in one of the visitor's parking spaces. Sophie and Cat declared the car cool, but Alice finds it cold and uncomfortable, and the smell of damp curdles inside her throat. It's locked, so Alice puts her violin case on the ground, leans against the rusting green passenger door and glances up at the building in front of her.

From the exterior, no one would realise that it is a school. It looks like a run-down old rectory house, with red-brick walls and a moss-covered tiled roof. The windowpanes are white with paint peeling, and in the corners, spiders' webs are congealed with dead insects. The extensions are all at the back of the property: 1970s add-ons in a paler brick with views into the woods behind. If anyone bothered to look or listen, it would quickly become apparent that this isn't an ordinary family home. To the right of the front door is a brass sign: Edstol's Music Academy. When she set up the establishment in 1959, Millicent Edstol proclaimed that it was to be so much more than a school. A place where music was integrated into every element of life; a place where musicians were made. She deemed the word 'school' too lightweight to meet her vision.

The practice rooms are at the rear. Nevertheless, the sounds of repeated bars from pianos and strings instruments weave around the single-glazed building, and if the air is still, can be heard both in the driveway and in the garden near the woods. The other reason that the word 'school' seemed inappropriate was because there have always been so few pupils attending the establishment. Maximum capacity is forty. Today there are only thirty-two young people deemed to have sufficient promise to be worthy of inclusion in the Edstol family. And three of those are Edstols, with Millicent's blood running through their veins. Funds from the school come from the UK government as well as endowments from wealthy benefactors.

Before she died, Millicent gave her blessing to her daughter Venetia's fiancée. 'Karl is everything I hoped for you,' she rasped. 'A fine violinist. I have every faith that the two of you will continue my legacy. I have just one request. He must take on my name. The Edstol name.' As her words faded, the breath rattled out of her and she passed away.

'ALICE, IT'S WONDERFUL NEWS!' Martha is hopping from foot to foot like a young child, her ruddy face lit up with a beaming smile.

'Why are you here? It's the middle of the day,' Alice says with a frown.

Martha inserts her key into the driver's door, clamours into the driving seat and leans across to open the passenger door. 'Hop in, love, and I'll tell you.'

Alice lays her violin case on the back seat and gets into the front passenger seat. The door doesn't shut properly, so she has to open it again and slam it closed.

Martha turns to face her daughter, eyes lit up with excitement. 'You are performing at The Cadogan Hall tonight!'

'What?'

'Karl called me to come and collect you. Cat won't be making the performance tonight and they're sending you in her place! We're going to London!'

'No!' Alice screeches. 'No! I'm not ready. There's no way that I'm going!'

Immediately, Martha's face hardens into a scowl. 'Oh yes you are.'

'No!' Alice says, wailing and burying her face in her hands.

'Pull yourself together, missy. We have worked for this moment for the last sixteen years, scrimping and saving. Think of all the hours you have put in; me too. You are not going to let us down.' Martha's eyes narrow. 'The plan has always been for you to step into Cat's shoes. And now the opportunity has arisen, you are going to grasp it and be successful. This will be your debut. When they realise you've got even more talent than the wonderful Cat, you'll be lauded as the best young violinist in the United Kingdom.'

'Where's Cat?'

'That isn't your concern. Right now, we need to focus on going home to collect your dress and getting ourselves up to London.'

Alice stifles a sob, watching her mother as she inserts the

key into the ignition slot. The old car starts up with a loud
cough and a rumble.

FIFTEEN MINUTES later and Alice is sitting on the edge of her
bed, frozen with terror. She knows the pieces. She's been
learning the first violin part of Schubert's String Quartet No. 14
for the past year and she's stepped in for Cat, playing with the
others on two occasions. Neither performances went that well,
but it hadn't mattered, as Veronica and Karl had been the sole
members of the audience. It's a fiendishly difficult piece for a
mature professional let alone a sixteen-year-old student. And
she doesn't even like it. Cat can play it beautifully because she
understands passion and heartache and sorrow; the dramatic
shifts suit her personality. But Alice knows that she doesn't
have the depth of emotion and worldly experience to do the
piece justice. She wants to be playing beautiful melodic pieces
that make the heart sing, not funereal chamber music written
when Schubert was dying from tertiary stage syphilis and with
the creepy name of 'Death and the Maiden'.

A door slams downstairs and Alice can hear voices. Her
dad. She recognises his heavy footsteps as he climbs upstairs.

'Congratulations, Pudding!' Bill says as he leans on the
doorframe in Alice's bedroom. He's wearing a short-sleeved
white shirt and dark grey, shiny suit trousers. All Alice knows is
that her father works in an office doing something in accounts
in a job he hates.

'Why are you here?'

'Mum rang me and told me the news. Thought I'd nip
home in my lunch hour and wish you luck.'

'I can't go, Dad! I can't do it!'

'Don't be silly, Pudding. They wouldn't be sending you if
they didn't think you could do it!' Bill says.

'Please don't make me go!' Alice can't stop the shuddering sobs.

'Come here, love,' Bill says, opening his arms out wide. She rushes into her father's arms and he hugs her hard. It's the first time he's done that in years.

'Now wipe those tears away and remember what a great opportunity this is. I know you'll be brilliant. Do us proud, Alice.' He grasps her shoulders, then steps away from her.

Alice turns her back on her dad and walks towards the bed. She is startled by her mother's voice. Martha does that: creeps around without shoes on.

'Venetia wants you to wear the silver shift dress,' Martha says.

'No! I hate that dress!'

'Fortunately it isn't about you or what you like. Venetia knows best, so you'll put on whatever she tells you to wear.'

'She's got terrible dress sense.'

'That may be, but she also has a lifetime of experience. Besides, you haven't got anything else.'

Alice watches her mother take the dress out of her small wardrobe and carefully carry it out of the room. She sits on the edge of her bed, and hears every word Martha whispers to Bill at the top of the stairs. 'Can you imagine? We might actually get out of this hovel! Now you've been passed over for promotion yet again, there's a light at the end of the tunnel! Thank God for Alice!'

3

I have spent a pleasant afternoon wandering up and down King's Road, browsing the shops and, stunned by the prices, buying nothing. The Cadogan Hall is conveniently tucked away just off Sloane Square, and now I am in the foyer waiting for Joe. There is a big crowd, and briefly I wonder if I'll miss him. But then he is there, striding in, his sharp eyes dancing around the room, looking for me. When his face lights up with recognition, clichéd though it is, my stomach does a somersault. People notice Joe. Yes, he's tall and good-looking, with ebony skin and sparkling eyes, but there's more to it. He has an assurance about him that garners respect, a unique presence that, despite all my psychological training, I haven't yet been able to adequately describe. He is everything I imagine a policeman should be.

'Darling, where are the shopping bags?' He laughs as he bends down to kiss me. Now that I am a consultant psychologist to the police, we have to keep our distance and maintain a professional relationship, so it is rare that he shows his affection for me in public.

'Are you ready for Schubert?' I ask.

Joe grimaces, and then the bell rings and it's time for us to move into the auditorium. We have good seats in the Stalls, just a few rows back from the stage. As people are settling into their seats, I glance around the building. There is an austerity about it, bringing back memories of church and upmarket school halls. Nevertheless, the seats are plush and comfortable. Joe takes my hand as we leaf through the programme.

I am just about to tell him that I met the performers on the train when the lights dim and a voice booms through the speaker system. 'Ladies and Gentlemen, I regret to announce that due to unforeseen circumstances, Catherine Kingsley has been unable to join us this evening. Instead, we are thrilled to announce that rising star, sixteen-year-old Alice Jones, will take her place. We are honoured that Alice will be debuting with us tonight. Please put your hands together for Alice Jones on first violin, Vadim Maximovich on second violin, Sophie Buck on viola and Christophe Barnet on cello!'

A lone 'boo' echoes above the half-hearted clapping and the low-voiced murmuring that ripples through the crowd. I wonder what happened to the girl who didn't make the train.

The energy drops away immediately. The two boys and Sophie take their seats, and then a young, slight girl walks gingerly onto the stage and then stops like a rabbit frozen in headlights.

Alice.

Christophe, the young cellist with the mop of dark hair, beckons her forwards but she doesn't move. The audience is confused and the clapping fades away to silence. Christophe places his cello and bow on the floor and runs towards Alice, grabbing her hand and pulling her towards the centre of stage. He whispers something in her ear, turns his back to the audience and then sits down again, picks up his cello and bow and positions the cello between his knees.

Alice is wearing a floating, silvery dress, cut like a night dress, that accentuates her skinny, boyish frame and makes her bare arms look like the fine branches of a silver birch tree. She sits down on the empty seat to the right of Vadim, lifts her violin onto her shoulder and tunes it. The others follow suit. Then Alice shuts her eyes. The moment seems very long. Eventually she opens her eyes and the other players look at her. They all raise their instruments slightly and play the first chord and the second. And then they look again at Alice, who is clearly meant to be leading, but the only notes played are those coming from Sophie on the viola. Realising something is very wrong, Sophie stops playing too.

Christophe whispers loudly, 'Start again!'

But Alice gets up, violin under her arm, the bow dangling off a finger, and rushes off the stage like a wisp of steam. There is a collective gasp. The three remaining players glance at each other, eyes wide and darting around like frightened deer. Then Vadim, the second violinist and a good-looking young man with hair as dark as Sophie's, gets up and hurries off stage. The other two follow shortly after.

The boos start quietly at first and then crescendo. I have clients who are musicians and I know that it is sacrosanct: whatever happens, the music must go on.

After three or four minutes of silence, the auditorium lights come back on. People don't know what to do. Will the performers return to the stage? Should the audience leave? It must be a further ten minutes before a voice booms again through the loud speakers. We are deeply sorry; the show is cancelled; your money will be refunded; we will rearrange a date. People start collecting their belongings, standing up, edging into the aisles.

'We can have a drink at the bar here and I'll give the restaurant a call to see if we can have an earlier table for dinner,' Joe says.

'I've got a bad feeling about this,' I say, and repeat the conversation I had with Sophie on the train.

'Well, I haven't!' Joe says, kissing me on the nose. 'Come on, let's get a drink.'

4

Alice is sobbing so much, she throws up. As the other female member of the quartet, Sophie hurries to the Ladies to comfort her.

'Come on, Alice, pull yourself together.'

Sophie leans against the back wall, her arms crossed. She is trying to suppress her fury, but it's hard. She blames Cat, not Alice. If Cat hadn't done a runner, then they wouldn't have had to pull in Alice, who is nowhere near ready to take centre stage. And then she wonders whether perhaps something bad has happened to Cat. Would Cat have walked away from a performance as prestigious as this? She also blames Karl and Venetia. What the hell were they thinking, sending a sixteen-year-old novice to step into the shoes of a seasoned performer? Vadim could have played first violin and Alice second. But, as always, when they decide someone is going to be a star, nothing will deter them from that course, and Alice is being groomed to be the next Cat. Sophie is also angry with herself, Christophe and Vadim. They could have carried on. They *should* have carried on. The consequences will be catastrophic, and not just financially. Their reputations will be massacred. She's a good viola player, in fact one of the best, so in theory it shouldn't be hard to sign up with a new quartet or preferably a band. The trouble is, like everyone in the Edstol 'family', she's committed. And how she wishes she wasn't. She's dreading facing Karl.

'Look, these things happen to the best of us, and you're only a kid. They shouldn't have put you out there,' Sophie says to Alice.

'What will happen to me now?' Alice says, snivelling.

Sophie shakes her head. 'Honestly, I don't know.'

'Has it ever happened before? To someone else, stage fright like that? Is it true about Sarah Bellingham?'

Sophie is glad that Alice is inside the cubicle and can't see her face. It has happened before. Alice is right about Sarah Bellingham. It didn't end well. Not for anyone.

The toilet flushes and Alice comes out, her cheeks ghostly pale, her eyes red.

'You need to get out of that dress!' Sophie says, scowling. She knows what Venetia's reaction will be if the dress gets ruined. She hands Alice the bag stuffed with her day clothes.

Alice hesitates and then accepts it. She turns away from Sophie as she gets changed, unzipping the dress at the side and sliding the spaghetti straps off her shoulders. As she's slipping on a long-sleeved T-shirt, the dress shimmers down her legs and falls to the floor in a puddle of silk. Sophie rushes forwards to collect it and as she stands up, finds herself just inches from Alice's legs. Alice tries to cover her thighs with her jeans, but it's too late.

'Alice! What the hell is that?' Sophie's voice is low and wavering.

'It's nothing. None of your business!' Alice sobs, and tugs her jeans on as quickly as possible.

'Those scars. That plaster.' Sophie knows exactly what those silvery snakes and inflamed red sears on Alice's legs are. 'You're cutting, aren't you?'

'Leave me alone!' Alice yells.

'If you boarded at school, someone would see and tell Venetia. She may be a battle-axe, but she'd help you. Alice, you shouldn't have to deal with this by yourself.'

Alice sniffs. 'You don't understand.'

Sophie sighs as she puts her hands on her hips. 'Actually, I do. Come on, let's go and find somewhere to eat.'

'I can't. My mum is here. Besides, I haven't got any money.' Alice shifts the violin case onto her back.

'No worries,' Sophie says. 'Either way, we need to get a move on.'

They come out of the performers' toilets, Sophie first, a reluctant Alice behind her. Sophie walks along the backstage corridors towards the main foyer. She needs to get this over and done with. Karl will be incandescent with rage, and rightly so.

It isn't until she reaches the door that she turns around and realizes that Alice isn't following her. She glimpses Alice pushing down the handle on the fire exit door and slipping away outside.

'Stupid bloody cow!' Sophie murmurs as she comes face to face with Karl Edstol and Jonno, Viscount Sneddon.

JONNO IS Edstol's greatest benefactor, Cat's personal sponsor and the owner of the priceless Guarneri violin she plays. Edstol's Music Academy would cease to exist without the financial support of its benefactor. Five years ago, he declared himself enchanted with young Cat Kingsley and asked Karl if he could sponsor her, paying for her tuition, her travel, and loaning her the violin in return for a number of private concerts he would host in his somewhat run-down stately home in the Surrey Hills. Needless to say, Karl leaped at the idea. Hardly any of the string instruments the Edstol's pupils play on belong to either the pupils or the Academy; they are on loan. That's the norm with expensive musical instruments, violins particularly. They make good investments for the super-rich, and have the added advantage of boosting their reputations and street cred by being associated with some of the world's best artists. But of equal benefit to Edstol's are Jonno's connections. A failed musician himself, he knows everyone from Yo Yo Ma to Howard Shore, from Karl Jenkins to Placido Domingo. His network of contacts extends equally to the pop world, and he counts Bono, Jessie J, Elton John and Beyoncé amongst his closest friends. He also claims to know the influencers in music, having been on holiday with Simon Cowell and spent New Year with Valery Gergiev. Not that any of these famous people have visited Edstol's Music Academy. Every concert Cat plays in, Jonno funds. Unsurprisingly, Karl and Venetia are in awe of Jonno and terrified of the implications of falling out of his favour.

Karl watched the debacle of the non-performance with horror. In all their years, he has never had performers bolt off the stage. And because Jonno arrived as the lights were dimming, he hasn't even had a chance to talk to him.

'Outside, now!' Jonno says.

Karl follows him out of the auditorium. When they are standing on the street, Jonno shrugs on his black leather jacket, ties his royal blue cashmere scarf into a knot at this neck, then lights a cigar. He stands with his left hand on his hip and puffs on the cigar with his right hand.

'What the fuck happened?' His voice has a rasping edge, the result of a lifetime of smoking.

'Cat disappeared, so we sent Alice instead. It didn't work out,' Karl says. Anyone watching might wonder why such a big, broad man who is normally brimming in self-confidence appears deflated and subservient to a man half his size.

'Who authorised you to substitute Cat?'

'We rang your office, but your assistant said—'

'I know what she said! So Catkin has gone missing?'

Only Jonno calls Cat 'Catkin'.

Karl nods.

'Why didn't the rest of them carry on?'

Karl is a shouter when he gets angry, so he finds Jonno's quiet, steely tone and narrowed eyes disconcerting.

'Taking into account the refunding of tickets, the costs of the tour, the lost revenues from merchandise and the future lost revenues, you owe me...'

Karl interrupts. 'What future lost revenues?'

'You don't expect me to continue supporting you and your precious little non-performers, do you?'

'Is that how you do business? One hiccup and we're chucked out the door?' Karl takes a step towards Jonno.

'The real issue here is Catkin. Where is she?' Jonno deflects the question.

Karl stops still.

Jonno's eyes narrow as he stares at Karl and blows a puff of cigar smoke straight into Karl's face.

'Please don't tell me the Guarneri violin is missing too?'

Silence.

Jonno paces now, backwards and forwards, the leather of his patent black ankle boots creaking as he walks. He tugs at the diamond earring in his left earlobe, at the lapel of his jacket, and runs his fingers through his thinning hair.

'I...It's insured, isn't it?' Karl says, stuttering.

'It's priceless,' Jonno spits. 'It's the pinnacle of my collection. No money can be put on an instrument of that calibre. You know that as well as I do.' He turns, his narrow back and sharp shoulder blades facing Karl.

'You will find Cat. And you will find the Guarneri. I cannot begin to tell you what hell will break out if you don't. Do you understand?' He twizzles around. 'Do you understand?'

Karl whispers, 'Yes.'

5

T he restaurant is small and intimate, tucked behind a mews off Sloane Square. I wonder what it would be like to live here, with a pastel-coloured front door and two large, twisted olive trees carefully positioned on the front steps. Joe cuts through my musings as we sit down at a table for two, set with gleaming silver cutlery on a white tablecloth. A waiter with a strong Italian accent hands us the menus.

'I'm sorry the concert didn't work out.' Joe's expression suggests he is anything but sorry.

'I *will* get you to a classical music concert,' I say as I unfold the napkin onto my lap. 'I just feel sorry for the young performers.'

'Quite. I wonder what the consequences are for bolting off the stage?'

'I sat next to the violist on the train up to London. She seemed quite concerned about the disappearance of their first violinist, Cat Kingsley. I suppose substituting that waif of a girl was a last-minute decision. I wonder if they'll report it—'

'Don't go there,' Joe says, throwing me a piercing stare.

'It's just that whenever a young person goes missing...' My words peter out.

We are interrupted by the wine waiter. Joe orders a bottle of Barolo. The waiter uncorks it at the table and pours us large glasses.

'I get the feeling that something bad has happened to Cat. Sophie implied that she was reliable and would never bunk off a performance.'

'Come on, Pippa. She's probably gone to stay with her boyfriend. Do you know what the statistics are for missing persons?'

I shake my head.

'Seventy-seven per cent of missing adults are found within twenty-four hours and eighty-seven per cent within two days.'

'And what about the remaining thirteen per cent? What happens to them?' The pitch of my voice is rising. It always does when I struggle to contain my emotions about Flo. 'How do you know that something bad hasn't happened to the violinist?'

'We don't. But this isn't about them, is it, darling?'

Joe is getting to know me.

'Would it upset you too much to tell me about your daughter?' he asks.

'No, it's fine.' It will be a relief for Joe to know everything. He leans across the table and reaches for my hands.

'Florence—Flo, we called her—was on her gap year. She wanted to change the world, and if you can't aspire to change the world at eighteen, you never will. We supported her. She had a place at Durham University to study Sociology. She'd talked about going on to do a Masters in Criminology.'

'She took after you then?'

I nod, glad that his eyes don't cloud over with pity. 'Anyway, she signed up with one of those Community Development programmes. She had her heart set on going to South Africa to help kids in townships. It was expensive but Flo was deter-mined. She raised money, did holiday jobs, and in the end all Trevor and I did was give her pocket money. We were really proud of her.'

'You were still married then?' Joe asks.

'Yes. Although things were far from great between Trevor and me, but that's another story.

'Flo loved it. The programme was brilliant and she fell in love with Cape Town and the children, so much so that, when the eight weeks were up, she begged us for permission to stay on for another month. I was scared. It's one thing having your teenage daughter being part of an organised programme, quite another her being out on her own. But she reassured us. She said she had found somewhere to live and that she was bunking up with another girl, an American. That they were in a safe part of the city and that she knew her way round by then. I had a few conversations with the English couple who ran the programme and they reassured me that Flo was one of many who wanted to stay on afterwards. They said what a special girl she was, how she had created these amazing bonds with the kids. Trevor didn't hesitate. I did, but eventually I agreed. She could stay on.' I blink hard to stop the tears from overflowing.

'And she never came home?' Joe asks, tenderly.

I close my eyes. 'She never came home,' I whisper. 'There were investigations. The Foreign Office helped a lot, but it was as if she had vanished off the face of the earth. They never found a...' I still can't bring myself to use the word body in rela-tion to my little girl. 'And so they shut the case.'

'Oh Pippa, I'm so sorry.'

'Our marriage didn't survive. George went off the rails. When Trevor left me, George vowed to never speak to his father again. Our family was destroyed. After three years of hopeless investigations, both Trevor and George—separately of course, as they didn't communicate—decided Flo must be dead. They began to mourn. But I refuse to mourn. I would know if my daughter was dead, I am sure I would. So, with my divorce settlement I took out a mortgage on the cottage in Storrington and set aside a lump sum for paying for a private investigator. Ulrik Naidoo, the private investigator, has been on retainer, working for me for four years.'

'Has he uncovered anything?'

'Bits and pieces, but rarely now.'

'You know I will do whatever I can to help you. I've never been to South Africa but...' His gentle smile melts my insides and I blink away the tears welling in my eyes. Every time I see this man, my feelings for him grow. Right now, I wish we could pass on the food and find a hotel room.

But then our starters arrive: Tagliatelle pasta with Porcini mushroom sauce for Joe, and Beef Carpaccio with rocket and parmesan cheese for me, and I find that I am hungry after all.

'Is that your phone that keeps on ringing?' Joe asks.

My concentration is so focused on Joe and the delicious food that I have zoned out from the faint ringing of a phone. Startled, I drop my fork onto the plate and reach down into my handbag. I have two missed calls from a telephone number I don't recognise.

'It can't be that important,' I say, hoping it isn't a client facing some emotional emergency. Just as I am about to put the phone back into my bag, it pings with an incoming text. I look at it and glance up at Joe.

'Read it,' he reassures me.

Hello Dr Durrant, Sophie here - the viola player. Can I see you, urgently? Thanks, Sophie B.

I can't see her. I am out on a date with my lover, the first time we have been to London together. I text back.

Sorry, Sophie. I can't see you this weekend. Why don't you book in with me next week?

A message pings back almost immediately.

Alice has disappeared. I'm really worried about her. Please can you help.

I hold up my phone so that Joe can read it. He sighs and leans back in his chair. 'Pippa, this doesn't mean anything. The first girl has been missing for less than a day, and the second one for an hour. I think Sophie is a member of the snowflake generation having a meltdown!'

I shake my head. 'I disagree with you. I've got a bad feeling about this. Think of the pressures put on young musicians. The need to practice day and night, of having to compete against your contemporaries for those few-and-far-between gigs, the need to achieve perfection. It must be horrendous.'

'Possibly, but it's not our problem. Come on, darling, have another glass of wine.'

'No, Joe. I can't.' My throat constricts. 'If someone had gone looking for Flo as soon as she disappeared, things would have turned out very differently.'

'Pippa—' he says.

But I ignore him and bend down to pick up my handbag. 'I'm sorry Joe, but I need to go and help.'

He throws his arms up in the air. I stand up. Is he going to come with me or is he just going to watch me leave? I turn around and start walking towards the door.

'Pippa, wait! I'll get the bill and we'll go together. But in a personal capacity. This isn't a police matter.'

6

Alice has no idea where she is. She hasn't stopped running, her skinny legs pumping hard and the violin case on her back bouncing up and down, carving into her bony shoulders and jabbing her spine. She doesn't care where she is, and has no idea where she's heading. She just needs to get far away, to clear her head. Eventually she gets a stitch and has to stop, but she doesn't mind the pain. Pain is good; it helps numb the hurt in her soul.

She knows her mother and Karl will be furious. The anger, she can cope with; it's the disappointment that will be too hard to bear. She will go back and face them at some point. She will have to. But for now, she needs solitude. The air is bitterly cold and catches at the back of her throat, her breath making clouds of steam. As she doubles over, she hears footsteps coming to a halt behind her.

Wiping the tears from her eyes, she tries to stand up and turns around. She thinks she sees a shadow in a doorway. Now fear mingles with desperation. 'Who's there?' she whispers. But her faint words don't carry.

She forces herself to move forwards, faster, faster. And yes, she is sure there are footsteps now. But it's London and there are people around. Of course there are footsteps. It's hard to look over her shoulder with the violin case on her back. She runs faster again and then she is on a bigger road with smart-looking shops. Despite the darkness and the closed signs in the boutique windows, there are too many people around. She needs to lose herself in this metropolis. Is that even possible in central London?

Alice doesn't look. She just knows that she needs to cross over to the other side, where there are tall, dark houses and narrower streets. She dashes out. The screech of tyres and the sounding of a horn make her freeze in the middle of Sloane Street. A black cab swerves around her, the driver of a red London bus hoots at her, making gestures, and eyes, so many pairs of eyes, stare at her from the inside of the bus. She hears a voice and for a moment she thinks she hears her name being shouted. A female voice, screaming 'Alice!' Please, not Martha! So then she is off again, the lure of darkness and solitude wrenching her across the road to safety on the other side.

It is quieter here, the rows of tall, imposing red-brick houses all dark as if it's a ghost town. She can see gardens on the other side of the street, just ahead. That's what she needs: to sit alone in amongst the bare branches of trees and the empty flower beds. But when she reaches it, there are railings, tall black wrought-iron railings as far as the eye can see. She scampers forwards. She reaches a gate, her breath loud, her body riddled with pain. Everything hurts. Inside and out. And then she hears the panting of breath, so close it seems as if the person is right behind her, footsteps heavy. She thinks of Cat. Was Cat chased? Did someone take Cat? What have they done to her? Is she still alive?

She fumbles with the gate, but it doesn't open. Why? There is no padlock. But then she realizes it is locked with a sophisti-cated electronic device, one of those fancy systems that require a swipe card to open it. Where can she go? Where can she go so that she can stop the hurt? Alice's heart is hammering hard, her breathing so shallow it doesn't fill her lungs.

The houses all have steps leading down to basements with dark windows: nobody at home. She sees the house number 34. It's a good number, three four being the beat of a waltz: happy music. She stumbles towards the steps, but the heavy violin case on her back and her shaking legs put her off balance, pushing her forwards. Or was it a hand giving her a gentle shove, just enough so that she trips, the thin soles of her trainers offering no grip. The sharp edge of the concrete steps come up to meet her.

In that moment, she doesn't think about herself but about the violin. That the violin should be saved for someone else, for someone who will love it as much as she does. It will make everyone happy that the violin is safe. She can see Venetia's beatific smile. And then she thinks of Martha and Bill and how angry they will be that their dreams have been dashed, that they will have to stay in their crumbling home.

Alice hits the hard concrete and something inside her goes crunch. Fireworks explode within her head. Is it seconds or minutes that she lies there? She grapples to stand up but there is something wet and slimy, and she stumbles again. But she can't hear the footsteps now or feel hot breath on her neck. She just hears screaming in her head and pain, such pain, in her body.

'Help!' she cries as she reaches up to grab the handrail. She glances around her, peers into the darkened window, but it is covered by internal shutters, so she has no idea what is inside. Then she wonders, can someone see her but she can't see them? As the panic rises, she thinks she hears the click of a door unlocking, someone coming to get her. She glances in terror at the house, but it's too dark to see anything. Alice turns and scrambles back up the steps. She needs to get to the road, to stop a car, to get help. She runs. Past the gardens, along the expensive Knightsbridge streets, past fancy parked cars. And then she realizes. Something feels different.

The violin case has gone.

'My violin!' she screams. It's not a multimillion-pound violin like Cat's, but it was chosen by Karl from their extensive 'on loan' collection and deemed by all to suit her personality perfectly. Alice loves that little Klotz violin. But now her back is light. Her eyes track her surroundings, manically looking, but the violin case isn't there and she has no time to search. She needs to get back to The Cadogan Hall, to find Sophie. Sophie will help her. She's up by the main road again and luck is on her side. The traffic lights are red and the cars have stopped, opening up space for her to sprint back across a main road. A different road this time, one she doesn't recognize. But then the footsteps are there. Again. Closer and closer. Pounding. Searing pain courses through Alice's legs. She puts her hand up to her head and her fingers come away sticky with blood.

A couple, arms entangled, are walking towards her. Their eyes flash with concern and fear.

'Are you all right?' the man asks.

But Alice ignores him and darts across the road again. Limping as fast as she can along the other pavement, she spots a narrow side road with smaller, shorter houses. It's dark, some-where perhaps where she can sit down and take stock. Her breath is so loud, her whole body throbbing with pain, she wonders if it would be better just to collapse on the pavement and die. Right here. Let them take her. She can't do this anymore.

The bright headlights of a car are coming towards her, faster and faster. Alice turns away, tries to shield her eyes but the lights are too strong. And she stumbles again.

This is the end, she thinks. Relief.

7

S ophie is standing on the corner of Sloane Terrace and Sloane Street, hopping from foot to foot, blowing onto her hands.

'Where are the others?' I ask. I expected Vadim, Christophe and various teachers to be with Sophie. Where is the search party?

'We all looked for her earlier but then Karl, our teacher, insisted we leave for Victoria Station and catch the train back to Horsham. He crossed his arms and refused to answer any of my questions, so I walked away and said that I was staying in London. I gave my viola to Vadim to take back to the Academy. I'm not a kid anymore. I can do what I want. I'll be in trouble, but I don't care. It's not right leaving Alice all alone in London.'

'Doesn't Karl have a duty of care?' I direct the question to Joe.

'Only if her parents weren't with her. If it was your child performing at a venue like The Cadogan Hall, you would be in the audience, wouldn't you?'

I nod. 'Were her parents in the audience?' I ask Sophie.

She shrugs. 'Dunno. But I still don't think it's right.'

'Perhaps we could call Karl to double-check?' I suggest.

Sophie recoils, her eyes wide. 'No. No you mustn't do that! Please just help me look for her! Please!'

I catch Joe rolling his eyes at me. I ignore him. If Alice really is missing, then I must help. 'Where have you looked for Alice?'

'Over there!' she says, pointing towards Sloane Square.

'Let's split up. Sophie, perhaps you could go along King's Road. It's the safest area, as it's all lit up with plenty of people around. I'll go over the road towards all those posh houses, and Joe, you can go north, towards Knightsbridge. Let's meet in front of The Cadogan Hall in thirty minutes.'

Joe raises one eyebrow, but there isn't time to debate the issue.

Sophie starts jogging away, but before I can move, Joe reaches forwards and places his hand on my arm.

'She's not Flo,' he says.

'I know.' I glare at him for a moment, adjust my bag across my body and then dart away over Sloane Street, towards the darkened residential roads ahead.

I'm quickly out of breath and as I slow down, I realise how ridiculous this is. We have absolutely no idea where Alice is. I am sure Joe thinks I'm crazy, and am surprised he didn't try harder to stop me. This certainly isn't a well-organised search. As my eyes dart from one side of the road to the other, I spot a waif-like figure with an oblong box attached to her back on the other side of the road. It must be Alice!

I ignore the stabbing in my side and my ragged breathing and race towards her, but she is nimbler than me. She rounds a corner and then she is gone. How could she have vanished? Or perhaps it wasn't Alice after all, just another young person on their way home? I don't know where to go now. The streets all look the same, with tall red-brick buildings, white window frames and black wrought-iron-trimmed balconies. It is so quiet. Unnaturally quiet for a capital city. I suppose it is too expensive for most people to live here.

After a while, I'm lost. I stop and take out my phone. I go to Google Maps and work out how to get back to The Cadogan Hall. I must have gone around and around in circles because I'm not as far away as I had thought.

I can't stop myself from thinking about Flo. Did she call out for me? Was she terrified? I do my breathing exercises and try to still my mind, but the adrenaline is still pumping around my body. I mustn't think about Flo.

And then I see Alice. There is no doubt it is her. She is on the other side of the street, standing stock still, staring at the headlights of a car that is zooming towards her, her face lit up, her eyes in dark shadows as if they have shrunk into her skull.

'Alice!' I yell. 'Move!"

But it is as if she is frozen to the pavement. She doesn't hear me, or she ignores me. Is the car going to mount the pavement and hit her? I run, screaming. And then the car screeches to a halt adjacent to her. The driver's door flings open and someone jumps out, but I can't see properly. The headlights are on full beam and glaring, blinding me. Just as I come up level to the car, the driver's door is slammed shut and off the car roars. I jump back onto the pavement, my heart thumping with terror as it passes by me with just a whisker of an inch to spare.

The driver of that car nearly killed me.

And Alice is gone.

I am shaking as I walk back towards our meeting place. Who has taken Alice?

Joe and Sophie are already there, their heads bent close, talking to each other. When Joe catches sight of me, he strides forwards.

'What's happened?' His firm hands grab my shoulders.

'She was taken,' I murmur. 'And the car nearly hit me.'

'But it didn't?' he asks, peering into my eyes.

'No. It didn't.'

'Did you get the registration number? The model or make of the car?' Joe asks.

I shake my head. 'It was all so quick, so dark, and the head-lights blinded me.'

'I'll talk to the station. Let's see if we can track down Alice's parents and put your mind at rest. I'm just so relieved you're all right.'

8

It is Sunday morning and Karl and Venetia have convened a meeting with all twenty of the Edstol's Music Academy's string players in the Common Room. Most of the youngsters are perched on mismatched sofas and armchairs that have exposed springs and torn covers in a variety of faded colours and floral patterns. Christophe, Vadim and Sophie lean against the back wall in the space between the bookcase that houses numerous CDs and books, mostly on the subject of music, and the antiquated television in the corner of the room. No one has suggested it be replaced with a modern one, largely because the students rarely have free time to watch television. The occasional snatched moment is spent on their mobile phones browsing YouTube videos and dreaming of the day when they might be stars with millions of followers.

'We're very concerned about Cat,' Karl says. 'We've spoken to the police. Does anyone know anything?'

There is silence, but Vadim shifts uncomfortably. He hasn't shaven, and the contrast between his pale skin and dark stubble is even more pronounced than normal. His eyes appear sunken and red.

'She send me text,' Vadim says quietly. His usually flawless English tends to desert him when he is emotional or under pressure.

'What! When? What does it say?' Venetia leaps forwards, narrowly avoiding tripping over a young girl's outstretched legs.

'It's here.' He pulls the phone from his pocket and holds it out in front of him. Venetia grabs it.

I've run away. I've had enough. Don't come looking for me. Cat x,' Venetia reads it out aloud.

'Why the hell didn't you tell us that before?'

'It only came through a couple of hours ago. I was practising, so didn't hear my phone beep.' Venetia hands the phone back to him and he slides it into his jeans pocket. 'I don't believe it,' he says quietly.

'You don't believe what?' Karl asks.

'She wouldn't just run away.' Vadim bites the side of his lip and keeps his eyes to the floor.

'Perhaps she's gone off you!' Christophe whispers so quietly only Vadim can hear. He is wearing a short-sleeved black AC/DC T-shirt and has goosebumps along his arms. A curtain of hair covers his eyes.

'Where would she run to? It sounds like nonsense,' Venetia says.

Karl frowns. 'It does put rather a different perspective on things.' He pauses. 'Sophie, what are your thoughts? You spend lots of time with Cat.'

Sophie shrugs. She doesn't want to be having this conversation. There is no way she can tell Karl and Venetia what she really thinks. They would go apoplectic. Things are tough enough for her as it is. And then there's Dr Durrant. She hopes that the psychologist will step in, especially after last night and their fruitless search for Alice. But perhaps the real reason she doesn't want to say anything is because she's jealous. If Cat managed to get away, then good on her. Sophie would love to do the same, but she hasn't got Cat's spunk, that little edge that pushes her from good to brilliant. Like many musicians, Sophie can recognise it in other performers, but she can't distil or copy it. Charisma, stage presence, call it what you will, Sophie reckons you're either born with it or you're not.

'Sophie?' Venetia urges.

'Sorry. I can't think of anything out of the ordinary. She was looking forward to playing in such a prestigious concert. We all were. You haven't received a ransom note or anything, have you? So she's probably fine.'

'Are you worried about Cat or about the Guarneri violin?' Christophe spits. 'I bet Viscount Snodface was down here in a jiffy! Or was he at the concert last night?'

Fifteen-year-old Ellis sniggers.

Red blotches appear on Venetia's neck, and Karl erupts.

'That's quite enough! Get back to your practice rooms, now!' He claps his hands together, which makes them all start. Vadim is out of there first, but just as Christophe is loping out of the door, Karl calls out, 'Christophe. Stay behind.'

Karl leans back in his chair. 'This is a fucking disaster, and most of it is your making!'

'How so?' Christophe crosses his arms.

'You are the eldest. You were meant to keep an eye on Cat.'

'She's a grown woman! She's not my responsibility! Anyway, perhaps she's just had enough of your rules and regulations and wants to go off and do something proper with her life!'

'How dare you!' Karl jumps up and strides towards Christophe, who takes a step backwards and stumbles over a magazine rack. Karl grabs Christophe by the neck of his T-shirt, hauling him in.

'You scumbag! You've been smoking pot again! You don't deserve to be part of this establishment!' Karl lets the young man go.

Christophe's lips curl into a sneer. 'Fire me, then! Expel me from your precious school!'

Karl's thick jaw trembles with rage. But they both know that there is nothing either of them can do. Karl cannot get rid of Christophe. Money talks. Christophe's father is too influential in the world of music. And Christophe can't walk away from Edstol's. Instead, he shrugs nonchalantly and, as if nothing has happened, ambles out of the room.

CHRISTOPHE FALLS ASLEEP FULLY CLOTHED on his bed and later awakes with a start. The room is dark and he is disorientated. There's a knock at the door. He fumbles to find the switch on his bedside table, sits up and rubs his eyes with his knuckles. The effects of the pot have worn off and he has a pounding headache.

'Yeah,' he mutters.

Ellis pokes his head around the door.

'What do you want?' Christophe spits.

'Everyone's talking.'

'About what?'

Ellis shrugs his bony shoulders. 'Cat's disappearance. Is it true?'

'It's bloody Vadim you should be talking to.'

'Christophe?' Ellis's voice is still high-pitched, although every so often it slides into a croak.

'What?'

Christophe swings his legs over the side of the bed. He strides over to the sink on the far wall and drinks from the tap, even though the water tastes of chlorine and other unpleasant chemicals. He stares at himself in the mirror and runs his fingers through his hair, trying to flatten the bouncing curls. He catches sight of Ellis, who is still hovering in the doorway.

'Spit it out,' Christophe says.

'Is Alice all right?'

'How would I know!' Christophe swallows a bit of tooth-paste, hoping it will freshen up his breath.

'It's just I overheard Karl shouting that Alice is being expelled.'

Christophe straightens up. 'Is that so?'

'I just...'

'I know, Ellis. You have a crush on Alice. Always have done. It's pretty bloody obvious!'

Ellis turns crimson so rapidly it is as if a valve has been released in his face, letting the scarlet blood rush to the surface.

Christophe paces over towards Ellis, who is looking every-where except at the older boy. He grasps Ellis's shoulder. 'It's ok, mate. It's normal.'

Ellis looks up, relief fading the blush. 'I think something bad is going on, don't you?'

'I think you've got a fertile imagination, young man!' Christophe laughs. He holds open his bedroom door. 'Go! I need to practice.'

9

When Alice awakes, she is totally disorientated. Everything aches: her head, her bones and her heart. She turns over, but she's lying on a sagging sofa and almost falls off the side. Where is she? What's happened? She is not at home, and wonders for a moment if she is at school. But, as her eyes adjust to the darkness, she remembers.

WHEN SHE IS PULLED into the car, she thinks it is the end of her life, that she is being dragged to hell. Her head feels all mashed up. As strong hands tug her into the back seat of the vehicle, she struggles. She tries to lash out, but is too tired and weak.

'Alice! Pull yourself together!' It's her mum! Martha slaps her cheek. It stings, and the shock wrenches Alice back into awareness.

'Mum!' she sobs. Tears mingle with blood. It is a lifetime since Alice called out for her mother. 'Mum!'

Then the door slams shut behind her. Martha climbs into the driver's seat and the car pulls away.

'Mum! Where are we? What's happening?' Alice says, gasping.

A set of traffic lights turns red. 'We're getting out of London.' Martha reaches into the driver's side door pocket and hands Alice a small bottle of water and a pill. 'Take this.'

'What is it?'

'A painkiller.'

Alice knows it isn't, because it is pale blue and small, but she takes it anyway, her hand shaking as she puts the pill into her mouth.

Everything hurts. Her head is pounding and her body feels as if she is bruised from head to toe.

'Where are we going?' she asks, but Martha doesn't answer. The lights turn green and they lurch forwards.

'How did you find me?' Alice leans forwards from the back seat. Martha's fingers are gripped tightly around the steering wheel and the tendons in her neck protrude with tension. But for Alice, the shock of being slapped gives way to relief, intense relief coursing through every vein in her body. 'You saved me!' That's what parents are meant to do, aren't they? Scoop up their children and protect them, save them from danger.

Martha rolled her eyes. 'Go to sleep. You've caused enough trouble tonight.'

'I'm sorry,' Alice whispered. Martha had witnessed her failure. The ultimate humiliation. She cried then. Big, overwhelming sobs that shuddered through her slender body.

'Pull yourself together, Alice. What's done is done and now we just need to work out how to fix things.'

'Someone was trying to kill me,' Alice sobbed.

'Don't be so stupid. Get a grip.'

'Someone has taken Cat and someone was following me. I think I'm going to be next.'

Martha's jaw pushes further forwards and she sighs. 'Alice, you have a very active imagination. I assume that's what makes you such a good musician. There is nothing to suggest that Cat has been harmed. I'm quite sure the Edstols would have told us if there was any danger. Besides, we've got more important things to think about. Namely how to salvage your reputation and stop you from being chucked out of the Academy.'

'They're going to expel me?' Alice asks in a murmur.

'Speak up, I can't hear you.'

But Alice doesn't. She shuts her eyes, squeezes her legs together and tries to ignore the pain. All Martha ever cares about is how well Alice plays the violin, whether she is on track to be the best. She supposes she should be grateful that Martha rescued her and that she's in the warm and is safe.

She yawns and glances at her little Timex watch, given to her on her sixteenth birthday by her paternal grandparents. It's just gone 9 p.m.

'Are we going home?'

Martha doesn't answer.

'I've got a violin lesson,' Alice says. The more she thinks about it, the shallower her breathing becomes. Her heart pumps wildly at the thought of Karl's reaction. He will be incandescent with rage. 'Whatever happens, carry on playing' is the mantra they are indoctrinated with from a young age. As far as Alice is aware, no one has ever frozen and then run off the stage, particularly not in a major performance where the public was paying to attend. What shame she has brought upon herself and the whole school. She is certain Karl will do something much worse than step on her toes or rap the side of her head. Rumour has it he has an extra-long ruler that he uses on students who really misbehave. The more the terror mounts, the more Alice's urge to cut herself increases. She needs to dig in to her flesh to release a bit of pain, but there's nothing in the car. She tears off a fingernail with her teeth to make it more jagged and pointy and tries to dig it into the thigh, but she's wearing jeans and her nail isn't sharp enough. She wonders whether she should throw herself out of the car. At least then she will relieve the Edstols and her parents of the shame of being associated with her.

'Stop snivelling,' Martha snaps.

But the more the pain recedes, the more her memory comes back.

'My violin!' she screeches.

'Will you pull yourself together, otherwise you'll cause an accident!'

'I've lost my violin.'

'It's in the boot of the car. Now stop the histrionics. You're making me very angry.'

Alice tries to focus on what is outside, but her eyelids begin to feel heavy and she leans her head back against the headrest, her aching body giving way to slumber.

When Alice wakes, the car is still and she is alone. She hauls herself up in the seat. They are parked in a petrol station. She can see into the shop, but it is empty. The cashier is watching a television up on the wall. It's dark outside, and she has no idea where they are. And where is Martha?

Carefully she tries the car door and is surprised when it opens. She holds it ajar for a moment and then she hears Martha's voice.

'No Bill, we can't.' Pause. 'Just text me the address. We should be there within two hours.'

Alice holds her watch up to the light. It is 11.30 p.m. What is Martha talking about? It doesn't take that long to get home. Where are they?

'Of course it's costing a bloody fortune, but how else were we meant to get there?' Pause.

'How long shall we keep her there?'

Alice can't contain herself. Her parents have Cat! How could they do such a thing? Alice flings open the car door and jumps out. She grabs at Martha, who loses her grip on the phone. It clatters to the concrete.

'What the hell!' Martha says, stepping away from her trembling daughter.

'What's going on?' Alice is shaking from terror and the cold.

A large red car pulls up at the adjacent pump. A middle-aged man with a soft, flabby face and kindly doe-like eyes gets out. He is holding a can of Red Bull. He smiles at Alice before turning to the pump. Alice wants to scream at him: *Can't you see something is wrong?*

Martha bends down and picks up her phone. She glowers at Alice. 'Get back in the car!' she spits.

Alice has no choice. She has no money. She doesn't know where they are. And Martha is her mother, someone she has never disobeyed.

She is grateful for the darkness and the soothing motion of the car. She shuts her eyes and let her tears fall down her cheeks. She knew Martha had it in for Cat. She knew she wanted Cat out of the way so that Alice could be the best violinist in the school, but to take her? How could her parents do that?

AND NOW SHE is in a cottage in the middle of nowhere, and has no idea where.

10

'Wakey, wakey, rise and shine!' Martha claps her hands just above Alice's head.

Alice wakes up with a start, having gone back to sleep again. A clattering noise comes from downstairs and she sits up with a thudding heart. Is Cat being held here?

'Where are we?'

'The Peak District,' Martha says, pulling open the curtains.

Alice was so confused and sleepy when they arrived that she couldn't take in her surroundings. Besides, Martha refused to talk to her, saying she would explain everything in the morning. Dark grey light filters through the window. Alice wonders what time it is.

'Get dressed and come downstairs,' Martha instructs.

Alice looks around her. She is in a tiny room just big enough for the small sofa on which she slept. She pads over to the window and looks outside. It's cold, so she clutches her arms around herself. Even though it is only just beginning to get light, she can tell that the views will be magnificent, with undulating hills and rocky outcrops that stretch for miles. The cottage is surrounded by fields edged by dry-stone walling. Her warm breath condenses on the window panes. As she turns around to face the room, she sees a small suitcase on the floor with her violin case perched on top.

As she recalls the previous evening, her mind becomes foggy. How is it here?

'Hurry up!' Martha shouts from downstairs.

Alice unzips the suitcase and pulls on some old jeans and a thick wool jumper. Martha must have packed it. She hears footsteps coming back up the stairs and then Martha is standing in the doorway, hands on her hips.

'Why are we here?' Alice asks.

'We are somewhere remote so you won't have any distractions. You can practice all day long and the only living things that will be disturbed are the sheep.'

And you, Alice thinks. *Are you not a living thing*?

'Who lives here?' Alice asks.

'No one. It's a holiday cottage.'

'Are we on holiday?'

Martha turns and walks back down the narrow flight of stairs, Alice following closely behind. 'Don't be bloody stupid. You're here to work, to redeem yourself.'

They walk into the kitchen and there is Bill, standing in front of an antiquated stove.

'Daddy!' Alice cries, throwing her arms around her father.

'How are you, Pudding?' He holds her tight.

'Enough of the emotion. Let's get sorted,' Martha instructs, pushing past them and sitting down at the small pine table.

Bill pulls away from Alice, and it is only then that she actually looks at her father. Her hand rushes to her mouth.

'Daddy, what happened to you?' she asks, as she takes in the florid bruises across Bill's left cheek and his scarlet left eye, where blood vessels have burst.

'It looks worse than it is. Don't worry, Pudding. Come on. Let's get you and Mum some breakfast.'

'Did you have an accident?' Alice asks.

'Stop with the questions and sit down,' Martha says. 'Bill, love, hurry up. I'm starving.'

Bill pours them all a glass of orange juice from a carton, then places a single sausage along with some baked beans on each of the three plates, all of which are chipped and cracked. There is a small knife lying on a bread board, but no bread.

'Is Cat here?' Alice asks quietly as her parents munch on their over-cooked sausages.

'What?' Martha frowns. 'Why would Cat be here?'

'Never mind,' Alice says, pushing her beans around her plate.

'Do you know something about Cat?' Bill asks.

'Not now,' Martha growls, her eyes narrowed at Bill.

'How long are we staying here?' Alice says.

'As long as it takes,' Martha replies.

'But not me,' Bill interjects. 'I've got to go home.' He is talking with his mouth full.

'Why?' Alice groans.

'Someone has to work to pay for the food on your plate and the strings on your violin!' Martha says.

'Why didn't we all just go home?' Alice asks.

'I've already told you to stop with the bloody questions!' Martha thumps her cutlery onto her plate. 'Look on this as a bootcamp; a time to prepare for auditions.'

'What auditions?'

'You, Alice Jones, have been expelled from Edstol's. You will need to apply to other music schools.'

Alice doesn't know whether to laugh or cry. Hysteria grips her chest and she lets out a strange moan. And then the words come tumbling out. 'I'm glad I've been expelled. I hate it there! I'm glad I don't have to go back!'

'Karl Edstol—' Martha says, but Alice interrupts her.

'Karl Edstol is a creep! He's a dodgy paedophile who makes passes at us girls and is responsible for the death of Sarah Bellingham. Did you know that? She died because of what he did to her. Thank God I'm not going back there!'

Martha stands up. Her chair topples backwards and makes a cracking sound when it hits the stone floor. She leans onto the kitchen table, which wobbles precariously. She narrows her eyes and speaks quietly. 'Help your father wash up whilst I use the bathroom.'

Alice waits until she can hear her mother pacing around upstairs.

'I don't want to be here, Daddy.'

Bill clears his throat. 'Your mother thought it would be a good idea to have some time out to recharge your batteries and refocus on your playing. The unfortunate incident last night is going to need sorting. You're going to have to apply to new schools. I'm sorry you got spooked, Pudding. What happened?'

'I don't know.' Alice's bottom lip quivers and she wraps her arms around her slender body. 'Daddy, I don't think I want to be a violinist anymore.'

Bill stands very still. The knife he is holding trembles mid-air. His shoulders sag. He sighs deeply and then turns around to face her. 'You don't mean that, Alice. It's a natural reaction from a bad experience, a bit like getting back on a bike after you've fallen off it.'

'I do mean it. I've been thinking about it for ages. I can still play the violin without being a violinist. I don't want something horrible happening to me like what's happened to Cat. And I don't want to be like Sophie, who is bitter about not being a star. I just want to be normal and go to a normal school and have an ordinary life.'

Bill places the cutlery in the sink and wipes his hands on his grey trousers. 'Darling, you are special. You have the potential to be one of the greatest violin players in the world, and the opportunities that Edstol's presented you with are unsurpassed. Either we persuade Karl and Venetia to take you back, or we get you into another school. This is not something you can walk away from. You would regret it for the rest of your life.'

'But I don't even like playing the violin anymore. I used to love the sound and the feel of playing, and now it's like a wooden lump digging into my shoulder, so loud it hurts my ears. I hate everyone looking at me and I'll never be good enough. Never.' Tears spill from Alice's eyes. Bill stretches out his arms.

'William!'

Both Bill and Alice jump.

'Yes, love?' He steps back from Alice as he swivels to look at his wife.

'Outside. Now.' Martha strides down the stairs and pushes past her husband and daughter. She flings open the front door and cold, damp air curls into the small house. 'Now!' she shouts. Bill turns away from Alice and raises his eyebrows. With his bloodshot eye and massive bruise, it makes him look grotesque.

Alice slopes out of the kitchen into the small living room and slumps down onto the single sofa. She can hear her parents shouting at each other, but their voices become increasingly indistinct. When she can barely hear them, she gets up and creeps towards the window, pulling the yellow and brown floral curtain to one side so that she can peek out. But the clouds are hanging low and all she can see are brown and greyish-green fields stretching away as far as the eye can see.

Going upstairs, Alice goes to her violin case and unzips the side pocket where she keeps her mobile phone and wallet. To her relief, the phone is still inside. She tugs it out and switches it on. It has only ten per cent battery left. She isn't sure who to call because she doesn't have any friends. Not real friends, anyway. She decides to ring Sophie, but there is no dial tone. Alice peers at the phone, wondering if perhaps there is no reception out here in the middle of nowhere. She feels like a prisoner, held captive by her own parents.

She tucks the phone down the front of her jeans so that Martha won't see it, in the hope that she can send Sophie or someone a text message later. Perhaps there is better reception elsewhere in the house, or outside. Then she goes downstairs to the front door and flings it open. Martha appears on the brow of the hill, striding towards the house, her features tight, her forehead in a frown.

'Get back inside,' she shouts at Alice. 'You'll catch a cold standing there without a coat on!'

Alice wants to retort, 'But you're out without a coat,' but instead she steps back into the living room.

Martha marches in and slams the front door behind her.

'Where's Dad?'

'He's gone.'

'But how can he go? He hasn't said goodbye! He hasn't got any of his stuff with him!'

Martha rolls her eyes. 'Your father's suitcase is still in his car. He needs to get back before the traffic gets too bad. He needs to go to work.'

'But where's his car?' Alice waves her arms around.

'Around the back of the house. Anyway, he's taking the Defender. We'll have his car. It's much nicer to drive.' On cue, they hear the spluttering start of an engine.

'But he hasn't said goodbye!' Alice wails. 'He always says goodbye!'

She dashes back to the door, flings it open and runs outside. But Alice is too late. The tail lights of the Defender disappear over the brow of the hill.

'Daddy!' Alice screams. And then she sinks into her knees and lets the tears fall.

When she returns to the little house, her cheeks blotchy and eyes red, she waits until Martha is looking the other way, then slips the small knife lying on the kitchen counter into her front jeans pocket. Pulling her jumper down low to cover the bulges of her phone and knife, she hurries upstairs to the bathroom.

11

I am curled up on the sofa reading the Sunday papers. Mungo, my faithful black Labrador, is snoring quietly at my feet, although I know it won't be long before he starts nuzzling me, requesting a walk. Joe left earlier this morning to run some errands. Despite his loving attention, I couldn't relax properly. The escapade with Alice has put me off kilter and Joe sensed it. I already miss his presence. It's crazy how he has embedded himself in my life within such a short time. Sometimes I wonder if I'm opening myself to hurt, and then other times I remember that it's Joe. He would never play games.

I can hear my phone ringing from the kitchen, where I left it on the table. In the hope that it might be my son, George, calling from Switzerland, I race from the living room and answer it before checking who is calling.

'Hello!' I say breathlessly.

'Dr Durrant?'

My heart sinks; it's a young female voice.

'I'm sorry to disturb you on a Sunday night, but can I make an appointment to see you? It's Sophie, the viola player. Neither

Cat nor Alice have been found. Actually, I think you should come to the school, if you can?'

I roll my eyes and try to remember that she is young, and the young often have unrealistic expectations. Swallowing a sigh, I say, 'I'm sorry Sophie, but it doesn't quite work like that. If you'd like to see me, then you have to come here. Besides, their disappearances are a police matter.'

'Oh.' There is despondency in her voice.

'But we *all* need your help.'

'Who is all?'

'Christophe, Vadim, Ellis—all of the music students at the Edstol's Academy.'

'In that case, I would need to be officially appointed by the school. If you can engineer that introduction, then perhaps we can sort something out.'

There is a long silence. 'Can I see you anyway? But I haven't got much money. I could play the viola for you if you like? Any pieces you want? I could do a soirée for you and your friends.'

I laugh. No one has ever attempted to barter musical services with me before.

'If you're that concerned, come and see me at 6 p.m. tomorrow. I'm in Storrington, near Pulborough.'

'That's great. I'll get the bus. We're only twenty minutes away. I could probably even walk. Thank you, Dr Durrant.'

Joe calls me at 8 a.m. on Monday morning. 'I have an apology to make. Young Alice Jones and her parents have been reported missing.'

'The whole family?'

'The grandfather reported it. To be honest, we would have dismissed it if we hadn't gone on that wild-goose chase on Saturday evening and if the other violinist, Cat Kingsley, hadn't been reported missing as well. But I think we need to investigate what's going on at that school. I was wondering if you could join me so we can interview some of the staff and pupils?'

This is the downside to becoming a consultant to the police. The work is irregular, and I can't shift my private clients around. I try to leave myself long lunch breaks for my police work, but invariably it involves working in the evenings and very early mornings. Long term, this isn't going to be sustainable, but right now I'm in no mood to grapple with the conundrum. I would rather have too much work than too little.

Monday morning is jam-packed with clients, three face-to-face in my consulting room and one via Skype. The synchronicities in my life seem to be coming into play yet again. My new client is an actor, a rather dashing young man who, after excelling at RADA and landing the role of Prospero at The Globe Theatre in London, has over the past few years had a career that, as he describes it, has 'gone nowhere'. He assumes that he 'peaked' aged twenty-five and is now consumed with self-doubt and edging into depression. I think of the pressure that was put on him and the pressure he put on himself at a young age, and wonder whether his experience as an artist and performer is similar to that of musicians.

After a hurriedly-consumed sandwich, Joe arrives shortly after 1 p.m. and we're off to Edstol's Music Academy.

'The world of artists, actors and musicians must be so stressful,' I say. 'It's all about being the best, winning competitions or auditioning for roles. It's not like my job, or yours, where we just have to do a good job. My success is based upon how much I help my clients, and I suppose yours is based on how quickly you solve a case. If we want to apply for a promotion, we just go for it. It's not feast or famine.'

'You're in a very contemplative mood today.' Joe grins at me. 'Actually, I've declined a promotion three times.'

'You have?' I look at him with surprise.

'In all the British police procedural books and the television shows, the likes of Morse and so on are Detective Inspectors. The reality is, if you're a DI, you don't get to do the real policing, the interviewing and all the stuff I enjoy the most. It's about directives and meetings and budgets, reviewing investigations and deciding whether or not to continue with cases. They asked me to apply to be a DI again earlier this year. I turned it down.'

'Do your bosses mind?'

Joe laughs. 'No. They know I like to do the legwork, get my hands dirty or whatever cliché you'd like to come up with. The day I can't interview a suspect is the day I leave the police force.'

We pull up in front of a large red-brick house. It looks nothing like a school. Perhaps it's the way the trees are packed in tightly, shrouding the place in shadows, or perhaps it's because the place is so run down, but it sends a chill up my spine.

12

‘What is it, love? You look so miserable.’ Her words sound jumbled up, as if she has a mouthful of marbles.

Jonno jumps. 'What are you doing here?'

'The music stopped.'

'Right. Let's go and switch it back on again. Where is Kaya?'

'Dunno.'

The Viscountess Sneddon has full use of her eyes, but little else. Every day, Jonno is grateful that he can gaze into those beautiful chocolate brown eyes and see the soul of his wife. He turns the wheelchair around and pushes her out of his office, along the corridor to the small drawing room. It used to be called the Music Room, but after Marissa got her diagnosis and the disease took hold of first her fingers and her coordination, and then every muscle in her body, it seemed cruel to call it the Music Room any more. During one of her many hospital stays, Jonno got the Steinway and her three harps moved out of the room and into the ballroom. In their place he wheeled in a large, ancient television, the one with a chunky back, and got the chimney cleaned and the three dead crows removed. He threw an old rug over a tattered sofa, brought in a couple of standard lamps and tried to make it warm and cosy, a room where Marissa would feel comfortable and not be reminded of how very much she had lost.

But when he wheeled his wife into the reconfigured room for the first time, she sobbed. And so that night, when she was asleep, he opened up the frigid ballroom and pushed her favourite harp back along the corridor, placing it in the corner of the wood panelled room, where it had always lived.

She didn't say anything the next morning. She didn't need to.

The real fire has died down and the electric fire emits a burning smell rather than any effective heat. He settles Marissa's chair next to it and walks over to the old CD player.

'Would you like the Debussy again, or something else?'

Jonno can't make out her response but he won't ask her to repeat what she just said. That is too cruel. So he guesses and puts on Mozart's *Concerto for Flute, Harp and Orchestra*: the version where Marissa was the harp soloist, of course. His wife sighs contentedly and lets her eyelids close.

Jonno walks out into the corridor. 'Kaya!' he yells. 'Kaya!'

'Yes, sir.' The woman hurries out of the kitchen, wiping her hands on a tea towel, her hair tight to her scalp in cornrows.

'What are you doing?'

'Making lunch, sir. Will you be eating with madam today?'

'You mustn't leave her alone. How many bloody times have I told you that?'

'I know, sir. But I have to. She was comfortable listening to music and I had to make lunch.'

'Just get on with it then!' Jonno shakes his hand at her, the large gold signet ring inset with a ruby on the little finger of his right hand flashing in the low light.

Kaya scuttles away and Jonno sighs. It didn't used to be like this. When he first married Marissa, they had staff. A cook, a housekeeper, a butler and two gardeners. Nowadays they have Kaya, and no doubt she'll be like the others that came before her: hanging around for a couple of months—six has been the longest they've been able to keep someone—and then she'll be off bitching to the agency that the work wasn't what she expected, that the house is too big, too cold, that Viscount Jonno is too demanding and that Viscountess Marissa is too sick.

Marissa was a harpist. Sometimes Jonno thought she loved the harp way more than she loved him. She would hold the instrument with such tenderness, her fingers plucking the strings with passion, dancing up and down, coaxing it to do whatever she wanted. Music was her life. Music was their life. Jonno had been a young, thrusting agent in the agency to which Marissa was signed. When, as a twenty-something, she danced into the offices, his heart (which he had, up until that point, assumed was a part of his anatomy that was missing) soared. He fell deeply and hopelessly in love. For a long while, it was a secret that he nurtured, a love that he believed could never be requited. What would The Right Honourable Lady Marissa Arbuthnot, expected to be appointed as the official harpist to the Royal Family, want with plain John Sneddon from Croydon?

But Jonno got that one wrong. Lady Marissa found him exciting, so different to the privately-educated toffs she had been surrounded by during her elitist upbringing. But when they announced their engagement, Viscount Arbuthnot flew into an incandescent rage, swearing he would disinherit Marissa, that she was bringing shame upon the family. As the words petered out, his face went tomato red and he stormed out of the dining room to take refuge with a bottle of port in his study. Two hours later, his wife, an ineffectual and plain woman with twice as many titles as her husband, found him dead from a massive heart attack.

Not long after the death of her father, Marissa and Jonno married at Chelsea Registry Office, accompanied by Marissa's best friend from The Royal College of Music, and Jonno's brother, Milo.

Marissa and Jonno didn't expect to inherit the big house. She had an elder brother who, like all the males in their family, had joined the army. But he went to Afghanistan and never came home. Jonno was a hustler, a wheeler dealer who got caught up in all sorts of get-rich-quick schemes, some of which worked, most of which didn't. Marissa was happy to leave their financial affairs to her husband. Whenever he could, he followed her around the world as she charmed the international stage with her exquisite harp playing. There had been some initial disappointment that she wasn't appointed the royal harpist (more so on Jonno's part than Marissa's), but she was still world-famous and fêted by the musical elite. Of course, it wasn't all a perfect life or a perfect marriage. Secrets have to be kept, even between partners. Jonno primped and talked himself up to fit in with Marissa's crowd. He called himself Viscount Sneddon, a title that he bought on the internet for £150, because the husband of a Viscountess is just an ordinary mister. And there was no way that Jonno was prepared to remain Mr John Sneddon.

If Jonno had known what his life would look like at fifty-eight, he might well have chosen another path. But he didn't have that crystal ball and now he just has to make do. His primary objective is to care for Marissa. And perhaps, just perhaps, his greatest wish might be able to come true.

HE SHUTS the door of his office, deadening the sounds of Mozart, and picks up the phone. He has already checked which police station to call, and has done some online research as to the best detective to ask for. There's no point in calling 999 for an issue like this.

'Good morning. Can you put me through to Detective Joe Swain.'

The woman hesitates. 'Please can I ask what it's regarding?'

'I'd like to report a serious crime.'

'DS Swain isn't available right now. I will transfer you to his colleague, Constable Mia Brevant.'

'No,' Jonno snaps. 'I don't want to talk to anyone else.'

'But sir, if you are reporting a crime, it will need to go through certain channels. We need to create a crime reference number.'

'I don't give a sod about your procedures.' Jonno has no time for gatekeepers and has learned that bloody-minded persistence is what gets results.

'Hold on one moment, sir,' the receptionist says.

A couple of moments later, the phone is ringing again and then voicemail clicks in. *'This is DS Swain. Please leave a message and I'll get back to you.'*

Jonno hesitates and then leaves a message. 'That girl, Catherine Kingsley, who has been reported missing by Karl and Venetia Edstol. She's not missing at all. She's stolen my violin. It's worth £3.2 million. Call me.'

13

'This doesn't look like a school,' I say to Joe as we get out of his car.

'I gather they only have forty pupils.'

'According to my Google search, they have produced some of the leading musicians of the day. They must be doing something right,' I suggest.

'Let's go and find out!'

Joe presses the brass-domed bell on the brick wall next to the navy-blue front door. Paint is curling off it, revealing that the door's previous colour was pillar-box red. I can hear minor scales being played on a piano, getting faster and faster. It does nothing to dull my unease.

'Let's not divulge that we were at the concert in London,' Joe says quietly, just as the door swings open with a creak.

'We are here to see Mr and Mrs Edstol.' Joe shows the woman his police badge and introduces me as a psychologist and consultant to the police.

'I am she. Venetia Edstol.' She does not extend her hand.

Venetia is one of those ageless women. Her face is relatively unlined with strong cheekbones and wide-set eyes, but she wears no makeup, clearly hasn't visited a hairdresser in years, and her clothes are old-fashioned. She is wearing a purple and grey tweed skirt that cuts off mid-calf, flat shoes, and a mauve jumper that has holes in the sleeves and fluff balls over most of the body. Uncharitably, in my mind's eye I give her a make-over. Cut the lank grey hair into a bob, give it a warm, mahogany colour, tidy the eyebrows and run some mascara over those lashes, tweezer out that long hair on the side of her chin, and, along with a swipe of lipstick, she would be transformed into an attractive woman.

'Dr Durrant has considerable experience of working with young people, so I felt it was appropriate for her to accompany me,' Joe says.

Venetia Edstol turns to glance at me, almost as if she can read my uncharitable thoughts. I pull my coat tighter around my body. It's as cold inside as it is out. The hallway looks nothing like any school I have visited, more like a jaded country house whose owners have run out of money and hope. We follow her along a wide corridor, past heavy oil paintings of nineteenth-century musicians.

'Please sign in.' She points to a visitor's book on a wooden table. Joe fills it in for both of us. Venetia then leads us into a room at the end of the corridor. It houses a baby grand piano in one corner and a desk at the far end, at which a large, stocky man is seated. A long piece of hair, which I assume has been coaxed to cover his considerable bald patch, drops down in front of his eyes.

He stands up with a start, shoving the hair back in place, but it doesn't quite achieve the cover-up effect he no doubt seeks. 'I didn't hear the bell ring!' he says, stepping forwards, his hand extended.

Joe does the introductions and Karl Edstol beckons for us to sit down on two armchairs placed in front of his desk. They look comfy, but they are not, and I have to shift to one side to prevent a wire coil jamming into my left buttock. Venetia drags the piano stool across the room. Joe jumps up to help but she bats him away.

'I gather you are reporting a missing person?' Joe says as we all settle down.

'Yes. Catherine Kingsley, known as Cat.'

'Have you notified her parents?'

Venetia and Karl glance at each other.

'She doesn't have any parents,' Karl says.

Joe raises an eyebrow. 'Her legal guardians, then?'

'That would be us. Her mother was my sister,' Venetia explains. 'When she passed, we brought Cat up as our own. She has been our child for the past eleven years.'

'Do you have any children of your own?' Joe asks.

A fleeting glance is shared between them again.

'No. We view Cat as our child, which is why her disappearance is particularly distressing,' Karl says. Venetia clasps her hands together and turns her upper body away from Karl. I deduce that the subject of children is making her feel uncomfortable. 'Of course, we view all the children at Edstol's Academy as family.'

'How old is Cat?'

Karl hesitates.

'She's twenty,' Venetia says.

'So she is an adult.'

'Indeed.' Karl nods. 'But it is totally out of character for her to disappear like this. She failed to turn up at a concert where she was meant to be the star performer.'

There's a knock on the door, swiftly followed by it opening.

'Karl, sorry to disturb but...'

Sophie looks at me, her eyes wide with surprise. 'Doctor

Durrant, I didn't know you were coming here, I thought...' Her words peter out and her hand rushes to her mouth.

'How do you know each other?' Karl says, frowning.

'Perchance, we were seated next to each other on the train to London. Sophie expressed her concerns about Cat's disappearance, so when DS Swain told me that you had reported Cat missing, it seemed particularly a propos that I attend this meeting.'

'What did you want to say, Sophie?' Karl barks.

'Um, nothing. It's not urgent.' She steps back into the corridor and lets the door swing closed.

'Please tell us about Cat,' Joe says.

'She is our star performer and is sponsored by a major benefactor. We expect her to be the next Janine Jansen or Anne-Sophie Mutter.'

Joe glances at me, his brows momentarily in a frown. As he only listens to rock, I assume he hasn't heard of these performers before. I stifle a smile.

'Has she already won international violin competitions?' I ask.

'We don't believe in competitions. They're all rigged,' Venetia says, twizzling the string of pearls at her neck. 'The judges select their own pupils, so it is never a level playing field. Instead we are using our own connections—and those of Viscount Sneddon, her benefactor—to launch Cat's career.'

'And what is she like as a person?' Joe asks.

'Single-minded about her violin playing. Hard-working, sometimes a bit hot-headed. There is no logical reason for her to have disappeared.'

'When was the last time anyone heard from her?'

'She was here for breakfast on Saturday morning and then went to her regular yoga class. Christophe, Vadim and Sophie were expecting her to join them at Horsham Station to take the train to London. None of them reported any untoward behaviour prior to that.'

'And you have had no contact with her since early on Saturday morning?'

Karl shakes his head. Venetia shuffles. I keep my eyes on her. There is definitely something she's not telling us.

'Are you aware of any problems that she might have?'

They both shake their heads.

'What about a boyfriend?'

Venetia's upper lip curls momentarily. 'We actively discourage our pupils from having relationships. It is a massive distraction, something that we can't countenance at this critical period of their lives.'

I am shocked by this naive perspective, but Joe is ahead of me.

'We would like to speak to her friends, both here and outside of your school.'

Karl answers. 'You can speak to our pupils here, but Cat didn't have any friends beyond these four walls. A musician's life is transitory, performing with different people from one night to the next, never staying anywhere long enough to develop true friendships. That is the price one has to pay for pursuing this vocation.'

'Is there anyone who might want to cause Cat harm?'

Venetia gasps. Karl scowls. 'Of course not!'

Joe's phone vibrates in his pocket. He ignores it, but when it starts again, Joe apologises and removes it. He reads a text message and slowly puts the phone back into his pocket.

'Mr Edstol, would you care to tell us about the police caution you received three years ago?'

Karl slaps the palms of his hands on the desk. 'Oh for fuck's sake, that is done and dusted and nothing came of it. It's a load of bullshit. It went to the NCTL...'

'The NCTL?' Joe asks.

'The National College for Teaching and Leadership and they threw it out, said there was no case to answer for, hence why I am still sitting here doing the job I was born to do. And a bloody good job too, if I can say so myself.' His jowly face is flushed.

'Please tell us what happened.'

'Can't you read it for yourself? Are you enjoying dredging up that all over again, upsetting my wife?'

I glance at Venetia. She looks remarkably composed. The only person upset is Karl.

'It is better if you tell me in your own words,' Joe says. 'Otherwise I might need to ask you to attend the station.'

Karl looks as if he is going to explode.

Venetia answers. 'There was a fracas between a parent and Karl. The parent was extremely aggressive, making unreasonable demands as to why their child was being looked over for leading roles. Karl tried to explain that the child wasn't ready, but the parent was having none of it. After attacking Karl, right here in this room, my husband swiped back in self-defence and the parent suffered minor injuries.'

'I would have preferred if your husband had described that,' Joe says, sounding exasperated.

'When the child's father learned what had happened, they dropped charges,' Karl spits.

'You hit a woman?' Joe asks.

'She bloody well attacked me! I received a caution and it has not affected anything about this school. I fail to see what this has to do with Cat?'

'Perhaps nothing,' Joe says. But I can tell from his tone of voice that he doesn't believe that. Not for one second.

'We would like to speak to all your pupils. Can you arrange that?' Joe directs the question to Venetia, who nods.

Just as Joe stands up, he asks, 'How is young Alice?'

'Alice?' Karl says, as if he hasn't got a clue who Joe's talking about.

'The girl who got stage fright in London.'

'She's fine,' Karl says, busying himself tidying up a few items on his desk.

'Can I see her?'

He keeps his eyes averted. 'No. She's having the week off.'

I am surprised that Joe is pretending we don't know about Alice and her family's disappearance, but it seems to be a tactic that has paid off. Why is Karl lying? If Alice hasn't turned up to school today, wouldn't he have investigated?

'THERE IS something not right about that place, and those two,' Joe says as we slide back into his car.

'I agree. They were both hiding things.'

'Really?' Joe glances at me with surprise. 'I thought it was only Karl?'

'No, Venetia too. I get the impression she's scared of her husband.'

'Not surprising. He is hardly the warm type.' Joe is looking at his mobile phone. 'Alice lives four miles from here. I'd like to pass by, see if anyone's at home. Is that all right with you?'

I have just under an hour until my next client, so I agree.

Alice's family live in a semi-detached house on the outskirts of West Chiltington, a sprawling village full of affluent houses. It looks like the poor relation on the street, with a bin overflowing with litter next to the front door and an unkempt front garden.

We can't find a door bell, so Joe raps on the front door. There is no answer. He tries again. Then he peers through the letterbox and puts his face up against the window in the downstairs room.

'Can't make out a thing,' he says. 'Let's walk around the back.'

I hesitate. It is one thing for a policeman to do this, but I feel uncomfortable. Nevertheless, I follow him. He opens a creaking side gate onto a narrow alley that runs between Alice's house and the one next door. The garden is small and as unkempt as their front patch.

'What are you doing?'

The voice startles me.

'Hello! We're looking for Mr or Mrs Jones, or their daughter, Alice. Do you know if they're around?'

'And you are?' The elderly woman shuffles towards the fence that provides an inadequate barrier between her neat garden and the Jones's mess.

'DS Joe Swain and my colleague, Dr Durrant.' He shows her his badge.

'Something bad happened to them, has it?'

She sounds resigned, which surprises me.

'We would just like to talk to them. Do you know what time either Mr or Mrs Jones will be home?'

'No, dear. They've been gone for a couple of days and it's been total bliss. None of that screeching.'

'You mean the violin practice?'

'Nah! I can cope with that. The kid plays beautifully. It's the screeching of voices that gets to me. Just as well I'm half deaf. If I take the hearing aid out, I can just about bear it.'

'Did they say they were going away?' Joe asks.

She shakes her head. 'We keep ourselves to ourselves. The longer they stay away, the better. Just hope the kid's okay.'

'Why wouldn't she be?' Joe frowns.

'Just a gut instinct. You know, woman's intuition! Anyway, nice to meet you and all but I must be getting on now.'

Joe digs into his pocket and produces a business card. 'Please, Mrs...'

'It's Miss. Miss Ethel Smith.'

'Please, Miss Smith, when the family returns, could you let me know? And if anything pops up that you think might be of interest to us, please call me.'

'To be brutally honest, Inspector, I hope they've gone for good!'

14

S ophie arrives just before 6 p.m. I invite her in and ask her to complete a new client form.

'You are over eighteen, aren't you?' I ask, suddenly concerned that she may still be a minor. She looks younger today, pale, free from make-up and almost gaunt.

She laughs. 'Yeah, I'm twenty. All grown up!'

'Tell me what you'd like to get out of our session?' I ask, as she hands me back the form and leans into the armchair.

'Something isn't right. Cat has disappeared, and now there are rumours that Alice has gone too. And I've got a bad feeling.'

'You know that we can only discuss you in our sessions. I'm not in a position to talk about Cat or Alice.'

'I know. It's just it's affecting me.'

'That's completely normal. If unusual things happen, we have to learn resilience to be able to cope with them. Tell me how you're feeling?'

'I want to get out.'

'Get out of what?'

'The clutches of the Edstols. Mum thought she was doing good by me getting me into the school, but if I had known then what I know now, we'd never have done it. I could have gone to the Menuhin School or Chetham's. I'd have got scholarships; I was good enough. But Mum liked that Edstol's is such a small school, that I could stay on there until my career was fully launched, and the fact it was near where we lived.'

'Lived?'

'I don't have a home anymore. Mum died eighteen months ago. Cancer.'

'I'm sorry, Sophie. That must be so hard for you.'

'Yeah. It was always her and me against the world. But as you say, I'm grown up now, so I should be able to make my own way in the world. But...' Her voice peters out and she sniffs.

'But?' I encourage her.

'Once you're part of the Edstol family—' She does air brackets around 'Edstol family'. '—you're tied in for life. I had no idea Mum signed that contract. I'm not sure she understood it.'

'What contract, Sophie?'

'In return for the very best education, which is free, along with all bed and board and performance opportunities, the Edstols take some great big percentage of their student's earnings. And then I can't earn anywhere else for five years after leaving them. If Cat got away, then good on her. Just wish she'd taken me with her.'

'Is this normally how it works in the arts sector?'

'No!' Sophie's laugh is bitter. 'But we weren't to know that. Mum worked in Tesco's and at night she did cleaning shifts at the hospital. What did she know about contracts? We thought my life was sorted when the Edstols declared what talent I had and begged Mum to let them teach me. All Mum wanted was for me to fulfil my dreams and have a better life than hers.' Sophie rubs her eyes.

'She must have been so proud of you,' I say quietly.

Sophie takes a tissue from the box on the side table and blows her nose.

'Is there no way you can be released from the contract?' I ask.

'I don't think so. If I try to leave, I'd never be able to play again. I'd lose the viola. They'd make sure that I don't get any performance opportunities. Everyone thinks the world of Venetia and Karl.'

'On a scale of one to ten, how much do you enjoy playing the viola?'

Sophie looks at me as if I'm insane. 'A million! It's my life! If I couldn't play the viola I might as well be dead. Music is everything to me. Everything.'

'If there was nothing holding you back, what would your life look like?'

She opens her mouth, but no words come out. For the first time, it's as if she's finding it hard to articulate her thoughts.

'Let's put that another way. If you were free of the Edstols, what would you be doing?'

'I'd be studying at The Royal Academy of Music in London and be playing chamber music...and perhaps I'd have the occasional solo with an orchestra. I'd be studying and earning money, and I'd be written up as the one to watch! And I would definitely play with pop bands as well, to ring the changes.' Sophie's face lights up at the thought, and then it falls again. 'But that will never happen. The only time someone leaves the Edstols is in a coffin.'

Sophie makes the comment as an insignificant throw-away, but I am deeply startled. I try to compose myself and not let it show on my face.

'What can I do to support you, Sophie?'

'Help me get out?' She leans forwards, her eyes beseeching.

'I'm a psychologist, not a lawyer or a detective. Haven't you got another family member? Your father?'

'He left when I was a baby. I don't know him. And no. There is no one else. It was hard enough for me to get away to see you. I said I was going to the doctors. Severe period pains. I know you don't want to talk about Cat or Alice, but if you want to help me...and you do, don't you...?' She peers at me.

'Yes, I do,' I say, wondering what I am getting myself into.

'Then we have to talk about them. Because I'm scared. It might happen to me too.'

'What might happen?'

'Being kidnapped or abducted.'

'But you said you thought Cat had run away?'

'That's what Christophe thinks, but I think that's bullshit. If she was going to run away, she'd have gone with Vadim.'

'Vadim being?'

'The guy playing second violin. They are in love.' Sophie sighs.

'Mrs Edstol said that they discourage relationships.'

Sophie nods. 'Strictly forbidden, more to the point. But they didn't know about Cat and Vadim. I used to cover for them. Cat would never have not turned up to a concert she was performing at with Vadim. I think they found out about their relationship and somehow got rid of Cat.'

This seems a little far-fetched to me.

'Vadim is distraught. And that's why I know something bad has happened to her.'

'Has Vadim spoken up about this?'

'No. He received a text from Cat saying she'd run away and that he shouldn't come looking for her. He doesn't believe that, and I don't either, but everyone else does. Vadim has to toe the line otherwise he'll be out on his ear. It's tough enough for us Brits, but Vadim is Russian, so he'd be chucked out of Europe as well. He'd go home with nothing.'

'And Alice. Why do you think something has happened to her?'

'The last time an Edstol student screwed up a major performance was in my first year there. She was called Sarah Bellingham. Look her up on the internet. Her body was found washed up on a beach somewhere near Brighton.'

I stare at Sophie. Am I dealing with a delusional young woman or are the Edstol's really as evil as she is making out? There is little doubt that she is genuinely scared, so it is up to Joe and me to discover if there is justification for her fears.

'By the way, I've brought you something in lieu of payment.' She reaches into her pocket and produces a delicate ring set with a tiny diamond.

'It was Mum's. It's all I've got to give you, but I've got a good feeling about you. I really think you can help.'

I hand it back to her. 'I couldn't possibly accept this, Sophie. You wear it and remember the happy times you had with your mother.'

After Sophie leaves, I go to the kitchen and pour myself a glass of wine. I sit for a long time, stroking Mungo and taking small sips. There Sophie is, out in the world, motherless. And here I am, bereft of a daughter. I need to save those families from going through what I been through. Not knowing where your child is, not knowing what has happened to them, that is worse than death.

15

'Sophie, what did the doctor say?' Venetia accosts Sophie upon her return from seeing Pippa Durrant.

'It's nothing much. Just period pains. Told me to take regular Paracetamol and Ibuprofen. Have you heard anything from Cat or Alice?' Sophie hopes her red cheeks don't give away the lie.

Venetia's face clouds over. 'No, I'm sick with worry. The police have filed a report, but they consider Cat low risk. No physical or mental illnesses, she hasn't been acting out of character and she's an adult. Frankly, I think it's because they're overworked and can't be bothered. I've asked Karl to call a meeting so we can pull our own resources together. But we need to look after you, dear girl.'

'And Alice? Any word on Alice?'

Venetia turns her back to Sophie and shuffles some music around on the desk.

Briefly, Sophie closes her eyes. She wonders how Venetia would react to what she wants to suggest.

'You know that psychologist? I think she's a good woman. How about we get her on side?'

Venetia chews the side of her lip. Sophie knows what the answer will be and, sure enough, her guess is word perfect. 'I'll discuss it with Karl.'

VENETIA AND KARL are screaming at each other. It happens on average once a month, which Sophie assumes is normal in a marriage. As neither she nor Cat had, or have, any other role models, it is difficult for them to tell. Usually the pupils would stay well away, terrified that Karl's temper might be taken out on them, but today things are far from normal. So, rather than retreating to her small bedroom, Sophie tiptoes along the corridor and stands outside Karl's office, her ear up against the door.

'You've done it again, haven't you?' Venetia sobs.

Karl's voice is low, too quiet for Sophie to make out the words. But then she hears something smashing, clattering against the wall, which reverberates on the other side. Sophie jumps, her heart slamming into her chest cavity.

'I bloody well have not! She's like a daughter to me!' Karl yells. 'I keep my promises, unlike you! How dare you accuse me. All I do is for this place and for you.'

'So where is she?' Venetia's voice has a pleading, desperate edge.

'How many times do I have to tell you, I don't know!'

'Now the police are aware of your background, if they find out about this, you'll be banned from teaching. We'll have to shut the school down. I can't believe you've been so bloody stupid!' Venetia is hissing now.

Sophie's hand is over her mouth. What has Karl done? And are their futures really in jeopardy? Sophie is torn. On the one hand, it would be wonderful to be set free. On the other, the prospect is terrifying.

'The two are totally different, Venetia. You are overreacting. As far as I'm concerned, Alice can go to hell! I don't give a fuck about her or her parents. She's cost us and Jonno a bloody fortune. If she's never seen again, that's a day too soon for me.'

'You really don't know where she is?' Venetia's voice sounds more controlled now.

'No, I do not!' Karl yells.

'How badly was he hurt?'

'I don't know. Stop being so melodramatic, woman. He had a black eye. Nothing more. Besides, no one saw me. We're perfectly safe. Let's just concentrate on what matters.'

'Finding Cat,' Venetia says quietly. There is a pause, and Sophie wonders if she should scarper before one of them comes out and spots her eavesdropping. But then Venetia speaks. 'You promise you haven't done it again. You wouldn't to Cat, would you?'

And this time it sounds as if Karl slams the piano lid down and kicks the stool across the room. Sophie doesn't hang around. She runs as quickly as she can, racing back towards her bedroom.

'What's the hurry?' Christophe says languidly. He is leaning against the wall in the stairwell just outside the downstairs corridor—the boys' corridor. The girls' rooms are upstairs.

'Venetia and Karl are having a massive argument.'

'What's new?' Christophe puffs out some air. Sophie smells the stale weed and cigarette smoke. She wrinkles her nose.

'Karl's hurt someone. It sounds like he's done something really bad.'

'He's probably got Cat,' Christophe muses, kicking the toes of his shoe against the skirting board. 'I bet he's a perv.'

'He wouldn't be allowed to teach if he was,' Sophie says, but then she remembers all of the historic sex abuse cases in music schools and she wonders. Karl has never been suggestive towards her, but then she is rarely taught by him and, besides, Sophie knows she's not a looker. Not like Cat, anyway.

'Are you serious?' Sophie says.

Christophe shrugs.

'For goodness' sake don't say anything to Vadim. He'll freak if he thinks Karl has got anything to do with Cat's disappearance,' Sophie says.

'That would be amusing.' Christophe smirks. 'I wonder what—'

'What would be amusing?' Vadim appears. Sophie hopes he didn't overhear the earlier part of their conversation.

'Nothing,' she says hurriedly.

'Any news on Cat?' His Russian accent is heavy today. Sophie can see why Cat fell for him, with his square jaw and inky hair and dark stubble that appears within a couple of hours of shaving. He mutters something in Russian which the others don't understand. Sophie would like to give Vadim a hug. In some ways, he plays the violin even better than Cat, especially romantic pieces and anything melancholic. But he's a boy and he's foreign, and he's not an Edstol. Sophie wonders if he minds that he is always on second violin, always the runner up to Cat.

'Tomorrow you're going to be meeting a woman called Doctor Durrant. She's a psychologist and has been sent on behalf of the police.'

They all jump at the sound of Venetia's voice. Not one of them heard her footsteps and as Sophie looks down at her feet, she realises why. Venetia is wearing her normal heavy-weight dark brown woollen tights but, most unusually, she isn't wearing shoes.

'Why?' Christophe asks.

'We had a choice. Either you are interviewed by an advanced suspect interviewer...'

'What's that?' Christophe interrupts.

'A senior police officer at the station.'

'Why the hell do they want to interview us?' Christophe scowls and crosses his arms. Vadim leans back against the wall and closes his eyes. Sophie peers at him, concerned he is about to faint.

'If you let me finish,' Venetia says. 'Rather than be subject to specialist interviews, they have suggested that you all speak to the police psychologist woman. Apparently she is worried about your wellbeing and also wants to get more information from you about Cat.'

'And Alice?' Sophie asks.

'I suppose so.' Venetia waves her hand dismissively.

'Do we have any choice in this matter?' Christophe can't stand still, whereas Vadim is as motionless as a statue, his eyes now closed.

'No, you don't. Lunchtime tomorrow morning in the Common Room,' Venetia says, swivelling around and padding silently back down the corridor.

16

The Viscount and Viscountess Sneddon live in a castle. It is quite the most extraordinary building, set deep in the Sussex countryside and approached by a long track interspersed with cattle grids. The building rises up out of the ground unexpectedly and, at first, I think it is a Norman castle with battlements at the top of the large stone walls and two circular towers either side of the entrance.

'It's a mock castle,' Joe says, glancing at me leaning forwards. 'Built in 1883 and it's been in Viscountess Sneddon's family ever since.'

'How do you...?' But then I stop. I have come to learn that DS Joe Swain does his research. When we were in Holland a couple of months ago, solving a murder case in the horticultural industry, Joe stunned me with his knowledge of history and all the places we visited. I assume that attention to detail and curiosity is what makes him such a successful police officer.

As we drive in through the central archway, I realise that this building suffers from the same lack of upkeep as both the Edstols' house and Alice's home. It is as if the money has run out. An old washing machine stands by a side door, rusted, looking as if it has been there for some time. A couple of planters either side of the front door contain dead plants.

'They used to call this place the mini-Glyndebourne,' Joe says. 'Marissa Sneddon was one of the world's leading harpists. All the good and the great would congregate here for house parties and soirées filled with music. It is said that their ball-room has some of the best acoustics in the south of England.'

'But no longer?'

Joe shakes his head. 'I can't find out why, but Marissa hasn't performed in years.'

The front door swings open before we are out of the car. He is a small man wearing startling orange corduroy trousers, a navy jumper and a necktie. I am surprised to note that he also wears a single earring, a small gold hoop.

'Thank you for coming,' he says, crossing his arms across his chest. His accent is definitely more south London than upper class aristocracy. 'It's a fucking disaster.' Viscount Sneddon directs all his comments and questions to Joe.

We follow him inside, past a full suit of armour on the left and an array of swords on the back wall. The space is dark, cold, and smells dank. I wish I was wearing gloves and a hat. He leads us into the kitchen. It is a large room, which must have been modernised in the 1960s, as every surface is covered in wood look-alike Formica. The large oven is also ancient, and I can't see a fridge. He gestures for us to sit at the round pine table. Disappointingly, the view out of the window is of a large grey stone wall.

'Kaya!' he yells.

A large woman with a kindly face bustles into the kitchen carrying a tea towel and what looks like a child's beaker. She is wearing an apron and has bare legs.

'Yes, sir,' she says demurely.

'Can you get us all a coffee.'

She nods and turns towards the counter, filling up the kettle. The tap makes loud gurgling noises as the water pours out.

'My Guarneri violin has gone missing. I expect Cat Kingsley has stolen it. It's more than expensive. It was last valued at £3.2 million. I'm putting in an insurance claim, but my broker said I need to let you guys know. I need a case number or something.'

'Isn't it rather premature to be claiming for it? There is every chance that Cat Kingsley will reappear at any moment, along with your violin,' Joe says.

Jonno scowls.

'Do you have an extensive collection of instruments?' I ask.

Jonno stares at me, as if noticing me for the first time. 'What has that got to do with anything?'

His aggression bemuses me. I wonder what this man is so angry about. Kaya deposits three cups of coffee on the table, along with a small, chipped mug of milk and a pot of sugar, and scuttles out of the room.

'I am a collector. I know everybody within the world of classical music. I make things happen. The Edstols are losing their way. It is a joke!'

'Are you suggesting that they and Cat Kingsley appropriated the instrument?' Joe asks.

Jonno puts his elbows on the table and leans forwards. 'How much do you know about antique classical instruments?'

'Very little,' Joe admits.

'It's all about provenance. It isn't possible just to sell my instruments. They are collector's pieces and they don't go onto the open market. The occasional Strad might be sold at auction by Christie's or Beares, but mostly they pass between people in the know. No one will be able to sell the violin I loaned Cat, or if they do, they'll only get a fraction of its real value. My view is, Cat has either willingly, or by force, sold it to a middleman who has been tasked with stealing to order for resale within the cabal of international collectors. Of course, it can never be played in public because too many questions will be asked. So it'll be kept in a room with perfect humidity and temperature and slowly but surely the instrument's soul will be lost. So you, Detective Swain—' He points his finger at Joe. '—you need to use all your skills to find the instrument for me. It's a piece of history and I want it back. And if I can't get it back, I damn well want the money, and fast.'

'You didn't answer the question as to whether you have a collection of instruments,' Joe says.

'I did have a collection.' He glances away and catches sight of Kaya hovering in the doorway. 'What is it?' he snaps.

'Madam is asking for you.'

Jonno's face softens. 'Tell her I'll be along as soon as I can.'

'I understand your wife is a fine harpist?' I say.

'Was.' Jonno stares at the window. 'She has a rare degenerative disease and can no longer play. Keep that one out of the press, okay!' He wags that finger at us again. 'We don't want anyone's pity.'

'How well did you know Cat Kingsley?' Joe asks.

'Well enough.'

'It's just you seem very concerned with the whereabouts of your violin, but haven't expressed any concern for the well-being of the young lady. And you've been quick to accuse her.' Joe tilts his head to one side.

'Why should I be worried about her?'

'It is normal to express greater concern about a person than an object.'

'Cat Kingsley is nothing to do with me and most probably a thief. Don't try and twist things to make me look like the bad guy here. Let's concentrate on the matter to hand. Take these.'

He shoves a pile of documents across the table towards Joe, who picks them up one by one.

'Certificate of authenticity, insurance documents, receipts

and photographs. You'll need all of those when putting information out to Interpol.'

'Interpol?' Joe asks.

'For God's sake, I thought you knew what you were doing!'

'Of course, we will do our very best to assist,' Joe says, collecting the papers and standing up. 'We will be back in touch when we have further information or require any more information from you.'

This time it is my phone that rings. I fumble in my bag, embarrassed, as I was sure that I had switched it off. I pick it up just as it stops ringing. And then it rings again.

'Excuse me,' I say. 'I need to step outside.'

I don't wait for any comment from either of the men and hurriedly walk out into the gloomy corridor.

'What's up, Sophie?'

'I didn't tell you and I should have done. Alice, she's been cutting herself and I don't think anyone knows. I'm just worried something bad has happened to her. I can't stop thinking about it.'

I pace farther up the corridor. 'Have you any means of getting hold of her?'

Sophie sniffs. 'I sent her a text message asking if she's ok, but she didn't reply. Besides, I don't really know her that well. She's a lot younger than me.'

I suppose four years between the ages of sixteen and twenty is a lot.

'The rumour is that she's been kicked out. I don't know, Dr Durrant. I've just got a really bad feeling.'

I can't work out if Sophie is being hysterical. 'Why don't you go and talk to Venetia?' I suggest. 'And call me back later when you have more news.'

'Okay. Thanks.' She sniffs and hangs up.

I am about to turn around the way I came when I hear a strange noise coming from an adjacent room with a door just a couple of inches ajar. Gently, I push it open. There is a woman sitting in a wheelchair, her eyes staring at me with a look of terror. She starts garbling, but I don't understand.

'I'm sorry,' I say hurriedly, leaving the room. And in my rush, I turn left instead of right and find myself in a vast room that, other than a sofa and a couple of chairs covered with dust sheets, is totally empty. Based on the parquet floor, tall windows and ornate chandeliers, I assume this must have been a ballroom. But now it has an air of sad decay and it sends shivers down my spine.

17

'What an unpleasant little man,' I say to Joe as soon as we're safely ensconced in his car.

'Quite. It's a strange set-up, isn't it?'

But before we can discuss things further, his phone rings. I wait, trying to work out who is calling.

'That was Miss Ethel Smith. It appears that someone has turned up at the Jones's house; someone she doesn't know. I think it would be worthwhile popping in on our way back to yours.'

'If we're quick,' I say, glancing at my watch. I do not want to be late for my next client.

❧

THE JONES'S front door is ajar.

'Hello!' Joe shouts. 'Can we come in?'

A couple of moments later, an elderly man shuffles forwards, his legs bowed at an almost impossible angle.

'Who are you?' he asks. His face is as wrinkled as a walnut.

Joe introduces us both.

The man pales. 'Have you heard anything? It's me that's reported them missing.'

'As far as we know, nothing.'

'My Bill, he rings me every morning at 8 a.m. and every evening at 6.30 p.m. to speak to his mum and me. She's got dementia, but it keeps us going having those phone calls. He hasn't rung since Saturday lunchtime. All excited he was that young Alice was off to London to play the violin. Nothing since then. I know it doesn't sound long to most people, but our Bill is good to us. We've never had a day when he hasn't called. Never. I've got their key, you see.' He holds it up. 'Bill hasn't told Martha he gave it to me. Sour cow she is. So I came over to check everything's all right. But they're not here.'

'Could we come in?' Joe asks.

The man dodders to one side and we walk past him.

'We understand that the performance didn't go quite to plan in London,' Joe says. 'And Alice hasn't been seen since. But if she is with her parents, then surely there is nothing to worry about?'

'Oh dear,' he says, his rough fingers scratching his face.

'Would it be all right if we have a quick look around, just to see if we can find their passports and such like? Perhaps they have gone on holiday for a few days.'

He shakes his head vigorously. 'They've got no money for holidays. Bill would never jet off without telling me. Never. And I rang his office and they say he hasn't been in and he hasn't rung. He's as regular as clockwork is our Bill. I can feel it in my bones, there's something amiss. You'll find them, won't you?'

'We will do our very best,' Joe reassures.

I feel this elderly man's pain and wish I could hug him and make all of that terrifying unknowing go away.

'Have a snoop round, see if you can find anything. If Martha objects, I'll deal with it. Me legs won't get me up those stairs.'

In contrast to the exterior, this is a scrupulously clean and tidy house, so much so, it feels unlived in. There are no pictures on the magnolia-painted walls, no little trinkets on the mantlepiece or the normal kitchen accoutrements on work counters.

'Is it always this tidy?' I ask.

'Martha likes things just so. Everything has to be put away, cushions plumped up. That's why me and the wife don't come here no more. We don't feel welcomed and the wife, well, she forgets where she puts things and Martha gets all up tight. Bill brings our Alice over to see us. It's much better like that. Not that we don't like Martha. Don't get me wrong. She's a good wife, a good mother; it's just she likes things her way. You know what I mean?'

I nod and follow Joe upstairs. It feels as if we are trespassing and I had assumed we would need a warrant to search someone's house. With the single bed covered with a pink throw and a music stand in the middle of the room, it's obvious which is Alice's room.

'Have a good look, Pippa please. I'll go around the rest of the house.'

'What am I looking for?'

'Anything to suggest where they might have gone.'

I am savvy enough about teenage girls to know that if I want to understand Alice, I need to find her diary. Trying to reassure myself that I'm not snooping but helping out, I pull out her bedside table drawers, look in her small wardrobe and then run my hand underneath the mattress. My fingers encounter a small book. It is exactly what I'm looking for. But it's one thing finding someone's diary and quite another to actually read it.

'Joe,' I call. He reappears. 'I've found this.'

'We'll bag it up and get Grandpa Jones's permission to take it away.'

We go back downstairs. The old man is sitting at the small kitchen table looking quite desolate.

'I assume you've tried calling their mobiles?' Joe asks.

'Of course,' he says. 'But the car's still here. And according to Miss Snoop from next door, it's been here for the past five days. It doesn't make no sense. My boy Bill would never just disappear.'

When Joe asks if we can take the diary, he just waves his hand. 'Do whatever you can to find 'em and bring 'em home safe 'n' sound. Especially my Bill and our precious Alice.'

When we're back in the car I tell Joe, 'Sophie said that Alice was cutting herself.'

Joe grimaces. 'Sounds like she was a very unhappy kid.'

'Most likely under a huge amount of pressure,' I suggest.

'We need to talk to the other kids at the Edstol's Academy. Whether it's sinister or not, something untoward is going on and we need to get to the bottom of it. Right now, it looks as if we have one missing young person, one missing family and a priceless violin that has gone walk-about. I'll request resources be put onto the case.'

Police Constable Mia Brevant, the young, highly competent policewoman who works for Joe, rings me later in the day.

'DS Swain has spoken to the Edstols and, rather than bringing in a specialist member of the policing team to interview the pupils, he suggested to the Edstols that you speak to the other members of the quartet in your capacity as a psychologist. At this point we have no evidence to suggest a crime has actually taken place, it's just a MisPer.'

'Misper?'

'Missing person,' Mia explains. I try not to shiver in response to her throw-away phrase, 'It's just a MisPer.' 'DS Swain would like you to go over to Edstol's this evening or tomorrow.'

I am annoyed with Joe. It's a cheek to think that I can just drop all my plans and be at his beck and call. On the other hand, I would like to help. There is something very odd going on and if I can lend some psychological support to a bunch of talented and committed kids, then that would be worthwhile indeed. But I'm too tired, too emotionally wrung out to meet them tonight. I promise Mia that I will visit the school again tomorrow.

When Mia says, 'Your normal rates will apply,' I smile.

'And Doctor Durrant,' she goes on to say. 'I've had a read through Alice Jones's diary. She is a very troubled girl. It sounds like she loves playing the violin, but there are some pages that are completely illegible, and I fear it could be from smudging from her tears. The boss has asked if you would read it and give us your thoughts. He mentioned that you are a graphologist as well.'

'Of course I will,' I promise.

18

I stand outside the locked door and listen. She's crying again. I didn't know anyone could shed so many tears. It's getting boring now. She needs to pull herself together.

'Are you there?' she shouts. 'Let me out! Please let me out!'

I hammer on the door and can hear her shuffling away. 'Shut up!' I yell. 'I need you to bloody well shut up!'

I pace backwards and forwards. She can scream and shout all she wants. No one is going to hear her out here, but it's doing my head in.

'My violin! Please give me my violin!' Her voice is softer now, hiccupping and plaintive. And I don't have any bloody violin. I walk back upstairs, blinking hard as I adjust to the daylight. Perhaps I should get her a violin. If it will calm her down, make her more malleable, that would be a good thing. Because if she doesn't pull herself together, I will lose it. And if I lose it, then that will be the end of her. And that would be a shame, because I have bigger plans for her.

Yes. I will get her a violin.

I go back down into the basement.

'If you shut up, I'll get you a violin. But if I hear another word or sob, there'll be no violin. Do you understand?'

I put my ear to the door.

'Yes,' she whispers.

19

Vadim, Christophe and Sophie are waiting for me in what Venetia refers to as the Common Room. It is a large room with a haphazard collection of old sofas and armchairs, most probably charity shop rejects. There are posters attached to the walls, mainly artists' impressions of composers.

The three young people are sitting in different parts of the room as if in a doctor's waiting room and strangers to each other.

'Let's shift the furniture around a bit,' I suggest. 'A circle would be good.'

I push an armchair towards a cherry-red sofa with fraying fabric on the arms. Sophie pushes a green armchair. The boys stand there, not helping. When we have arranged things to my satisfaction, I sit in one of the armchairs and motion for them to sit on the sofa and the remaining armchair. Sophie flops into the armchair and then flicks her shoes off before curling her legs under her. This leaves the boys to perch on the sofa. I notice that they sit as far from each other as possible, each leaning onto their respective sofa arms to put maximum distance between their bodies. They don't need to open their mouths for me to know that there is friction between these two.

'I want to assure you that everything that is said in this room this morning will stay confidential and will not be passed on to anyone.'

'Not even the police?' Vadim asks.

'Unless I believe anyone is at risk or that the law has been broken, not even the police.'

'Or the Edstols?' Sophie whispers.

'Nobody,' I confirm. 'I would ask the same of you. What is said in this room stays in this room. Do you agree?'

They all nod.

'I have had the opportunity to speak to Sophie and get to know her a little, but Vadim, I haven't even said hello to you. Can you tell me a bit about yourself, please?' I smile at him.

He looks down at his brown leather loafers. When he speaks, he glances upwards through long, dark lashes.

'I am Russian, so my English is not so good. I came here two years ago. Karl Edstol found me when I won the Isayev Olegovich Violin Competition. I like it here very much.'

Christophe rolls his eyes.

'And when did you last see Cat?'

Vadim looks up at the ceiling now, through a black, silky lock of hair. 'Saturday morning at breakfast.'

'Really?' Christophe says sarcastically as he crosses his arms across his chest.

Vadim pales a little and, as he looks towards the floor, a large teardrop hovers on the end of his lashes and plops heavily onto the knee of his midnight blue cotton trousers.

'Are you close to Cat?' I ask.

He shuts his eyes and nods.

'Of course he is bloody close to Cat. He was in her knickers,' Christophe spits.

'She is your girlfriend?' I lean towards Vadim, but he keeps his eyes closed. I touch his knee, but he is motionless.

'He can't admit to it. It's against the rules,' Sophie says.

'You can admit to anything here. What you tell me is safe.'

Vadim opens his eyes and silently shakes his head. I decide to change track.

'Christophe, please tell me about you.'

He leans back into the sofa and also avoids eye contact with me, letting out his words in a monotone as if he is bored. 'Came here five years ago. Dad's a conductor, travels all over the world. Famous. Wealthy, thanks to his capitalist parents. Mother buggered off when I was a toddler. Wish I could get out of this hell-hole, but I can't. I tend not to bother with breakfast, so I didn't see Cat on Saturday morning.'

'What is your relationship with Cat?'

His laugh sounds strangled. 'What relationship?'

'Do you get on with her?'

'Everyone loves our Cat!' Christophe mocks.

'Except you?'

'I didn't say that.' His body language is all over the place; he is nodding when he says no, playing with his hair, his foot is jumping up and down. Christophe is at best very uncomfortable; at worst, he is lying.

'It's true what Christophe says,' Sophie interjects. 'Everyone loves Cat. You had your first kiss with Cat, didn't you Christophe?'

He glares at her and she smirks in return. Vadim shivers.

'Do any of you know who might want to harm Cat?'

'That's a bit dramatic, isn't it?' Christophe scowls. 'I expect she's just managed to do what we all dream of—making her big escape.'

'Christophe is probably right,' Sophie yawns.

'She wouldn't go without me,' Vadim interjects quietly.

'You're deluding yourself, mate,' Christophe says. 'Cat

couldn't risk you opening your big mouth. I'm sure she's just done a runner or maybe hooked up with another lover. Are you not up to it, little Cossack?'

Vadim jumps up, grabs the neckline of Christophe's T-shirt and hauls him up.

'Whoah!' Christophe shouts. 'Take it easy!"

'Vadim!' I yell. 'Let him go and sit down!'

I am shaken. I wasn't expecting violence. Vadim lets Christophe go reluctantly, but he spits before turning away.

'I leave now,' he says and strides to the door.

I let him go.

'Well, that was a great success,' Christophe sneers as he rubs at his neck, sinking back down into the sofa.

'Do you enjoy playing the cello, Christophe?'

He looks at me as if that is the most ridiculous and banal statement he has ever heard. 'Of course I do. It's the only thing I can do. It's my life.'

I nod. Sophie used almost exactly the same words when she told me about her love of viola playing.

'So although you all resent the contract under which you are here, music-making is your passion?'

'You couldn't do what we do if you didn't love it,' Sophie says. 'We each practice for six or seven hours a day. We dream with music in our ears. The only way we truly know how to communicate is with music. We want to change people through our playing. I would cease to exist if I couldn't make music.'

'And you agree, Christophe?'

He nods.

'Correct me if I'm wrong, but that attitude seems quite at odds with the atmosphere of fear that I pick up on here. Why do I sense a tension?'

'Because we're slaves,' Sophie says. 'We're slaves to the music, we're slaves to the Edstols, and even though we are born to express ourselves through our music, we're stifled. We have to do it the way our teachers tell us to.'

'Beautifully summed up,' Christophe says, nibbling at the edge of his thumbnail.

'And if you don't?' I ask.

Sophie and Christophe look at each other, their foreheads creased with frowns.

'Don't even go there,' Sophie says.

20

J onno is hunched over his laptop. His desk is covered in letters, many of which are final demands typed in red. But his concentration is on the latest article written by Doctor Geoff Snyder, a leading Canadian scientist researching gene transfer for Inclusion Body Myositis. It's difficult to understand for a lay person, but Jonno needs to comprehend the implications of the discovery. It could be the difference between life and death for Marissa.

They first noticed something was wrong when Marissa began making mistakes on pieces she had been playing since childhood. She was playing Chopin's Etude No. 13 in A flat major, Op. 25, arranged for harp, when the fingers of her left hand slipped as she played the opening arpeggios. Thinking she was overtired from too many concerts, and perhaps coming down with a virus, she stood up to wheel the harp to the side of the room, when her legs gave way. In those early weeks, as is so often the case with rare illnesses, Marissa trailed from doctor to doctor and received numerous misdiagnoses. When Jonno and Marissa were told that there was no cure, that she had IBM,

Marissa had laughed. 'For heaven's sake. Can't I at least have an illness named after an instrument, not a computer!'

Jonno didn't laugh. He was angry. Livid, in fact. Their life-style, their wealth, their fame, was all constructed around Marissa and her harp-playing. A year later and the disease had progressed with terrifying speed, reducing Marissa to life in a wheelchair, an invalid without the use of fingers or limbs. Jonno's anger eventually dissipated and he became single-minded. He would find a cure because Marissa must play again. And so he has dedicated the past five years to funding and spearheading research, ensuring that Marissa is the first in the queue for clinical trials, wherever in the world they might be taking place. That process has been all-consuming—finan-cially, emotionally and time-wise.

When Kaya knocks gently on his study door and says, 'DS Swain is here to see you,' Jonno ignores her. His mind is on Snyder, the man he believes is a miracle-maker.

'Viscount Sneddon?' Joe coughs as he enters the room.

'A moment!' Jonno holds his hand up and remains crouched over his laptop.

Joe paces around the study. It has dark oak-panelled walls and heavy dark-green brocade curtains, giving it the feel of a gentleman's club. Jonno's desk is littered with papers and scien-tific journals. There is a large picture in a silver frame of Marissa playing the harp, her blonde hair gently curling onto her bare shoulders, her face beatific. But the room is freezing cold and it smells damp and unused. Joe shivers. He wonders when they last heated the house.

Eventually Jonno slams the lid down on his laptop and turns to face Joe. He is wearing three thick knit jumpers. The red one hangs low onto his hands, the turquoise jumper extends below his waist-line, and the jumper on top is a thick, navy fisherman's rib.

'I trust you're here with news on the whereabouts of my violin.'

'Unfortunately we don't have leads as of yet.'

'What the hell have you been doing?' Jonno's lips curl. He huffs and waves his hands around again. 'So why are you here?'

'I would like to ask you some questions about the violin's valuation. That is why I requested the presence of your broker too. Will he be joining us?'

'Milo? He's a law unto himself. Might, might not.' Jonno has not passed on the request. The last thing he wants is his idiot brother tying them up in knots. He doesn't ask Joe to sit down, but the policeman sits anyway in the claret red leather armchair. Jonno is surprisingly intimidated by Joe's size but when they're sitting, the differential in bulk is less obvious.

'How did your broker establish the value of the violin?'

Jonno rolls his eyes. 'He's a valuer too. It's what the market can bear. A combination of what I paid for it, provenance, current auction values, etc.'

'What did you pay for it?'

'Can't remember exactly. Around the one-million mark, I think,' Jonno blusters.

'Rather a substantial hike in its value, then.'

As Jonno leans forwards on the desk, his elbows dislodge a journal that tumbles to the ground. Joe bends down to pick it up.

'Are you a scientist, Viscount Sneddon?'

'It's Lord Sneddon when addressing me in conversation.'

The grin Joe tries to suppress infuriates Jonno.

'I don't know what you're trying to insinuate,' Jonno says, 'but the valuation of the Guarneri is, if anything, understated. If you bothered to do some research, you'd know that the Vieuxtemps Guarneri was sold for over 16 million dollars in 2013. Both the Kochanski Guarneri and the Mary Portman Guarneri are worth in excess of ten million dollars each.'

'So why is your Guarneri worth that much less?'

'It's not like buying a bloody car that comes off a factory line. Each one is made by hand. They have different registers, deep, dark sounds that project through a concert hall, dramatic and lush, and sometimes an annoying wolf on the high C on the G string.'

'A wolf?'

'It's a beating sound that happens when the resonance frequency of the string and instrument interact with each other to produce another noise, but it's totally irrelevant to this conversation. Get to the point, will you? I've got a lot to do.'

'Has your broker submitted a claim for the missing violin?'

'Not yet, but as you've made no progress, I will tell him to do so.'

'Do you have any other valuable instruments?'

'Nope.'

'I note that there's a County Court Judgement Order against you. Could you explain that?'

'My personal financial affairs are none of your bloody business!' Jonno's face turns an alarming crimson.

'It seems that you are in some financial difficulty, and I was wondering why you haven't sold the Guarneri to pay off your debts?'

'For the same bloody reason I'm still living in this hell hole! It belongs to my wife. This place is her home and the instruments were, are, all hers.'

'Instruments?'

'There was a collection. I had to sell off some, otherwise the rain would be leaking onto your bloody head.'

'And your scientific work, does that bring in any income?'

'It's none of your damned business! But for the record, I am not a scientist. I am researching methods to cure my wife, working closely with some of the best brains in medicine.'

'Does that involve funding research?'

Jonno turns redder still. He stands, places his palms on his desk and leans forwards. Joe recoils slightly as a whiff of stale alcohol weaves towards him.

'Unless you intend to bring charges against me or unless you have some proper information for me on what has happened to my instrument, I would like you to leave. I don't appreciate your insinuations.'

'Have you committee insurance fraud, Lord Sneddon?'

'How dare you!'

Joe stands up. As he walks towards the door, he turns back to face Jonno.

'You haven't asked if we have any information on the where-abouts of Cat. Are you interested to know about your benefi-ciary? A young woman with a lifetime ahead of her, possibly one of the best violinists of her generation?

'Get out!' Jonno screams.

21

Christophe has been uploading videos to YouTube for nearly a year. He picked up a Fender Aerodyne electric bass guitar on Craig's List for a fraction of its real value, and keeps it hidden in the back of his wardrobe. It's not that they're forbidden to play any other instruments or even playing pop or rock; it's just that Christophe has plans that he intends to keep to himself.

His videos cut off his face, so all they show are his slender dancing fingers and occasionally a foot hammering the ground in time with the heavy beat. To begin with, Christophe recorded covers of popular songs, turning them into rock, adding head-banging beats via the computer. He's even slipped in a few classical numbers, modernising Bach and Mozart; although few would recognise them as such. The number of views has topped 119,000 but he's not earning any money from YouTube—he daren't risk it. And he still hasn't received that elusive message from the music agent interested in signing him. Christophe's head is in turmoil. What with everything that's going on—Cat, Alice and now the involvement of the psychologist woman—all Christophe wants to do is run. Instead, he rolls a joint, switches off the lights in his bedroom and draws the dope into his lungs, holding it there until he can feel his body relaxing.

Normally Christophe opens the window when he's smoking. His room is at the back of the house, looking over the gardens towards the area that was once the kitchen gardens and is now the compost heap and the place where the gardener (who visits twice a month in the summer only) burns garden waste. No one ever goes there, so the stench weaves it way out unnoticed. Or so Christophe assumes. But today he's not concentrating, and just as he's relaxing into a calming blackness, there is an almighty din as the fire alarm sounds off.

'Fuck!' he says, rolling out of bed and turning the light on. There is a blue-grey haze in his room, so he throws the window open as wide as possible before stubbing out his butt and chucking it out the window. He can hear the others scurrying along the corridor and down the stairs to congregate outside by the front door.

When he joins them, Venetia is there with her clipboard and a scowl across her face.

'Sorry, Venetia. It was probably me. No need to call the fire brigade,' Christophe says as he sidles up.

'What do you mean, it was you?' she asks, her left hand on her hip.

'I was having a smoke.' A grin creeps over Christophe's face, and then a giggle forms in his chest like a little bubble rising to the surface. How ridiculous that, at twenty-one, he has to abide by these petty rules designed for youngsters. 'I *am* old enough!' he says, smirking.

Venetia turns away from him and strides towards Karl. 'Go and check Christophe's room. If all is ok, you can cancel the fire brigade call-out.'

The other pupils are hanging around shivering, thin arms around slender bodies. The fire alarm goes off with great regularity so there is no sense of concern, just annoyance at the inconvenience.

After ten minutes or so, Karl returns. 'Everyone, back inside!' he yells.

'Not you!' He points a finger at Christophe.

Sophie raises an eyebrow and gives Christophe a little prod in his back. 'Good luck!' she whispers.

The fire brigade have had so many false call outs to the Academy that they are prepared to cancel on Venetia or Karl's say-so, which is contrary to normal protocol but a sensible use of resources. After Venetia has made the phone call, she follows Christophe and Karl back into Karl's office.

'Oh shit,' Christophe mutters as he sees what is on Karl's desk.

'Is this your guitar?' Karl asks.

'Yes. There's nothing stopping me from owning an electric guitar.' Christophe stands in a slouch.

'And is this your laptop?'

'Yes.'

'What are you uploading to YouTube?' Karl narrows his eyes at Christophe.

'That's none of your bloody business.' Christophe fidgets.

'Not the right answer!' Karl roars. 'You are forbidden from uploading any music to the internet without our express permission!'

'It is not classical music.'

'Is it any music?' Venetia asks, her voice quiet and calm.

Christophe squirms. 'Yeah. Just not your sort,' he says, mumbling.

'And what is our sort?' Karl shouts.

'Classical.'

'No! Under the terms of your contract, you are forbidden from sharing any music.'

'But this could do the Academy so much good!' Christophe sits down, perching on the edge of the chair.

Karl leans forwards onto his desk. 'I don't give a fuck!'

'Karl!' Venetia frowns.

Christophe leaps up again. 'Well, you should! I'm likely to earn more money playing rock than anyone does playing classical music. It's money you're after, isn't it?'

'You are to close your account immediately. In fact, do it now so I can be sure you've done it.' Karl's face has turned cherry red and a vein is pulsating near his left temple.

'No!' Christophe says. He is jittery and trembling. The effects of the dope have worn off. 'This is my life!'

'You and your father signed the contract—' Karl's voice is low and menacing. '—and you know perfectly well what happens to people who renege on our contract.'

'I'm not scared of you!' Christophe says, but his tone of voice and skittish movements betray him. 'I'll speak to my father—'

Karl laughs. There is a knock on the door.

'Come in!' Karl says.

The door opens and a young girl comes in; she doesn't look much older than thirteen. 'A parcel for you.' She holds the small package out in front of her, as if it is an offering.

'Thank you, Lisl,' Venetia says, taking the brown padded envelope. 'It's addressed to both of us,' Venetia says to Karl.

'Open it!' Karl waves his hand dismissively.

'You need to stop smoking that stuff.' Karl points a finger at Christophe as he sits down too. 'It's against the rules and sets a terrible example for the younger kids. Besides, it's illegal. How would you like it if the police found it? I assure, you jail would be a far worse place than here.'

'They're not going to send me to jail for smoking a bit of weed!' Christophe smirks.

Karl opens his mouth to reply but his words are cut off by

Venetia's scream. She is standing stock still, her eyes so wide and bulbous they look as if they might pop out of her head. The scream goes on and on.

'Shut up, woman!' Karl shouts.

Venetia does as she's told, but she is trembling and swaying from side to side. Then she crumples to the floor like a rag doll. But Christophe and Karl aren't looking at Venetia; they are staring at the small open box Venetia dropped on the edge of Karl's desk.

'What the fuck?' Karl says, peering at the box. A small finger—its delicate nail painted pale blue—lies inside the box, gently cocooned by fluffy cotton wool. Blood is congealed on the cotton wool. Wedged in the side of the box is a note. Karl grabs it.

'Fuck!' he says again. 'Is it real?'

Venetia is coming to, moaning on the carpet. She sits up.

'Are you all right, Venetia?' Christophe says as he bends down.

'Yes. Silly me. It was the shock of it. I'm just feeling a bit dizzy. Can you get me a glass of water, love?'

Christophe rushes out of the room. He runs down the corridor and into his room, slamming the door behind him. He has no intention of fetching Venetia a glass of water.

Venetia remains sitting on the floor. Her wool skirt has ridden up her legs.

'It's Cat's finger,' Karl says. He stares at his wife but makes no effort to bend down to assist her. 'There's a note. It says: "We have Catherine Kingsley. This is her finger. Give us five hundred thousand pounds in cash and we will let her go. If you don't follow our exact orders, we will cut off more of her fingers."'

22

'Will you come with me to the music school? There's been a development,' Joe says.

I have just waved goodbye to my last client of the day and was planning on taking Mungo out for a quick walk around the block. I hesitate. Joe is so matter of fact when we are working on an investigation. He is much better than me at compartmentalising his feelings, a trait that I suppose makes him excel at his job. But I miss his loving attention when we are working together.

'Has Alice been found?'

'No. I'll tell you all when I collect you in twenty minutes. Maybe you could come and stay at mine afterwards? Things will get a bit tricky next week. I'll explain.' Joe doesn't give me the chance to reply and hangs up.

As much as I want to see him, I need more than twenty minutes to sort out the house, pack a bag and walk Mungo. I stand in the middle of the kitchen, blinking rapidly. 'Guess we'd better get a move on!' I say to Mungo, who eyes me with his head cocked to one side.

Barely twenty minutes later, Joe is ringing my doorbell. I

grab the bag whilst Joe takes Mungo's bed and bowls and places them in the back of his car.

'What's happened?' I ask, sliding into the passenger seat and leaning over to kiss his cheek.

'This is no longer just a MisPer. It's a kidnap case and actual bodily harm. The Edstols have received a ransom note, along with what might be Cat's little finger.'

'That's horrible!' I shiver and pull my coat tightly around me.

'Mia is meeting us there. In fact, she's probably already arrived.' Joe puts his foot on the accelerator.

'Are you going to put the blue lights on?' I ask.

He turns and grins at me, then flicks a switch. Soon we are in the fastest car on the road and I grip the edge of the seat as I watch car after car pull over to one side to let us pass. I can't decide if it's terrifying or fun.

Lights are blazing from every window at Edstol's Music Academy. Mia Brevant has parked her marked police car at the front, and hops out when she sees us.

'Pippa, I'd rather you didn't say anything. Just observe, please,' Joe says.

I nod, but it never fails to irk me that one moment Joe wants my help, and the next moment I'm relegated to the third division.

Karl Edstol is already on the doorstep. There is something about his expression that is quite different to before. I need to get nearer to him to work out if it's fear or anger.

'My wife is lying down,' Karl says as he leads us into his office. 'She doesn't cope well with shock.'

He walks around his desk and points at a small white cardboard box. 'I put the lid back on. I can't bear to look at it.'

Joe pulls on a pair of white rubber gloves and lifts the top off. He grimaces.

'I assume from your expression that it's real?' Karl says.

Joe peers at it. 'Yes.' He lifts the box and shows it to Mia, who manages to keep her expression neutral. I wonder how many scenes of horror she has had to witness in her short life in order for a severed finger not to affect her. I glance towards the box, but quickly look away. I don't need to see it. Joe puts the lid back on and places the whole thing in a cellophane bag.

'Are you able to identify whether or not this is Cat's finger?' Joe asks.

Karl pushes his fists into his eyes. 'I wouldn't know, but from the reaction of my wife and Christophe, I think the answer is yes. Apparently she wore that particular shade of nail varnish. Not for recitals, of course. It's looks like the ring finger from her right hand. She will have to relearn how to use her bow.'

Once again, I am struck by the emphasis on Cat's skill and lack of consideration for the pain she must be suffering, the horror she must be living; assuming, that is, she is still alive. I shiver and try not to think about my own daughter. Did Flo have body parts removed? Or is she still intact?

'Can I see the package it came in?' Joe asks.

'Um, Venetia opened it. It was addressed to both of us. I'm not sure—'

'Could you ask her to come here. It's important that we speak to you both.'

Karl nods and walks out of the room. Joe picks up the note that was lying on the desk next to the box.

'It's handwritten,' Joe says, holding it up. 'Just as well we have a graphologist in our midst.' He glances at me. Joe places the note inside another evidence bag.

'I'll need the original if you'd like me to analyse it,' I say.

'We'll get it dusted for fingerprints first, and then you can look at it.'

Joe peers at Karl's desk. There is a pile of music manuscript paper, a cup holding an assortment of pencils and pen, and a messy pile of envelopes. Meanwhile, Mia is glancing around the rest of the room.

'In here,' she says, pointing at a raffia waste paper basket. It holds a number of envelopes and crumpled up papers. She slips on a pair of gloves, takes a piece of plastic from a bag she has with her and tips the basket upside down.

'What are you doing?' Karl makes all of us jump.

'Looking for the packaging the box came in,' Joe says, crossing his arms. 'I trust we have your permission for that.'

Karl doesn't answer but his jaw is clenched. 'Venetia will be along shortly.'

'Sir, I think it was sent in this envelope.' Mia holds the padded envelope up for Joe to inspect.

'How do you know that was what the box came in?' Karl scowls.

'A process of elimination. The writing matches that on the note. There is only one large brown padded envelope in your bin, three DL-sized paper envelopes and various torn up bits of paper, along with an old banana skin and several Kit Kat wrappers. If it didn't come in this, then what?'

We all jump again as Venetia says, 'That's the envelope the box came in.'

I wonder what it is with this couple and the way they creep around the building. Perhaps it's how they keep their pupils on their toes.

'We will take this away for finger printing and analysis. Was the package posted through your letter box or handed to someone?'

'I don't know,' Venetia says. I note she has large grey rings under her eyes and her skin has an unhealthy pallor. 'Lisl handed it to me. I'll call her.'

The child arrives a couple of minutes later. She is petite with a long, mousey fringe that she uses as a shield to cower behind.

'Tell these people how you took delivery of the envelope,' Venetia says.

Lisl speaks in a whisper. 'The doorbell rang and I was on duty, so I went to the door. When I opened it, there was no one there and the envelope was lying on the doorstep.'

Evidently none of the others are interested in the wellbeing of this girl, so I bend down and smile at her as warmly as I can manage. 'Thank you, Lisl. You've been very helpful.'

She gives me a bashful look. 'Can I go now?' she whispers.

I glance up at Joe, who nods. 'Yes, you can. And thank you.'

She is out of the room in the blink of an eye.

'We have already established that you don't have any CCTV on the premises, so I would be grateful if you could find out if anyone saw anything,' Joe instructs.

'They didn't,' Karl says. Venetia looks up at him with a fleeting expression of surprise. Karl turns away from her. 'I already checked. No one saw anything.

23

'Sarg, I think I should get this over to forensics ASAP,' Mia Brevant says to Joe sotto voce, placing the box with the severed finger and envelope—both now secured separately in see-through plastic bags—into a bag.

'I agree. Let's catch up later at the station.'

Mia Brevant excuses herself and sees herself out.

'I would like to have a tour of the school, talk to any other member of staff who might have seen something. Mr Edstol, perhaps you could come with me? Mrs Edstol, why don't you stay here and talk to Dr Durrant?'

I wonder what Joe is up to, but I nod. Karl scowls as he leaves the room with Joe close behind him.

'This is like a living nightmare,' Venetia says, letting out a loud sigh as she sinks into a chair. 'I am so worried about Cat. If that really is her finger, she must be terrified and in so much pain. Do you think she will have received medical attention?' Venetia's eyes are watery.

I am finding it difficult to distance myself from Venetia's fear. I was in her shoes; am still in her shoes.

'I don't know,' I say. We are both silent for several long moments.

'Aren't you meant to be comforting me? You're a bloody psychologist, aren't you? You must have something to say for yourself?'

I look at her in surprise, startled by the sudden aggression and anger. She stands up and paces around the room, her fingers walking up and down the tweed fabric on her thighs as if playing notes.

'Has there been any more news on Alice?' I ask.

'No.' Venetia avoids looking at me. 'She has a screw loose, does Martha Jones. It wouldn't surprise me one iota if she had something to do with all of this.'

'Alice's mother?' I ask.

'Yes. Her child has talent, but none of Cat's presence.'

'But Alice is only young. Perhaps she will develop that presence as she matures?'

'Pfft!' Venetia rolls her eyes. 'True star quality is evident from a very young age. Alice is good, but she will never be great. Not that Martha will ever accept that.'

'Sit down, Venetia,' I suggest, patting the arm of the chair next to mine. 'Tell me more about Martha.'

She sinks heavily into the hard-backed wooden chair.

'The archetypal pushy parent. We have seen many of them come and go through this institution. Some of them live their own dreams through their children, forcing them to attend Suzuki lessons from age two, breathing down their necks at every lesson, hovering over them whilst they practice, filling their children with all their hopes and dreams and never standing back and listening to what their child might want. Others take it to the next stage. Not only do they force their children to be the greatest, they attempt to eliminate the competition. There is nothing new about that. Think of Tonya Harding the ice skater, or Monica Seles the tennis player. It happens in the musical world too. Overly-zealous parents accidentally dropping a competitor's instrument or, in the case of Martha Jones, trying to break another child's fingers.'

'She did what?'

'Martha Jones dropped the piano lid on Cat's fingers.'

I gasp. 'Was she all right?'

'Yes. Cat was young and nimble, and pulled her hands out of the way just in time. The lid slammed down with an almighty crash, audible even in here. I thought the Steinway would be ruined. Fortunately they're well-constructed mechanical machines and there was no damage at all.'

'How do you know it was done deliberately?'

Venetia cocks her head to one side. 'A piano lid does not fall down. It has to be pushed. Cat explained to me exactly what happened. She was terrified, poor child.'

'I thought both Cat and Alice are violinists, not pianists.'

'All our students play at least two instruments. Cat was playing the piano, accompanying Alice, which is quite normal. What wasn't normal was for a parent to be present. We have very strict procedures regarding any adults coming in and out. Everyone has to be police-checked. We can never be too rigorous. But Martha is unusual. She is both a parent and a teacher. She is a piano accompanist. Did you know that?'

I shake my head.

'Piano accompanists are a rare breed. They have to play to the highest of standards and be utterly brilliant at sight reading. They also need to be willing to be second fiddle in any relationship, excuse the pun. The accompanist will never be the star, but the good ones raise the soloist to heights he or she could never achieve alone. Accompanists either have no egos or have learned to suppress them.

'Although she is a fine pianist, I always found the role of accompanist ill-suited to Martha. She was teaching Cat. For some reason, she lost her temper and slammed the piano lid down. Naturally, Karl fired her. She threatened to take us to the industrial tribunal and sent us a few solicitor's letters, but nothing came of it. It was more important to her that her daughter, Alice, be nurtured into a star.' Venetia stares out of the window.

I break a long silence. 'Are you saying that Martha might be complicit in Cat's disappearance?'

Venetia sighs. 'Perhaps. After all, that way, she got what she wanted. Her daughter stepping into Cat's shoes for a prestigious performance.'

'Have you shared your suspicions with DS Swain?'

Venetia shakes her head. 'Yes, but they're not taking me seriously. You have hit the nail on the head. They are suspicions only, and I have no proof. And now Alice has disappeared too.'

'Along with her parents,' I say.

'They are up to something, that's for sure,' Venetia mumbles. 'Dreadful woman.'

I stare at Venetia. I don't doubt that she is telling the truth. There is symmetry in her expression, she is sitting quite still and stringing words together in a straight-forward manner.

'I just want to find my Cat,' Venetia says, a sob making her words sound strangled.

'I know exactly how you feel,' I say, speaking without thinking.

'I doubt it. Unless you have lost a child yourself, I doubt it very much.'

'Actually, I have,' I state, surprised and disappointed in my unprofessionalism.

We look at each other. I am not sure which of us is more startled by my admission.

I am relieved that Joe returns to the room just then, obviating any need for me to offer Venetia further explanations.

'I need to get back to the station. I have agreed with Mr

Edstol that we will return tomorrow and carry out any necessary interviews.'

Venetia stands up and throws me a glance. She and I have a
bond now, however tenuous.

∾

WHEN WE ARE BACK in Joe's car, I tell him about my conversation with Venetia and her suspicions of Martha.

'I think it's a red herring,' Joe says. 'No charges were ever
brought against Martha, no official complaints made.'

'Yes, but—'

'We need to concentrate on the kidnapping and the
demands,' he says, interrupting me. He has a habit of doing this
and it is beginning to grate. He grips the steering wheel tightly.

'I don't understand why the kidnappers are demanding five
hundred thousand pounds in cash to release Cat. Why would
they want that when they have a Guarneri violin worth £3.2
million?'

'I agree it doesn't make sense, unless they don't realise the
violin is worth so much.' Joe bites the side of his lip as he
concentrates on steering the car along the narrow lane.

'Or unless two separate crimes have been committed,' I
suggest.

'The Viscount Sneddon explained that such a valuable
violin is very hard to sell. Perhaps the kidnappers need the cash
to tide them over and intend to try to dispose of the violin at a
later date?'

'It doesn't explain why they're keeping Cat hostage, though.
Why don't they just release her and hang on to the instrument?'

'Perhaps she knows too much.'

I can't help but draw parallels between Cat's disappearance
and Flo's. We waited and waited for a ransom note, year after
year. At times I was desperate to receive one because it would

have meant that my beautiful daughter was still alive, that someone thought her life had a value. But no one wrote to us. Our daughter simply vanished. Did Flo know too much? Or was hers just a random act of violence, the destruction of a life for no reason whatsoever? Or, as I still believe, or at least try to believe, is she alive but unable or unwilling to reach out to us?

'You're thinking about Flo, aren't you?' Joe says, interrupting my maudlin thoughts. He takes his left hand off the steering wheel and squeezes my knee.

'It's hard not to. I feel like a fraud. If I can't find my own daughter, what gives me the right to help find anyone else's?'

'I'm going to bring Viscount Sneddon in for questioning.'

'You are?' I'm surprised.

'I think he's got something to do with this, and at the very least is perpetrating insurance fraud.'

I disagree. I think Martha is involved and, somehow or another, I intend to find out. I cannot let another girl disappear, or stand by as yet another gets hurt or, worse still, murdered.

24

The next day, Joe persuades me to attend the interview with Jonno, the Viscount Sneddon.

'Kindly explain why I am here!' Jonno thumps his fist on the wooden table before Joe even sits down.

As on previous occasions, I am seated on a chair adjacent to the door, behind Mia and Joe. The position affords me a good view of Jonno. Seated alongside him is his solicitor, an obese man in a shiny suit with a jowly face, whose forehead and upper lip are dotted with beads of perspiration. It isn't even warm in the interview room.

Joe reads him Jonno's rights.

'Are you aware that Mr and Mrs Edstol received a package with what we must presume is Cat Kingsley's severed finger?'

'You what?' Jonno asks, his eyes opening wide with shock. I will need to study the recording of this interview, but I am almost certain that his reaction is genuine. He leans back in the chair, then immediately bends forwards. 'Bloody hell! Which finger? Which hand?'

Mia and Joe glance at each other.

'We believe it is the ring finger from her right hand.'

'Oh, thank God!'

'Thank God?' I can hear the frown in Joe's voice.

'Her right hand is her bowing hand. The only finger that isn't vital for bowing is the ring finger. The second finger, thumb and little finger are the most important. The second finger and thumb hold the bow. The little finger is used for balance and direction. It's essential for fluidity, essential for a good bowing technique. The loss of the little finger would mean a loss of clarity and the smoothness of the sound would be destroyed. The ring finger isn't that important. It will require some readjustment and relearning of bowing technique, but it shouldn't fundamentally affect her playing. What a relief!' He lets out a loud puff of air.

'Are Cat Kingsley's hand insured?' Joe asks.

Jonno glances at his solicitor, who is facing forwards, po-faced. Jonno shifts in his chair and his eyes skitter around the room.

'What relevance is that?' he asks after a long pause.

'We are investigating possible insurance fraud. Please answer the question. Are Cat Kingsley's hands insured?'

'Are you accusing me of insurance fraud again? Don't be so bloody stupid. I've done nothing wrong!'

'Please answer the question. Are Cat's hands insured?' Joe says.

'You would have to ask the Edstols. They're responsible for her day-to-day management, I'm just the benefactor.'

'So your answer is?'

'I don't know. Maybe they are, maybe they aren't.' Jonno's voice is steely. He is lying, and my bet is on Cat's hands being insured.

'If Cat's hands were insured, what would the payout for the loss of a finger be, do you reckon? Twenty thousand, two hundred thousand, a million?' Joe asks languidly.

'How the bloody hell should I know?'

'It seems to me that you are the person most likely to gain financially through Cat Kingsley's demise. You stand to receive over three million pounds for the loss of the violin, and quite possibly will benefit from the loss of her earnings. I would like to see the contract you have between yourself and the Edstols. Can you provide that?'

'How dare you!' Jonno stands up and his chair topples backwards to crash to the floor, making us all jump. 'Are you accusing me of something?'

'Sit down, Viscount Sneddon,' his solicitor urges.

Jonno bends down, rights his chair and sits again, arms crossed tightly across his narrow chest.

'I find it curious that you show no concern for the young woman's well-being. Your only interest appears to be monetary. The loss of earnings, the value of the instrument. If nothing else, it shows an alarming lack of compassion.'

'I am a benefactor,' Jonno spits. 'I am not her parent or her guardian, or even her friend. I am supporting her financially. Which suits me, because I earn money from her performances, money that I use to fund research into my wife's medical condition. I do not have any children and do not know how to react to them.'

At twenty, Cat is hardly a child, I think to myself.

'Unless you are going to arrest me, I would like to leave now. My wife needs me.'

Joe and Mia look at each other again, and I can't see if any words pass between them.

'Interview terminated at fifteen hours twenty-three minutes,' Mia says, switching off the recording equipment.

'MRS EDSTOL. Could you please tell me: were Cat Kingsley's fingers insured?'

When Mia accompanied Jonno and his solicitor out, Joe and I remained in the interview room. I am sitting in the chair Jonno recently vacated, and Joe has the phone on loud speaker so I can hear Venetia.

'Excuse me?' she says.

'Are Cat's fingers insured?'

'Yes, I believe they are.' She pauses for a moment, then lets out a small screech. 'Do you think someone cut off her finger because...?' Her voice fades, then returns with force. 'You are not accusing me of... What sort of monster do you think I am? Cat is my daughter! We would never do anything so horrific. Detective, I think you have a very warped mind!'

'I have been a detective for a long time. If her hands are insured, you would benefit.'

'I can't...I can't... This is too awful for words,' Venetia stutters.

'Thank you for your help, Mrs Edstol,' Joe says before hanging up.

'Why would Venetia or Karl kidnap a girl they consider their own daughter, demand ransom money from themselves, then claim for the loss of her finger on insurance? It doesn't make sense,' I say.

'It's a double bluff. Perhaps they need the insurance money?'

'But her fingers wouldn't be valued that highly, would they? It doesn't make sense.' I shake my head, trying to figure out Joe's reasoning.

He stands up and stretches. I follow him out of the room into the brightly lit corridor. 'Come back to mine for supper,' Joe says as he escorts me out of the police station to my car.

'I shouldn't, I—'

'Please.' He grabs my hands.

'What's the urgency?'

He looks away, shifting his weight from one foot to the

other. 'It might not be so easy to see you over the next three weeks.'

I shrug. 'Christmas is coming up. We all have commitments.' I try to sound light-hearted, but I dread Christmas and have no commitments. I am still hoping that George might relent and invite me back to Geneva to spend Christmas with my new grandson, but as the days slip past, I am recognising that it's unlikely. I wonder if my brother Rob will want to spend the day with me or whether it will be just Mungo and me, all alone.

'Holly is coming home from university tomorrow. I haven't introduced her to anyone since her mum and I split up, and it might be awkward.' He grimaces.

'Don't worry. I'll stay out of the way.' I stand on tiptoes and reach up to give him a quick peck on the cheek.

'Not here!' he says, glancing around furtively.

'Whoops!' I say, laughing.

'So will you come over later?'

'Yes.'

WHEN EITHER JOE or I ask each other for supper, we come prepared with an overnight bag. I wonder how soon it will be before we leave a change of clothes in each other's houses, and when my toothbrush will permanently reside in a mug next to his. We haven't got to the planning stage in our relationship, but I hope that he will suggest we take a holiday together some time next year. I am not sure whether it is love yet, but I have certainly fallen deeply into something with Joe. I return home, take a shower, wash my hair and dance around the house, singing in anticipation of a wonderful evening.

'Come on, Mungo,' I say. 'We're off to Joe's.'

The dog wags his tail and jumps up onto the back seat of the car. I switch on the radio and catch the six o'clock news. Cat Kingsley's disappearance has made the headlines of BBC Southern Counties Radio. No details are given, just that the police are increasingly worried about the disappearance of the twenty-year-old violinist who critics predict to be the next Nicola Benedetti. They then play an excerpt of a recording Cat made a couple of years ago. It's a simple piece, *Salut d'Amour* by Elgar, and it brings tears to my eyes. I jab my finger onto the dial of the radio and switch it off. My mood has changed in an instant.

Now I can't stop thinking about her, Alice and Martha. I recall how Sophie told me Alice was cutting herself. It is my duty as a psychologist and a grieving mother to do something to help. As I drive down the pot-holed track to Joe's small converted barn, I resolve to talk to him. I think the police are focusing on the wrong people. The Jones family are integral to this investigation. I bet that if we find Alice, we'll find Cat.

Joe takes my bag and hands me a glass of Chardonnay.

'You know me well,' I say, kissing him gently on the lips.

He drops the bag and pulls me towards him. I inhale his musky scent, but then peel myself away.

'We need to discuss the case.'

Joe groans as he lets me go.

'Have you got the handwriting for me to analyse?'

'Yes, but it can wait until tomorrow.'

'I think you need to throw more resources towards finding Alice,' I say.

'Pippa, it really isn't for you to dictate how we should investigate this case.'

'There's something very wrong. Alice was cutting herself; she is a troubled teenager.'

'We know that and we're doing what we can!'

'A bit like the police did what they could when trying to find Flo? If I had been taken more seriously at the time, then my daughter might be here today. You cannot let that happen again!'

'Darling, this case bears no similarity to the disappearance of your daughter.'

'How do you know?'

'I looked at the file.'

We stand and stare at each other, then both speak at the same time.

'I've got a sixth sense about this. You need to focus your energy on finding Alice.'

'Pippa, you know perfectly well that the police do not operate on a hunch or a sixth sense! We use proof and evidence and scientific data. Please don't let your emotional response get in the way!'

'Don't you dare tell me—'

We are speaking so loudly, neither of us hear the car pull up outside or notice the door opening. I jump and my heart pounds at the sound of a female voice.

'Dad? What's going on?'

We both turn around. 'Holly!' Joe exclaims. 'What are you doing here, love? I wasn't expecting you until tomorrow.'

She is obviously her father's daughter: tall, slender, with the longest legs, her thick, black and bouncy hair tied back with a scarf. She has the same dark, almond-shaped eyes and sparkling teeth as Joe.

'Who's she?' Holly asks, glaring at me with narrowed eyes.

'This is Dr Durrant. She's a psychologist, assisting me on a case.'

And your lover, your girlfriend, I want to say.

'Right. Can you help me with my suitcase?'

'Of course, darling. Dr Durrant and I have finished our discussion. Would you like to eat with us?'

'Us?' Holly scowls.

'Dr Durrant is staying for supper.'

Holly turns her back to me. 'I don't want to eat with her,' she says in a loud whisper.

'Come on, let's get your bag.' Joe places a hand on her back and they walk towards the door.

'Whose dog is that? You know I'm allergic to dogs,' Holly says.

'Since when?'

I can't hear the rest of the conversation. Joe picks up Holly's suitcase and they walk down the corridor towards her bedroom.

'Mungo, come here,' I say. I find his lead and attach it to his collar. Then I pick up my handbag and retrieve my overnight bag, which Joe has left on the floor to the side of the sofa. 'We're going home.'

When we're standing at the front door, I say loudly, 'I'm off now! I'll see you soon. Enjoy your Christmas holidays, Holly!' I speak as brightly as I can muster.

'Wait!' Joe says, hurrying out of Holly's room. 'Why are you going?' he whispers.

'You need to be with your daughter and I shouldn't be here.'

I lean up to give him a kiss, but Joe's eyes are on something behind me and he shifts to one side so that I almost topple forwards as my lips meet air.

'Thanks for coming over,' he says stiffly, opening the front door for me. 'See you soon, Mungo.' He scratches the dog's head.

I hold my breath as I walk towards the car, waiting for him to call out to me, hoping that he will say something, anything to acknowledge our relationship. When I have put Mungo in the car and am ready to turn on the ignition, I turn to look at the front of the barn, expecting to see a look of regret on his face, but the front door is closed, the outside is dark, and Joe is nowhere to be seen. As I drive back down the track, I blink away my tears, and when I'm back on the A24 dual carriageway, driving in the slow lane, I let out a loud scream.

25

Sophie is late for the rehearsal. They are meant to be performing at a lunchtime concert at The Wigmore Hall in January; a real accolade and another chance for them to be noticed by booking agents. After the disaster at The Cadogan Hall, this will be a chance to redeem themselves. The only chance, as Karl keeps telling them.

Since Cat has gone missing, they haven't practiced together, but this morning Karl sent Sophie, Christophe and Vadim an email telling them they should prepare for the possibility that Cat might not make the concert and, therefore, he was assigning them trio music to prepare. Sophie swallowed bile when she read that. To think that Cat might never be coming back is too awful to bear.

Sophie hurries down the stairs, her viola case over her shoulder, the music that she has just printed off in her hand. They have been assigned one of the larger rehearsal rooms, the one used by peripatetic teachers, of which there are few. She pushes the door open with her backside.

'Sorry I'm late!'

She turns around just in time to see Vadim punch

Christophe on the nose. A metal music stand goes flying across the room and crashes to the floor, sheets of music fluttering downwards around it.

'What the hell?' Sophie screams, dropping her case. She tries to ease herself between the two young men. Vadim only just misses punching her.

'Stop!'

Christophe breaks away and turns towards the window, blood pouring out of his nose. Vadim crumples to the floor and puts his head in his hands.

'What the hell has happened?' she asks, not sure who she should be caring for first. 'We are meant to be working together, supporting each other. Not beating each other up!'

'He is a liar!' Vadim says, raising bloodshot eyes to meet Sophie's. 'He says bad things.' His Russian accent is strong and, in the heat of the moment, he seems to be struggling to articulate himself.

'It is you who has done something bad! You who are tied up with the Russian mafia! Why don't you just accept that Cat doesn't love you anymore?' Christophe yells, hauling himself up from the ground. 'How dare you accuse me of something!' He steps aggressively towards Vadim.

'Calm it!' Sophie place herself between the two young men.

'He is trying to take over Cat's position!' Christophe says, jabbing his finger towards Vadim's chest.

'Are you high?' Sophie asks, recoiling from Christophe ever so slightly. He reeks of stale weed.

'No. Just sad.'

'We're all sad. Me particularly,' Vadim says. 'I love Catherine.'

'And I—'

Sophie tugs at Christophe's sleeve to stop him from throwing another punch at Vadim.

'Sit down, both of you!'

They do as she instructs, taking their places opposite each other in the semi-circle of three chairs that have been placed ready for their rehearsal.

'We all love Cat, and we all miss her. It's not going to do anyone any good if we fight each other,' Sophie says.

'He accuses me!' Vadim points at Christophe.

'Of what?' Sophie cocks her head.

'All I said was that Cat obviously doesn't have feelings for Vadim anymore and that I expect he organized the kidnap as payback. It's obvious that one of his henchmen chopped off her finger, or perhaps he did it for a bit of a laugh!'

Vadim jumps up. He grabs Christophe by the collar of his black T-shirt.

'Sit down, Vadim! Let go of Christophe,' Sophie says wearily. She bends to unzip her viola case. 'We all love Cat, and what we should be doing is working together to find her, not beating each other up.'

'Always the voice of reason!' Christophe says bitterly.

Vadim returns to his seat.

'Look. I think it'll be ok. That Dr Durrant is all over this like a rash. She's been really helpful in trying to find Cat and Alice. I think she's better than the police. Did you know she is a human lie detector? She solved a couple of murders,' Cat says.

'Murders!' Vadim says, shivering.

'She hasn't done much good so far, though. has she? How has she helped in the search for Cat?' Christophe says, sneering.

'Perhaps not yet, but I think she will.'

'It's speculation and nonsense. I can't rehearse now,' Christophe says. His cello is still in its case, leaned up against the wall. 'I can't.' He gets up, strides over to his cello case, picks it up and walks out of the room, letting the door slam behind him.

'Are you all right?' Sophie eventually asks Vadim.

Vadim runs his fingers over his face. 'Yes.'

They sit in silence for a few long moments.

'I hope this Dr Durrant will help. How do you know this about her?'

'She told me herself, and there's a load of stuff online about her. She's a consultant to the police.' For a few seconds they are both lost in their thoughts. 'Do you want to practice?' Sophie asks eventually.

'No.' Vadim studies his fingernails. 'I have done something.'

'What have you done?' Sophie's throat constricts. She leans forwards, her hands on her knees. 'I thought you just accused Christophe of doing something.'

'Yes. I think he has something to do with Cat's disappearance.'

Sophie snorts. 'Come on, that's a joke. He may be secretly in love with Cat and desperately jealous of your relationship, but Christophe couldn't organise a piss-up in a brewery. So, what have you done?'

'I went to Cat's room last night and took her diary and all the letters we had written to each other. And some other documents.'

'You've got her room key?' Sophie is surprised.

'We got copies made of each other's keys. Cat and I will be married.'

'You're a bit young for that, aren't you?'

Vadim scowls.

'We are having a baby,' he murmurs.

'You're what!' Sophie screeches and jumps out of her chair. She hadn't seen that one coming. 'Cat's pregnant?'

'Keep your voice down!' Vadim says. His face is ashen and his eyes are dark.

'Is that why Cat has disappeared?' Sophie speaks in a whisper now.

'No. We are happy. We talk about keeping the baby and

about getting rid of it. She decided to keep him. We were going to talk to Karl and Venetia. We are happy.' He scrunches up his eyes.

Sophie stands up and starts pacing the room. 'Well, that puts a different perspective on everything. She's probably taken herself off to get an abortion. That's what I'd do if I was stupid enough to get myself banged up at twenty.'

'No! Cat would never do that. She believes life is sacrosanct.'

Sophie huffs. 'Have you told the police?'

Vadim appears to shrink into the chair. 'No.'

'Well, you'll have to. Especially if a finger has been found.'

Vadim pales further.

Sophie sighs. 'I think you should talk to the psychologist woman, Dr Durrant. She's all right. It would be good for you to tell her everything. It might help find Cat sooner.'

Vadim looks away.

'Vadim,' Sophie says more forcefully, 'are you telling me everything? Are you telling me the truth?'

As the implications of what Vadim has said hits Sophie, a tremor runs down her spine. Cat must have told Vadim that she'd changed her mind about keeping the baby. Did she also want to break off their relationship? And in retaliation, Vadim must be holding Cat and demanding the ransom. Vadim is a sadistic kidnapper.

'What is it?' Vadim asks.

Sophie flees the room.

26

By the time I get home, I'm a mess, feeling sorry for myself and livid—angry with Joe, and perhaps a little bit jealous too. He has his lovely daughter. Mine is gone. The lost girls have stirred up something very deep inside me, and the grief I have managed to suppress for so long wells back up inside my chest. Whilst Joe and his team have thrown police resources into investigating what has happened to Cat, my immediate concern is for Alice and her mother, Martha. I know that Alice is in danger, and I feel a deep sense of urgency to do something for her.

I pour myself a large gin and telephone my brother, Rob. He is the only person I can talk to who won't judge me, who understands the horror of what I've been through.

As he answers the phone, I can hear laughter in the background.

'Have you got someone with you?' I ask.

'Just a couple of friends. How are you, sis?'

'Not too good.' Briefly, I tell him about the case and how I can't stop thinking about Flo. I can hear Rob's footsteps as he leaves his beautiful modern kitchen and walks out into the hall and then into the living room, where there is silence.

'You need to stay away from all of that,' Rob says. 'Look after yourself and stop getting wound up in other people's problems.'

'That's my job!' I laugh bitterly.

'No, it's not. You're a psychologist, not a detective.'

'I had an email from the private detective in Cape Town.'

'Ah. So that is what this is really about,' Rob says.

'He wants more money. He thinks he's got a lead.'

'What sort of a lead?'

'A gang that operates out of Bonteheuwel, a particularly violent suburb of Cape Town. Someone claims to know something. He wants another R20,000.'

'How much is that in sterling?'

'Just over a thousand pounds.'

Rob sighs. 'I'll give you the dosh if you haven't got it, but I don't think it's money well spent. It's been nearly seven years and this guy hasn't come up with one credible bit of information.'

I try to stop the tears and am glad Rob can't see me. My brother is right. But it doesn't mean that I'm going to give up on trying to find Flo.

'I was wondering if you fancy a trip to South Africa with me?' I ask.

'Why don't you ask your cop boyfriend to go with you?'

'It's over,' I say as I chew the side of my lip.

'What happened? Rob asks.

'It doesn't matter.'

But Rob knows me too well and recognizes the lie.

'I've got to get back to my friends now, but why don't you come over tomorrow?'

'Maybe,' I say unconvincingly.

'Are you all right, Pippa?'

'I'll be fine. You have a fun evening.' I put the phone down.
But I'm not fine. I haven't felt this miserable for a long time.

THE NEXT MORNING, I wake with a hangover and a deep sense of urgency. I check my phone, but there are no messages from Joe. Pushing away the disappointment, I decide to make the most of an empty early Saturday morning. After a quick shower and a hurried breakfast, Mungo and I set off for West Chiltington. I am hoping to catch Miss Ethel Smith, the Jones's nosey neighbour.

I pull up in front of the Jones's small semi-detached house.

'Stay,' I instruct Mungo, and try to avoid looking at his doleful eyes as I lock the car. I open the creaking wooden gate and walk up the short path to their house. I ring the doorbell but it doesn't seem to make a sound, so instead I knock. There is no answer. I stand back for a moment and then peer in through the window of the living room.

'Hellooeee!'

I jump. It is Miss Smith from next door, leaning over the sparse hedge that separates the two houses.

'You're back, then?' She leans heavily on a stick and is wearing a short-sleeved floral blouse despite the freezing weather.

'You'll catch a cold without a coat on!' I say, smiling.

'Us oldies are hardy types. Not like you young'uns!'

I am happy to be called a young'un.

'He's back is Bill Jones. But not seen sight of his wife or the girl.'

'Did you tell him the police would like to talk to him?' I ask.

She pulls herself up to her full height and large girth. 'Of course I did. I'm all about civic duties and doing the right thing. He didn't seem too happy though. He has a black eye. A great big bruise. I asked him what happened, but he didn't reply. Not like him, really. He's normally the nice one in the family.'

'Anyway, he left again in the old banger car. The big green Land Rover Defender that Martha normally drives.'

'What time did he leave?'

She looks at her wrist, but realises she's not wearing a watch. 'An hour or so? He was in a hurry. If you'd like to wait for him to come back, you can come in and have a cuppa with me. You'd be welcome, in fact.'

'That's kind of you, but—'

'I'm not taking no buts. In you come.'

I am saved by my mobile phone ringing from inside the pocket of my jacket. It's Sophie. I mouth my apologies to Miss Smith and walk towards the car.

'What can I do for you, Sophie?'

'I've had a message from Alice.'

'You have!' My heart pounds hard. That must be good news.

'It doesn't make sense to me, and she must be in danger. She says not to worry about her, but I am, and it's a half-baked message.' Sophie is garbling.

'Slow down, Sophie. Why don't you read me exactly what it says?'

'Ok. It says, *Don't worry about me, I'm with* … And then it cuts off. So of course I'm worried.'

'Have you tried calling her back?' I ask.

'Yes, but it sounds like the phone is switched off. It goes straight to voicemail. I don't even like Alice much. It's not like she's my friend or anything, but I'm worried. And the other thing is, I think Vadim has something to do with Cat's kidnapping. I don't want to tell the policeman because Vadim will know I've snitched on him. Then he might do it to me too.'

'Why do you think that?'

'Just things Vadim said. He's acting strange. I might be wrong, but...'

'You've done exactly the right thing by calling me. Why don't you send me Alice's mobile number and I'll try and call her too.'

'Okay. Am I safe?' There is a tremor in Sophie's voice.

'There is no reason to think you are in any danger whatsoever,' I say with a confidence I don't feel. I would like to tell her that I think Alice's mother has something to do with this all but that would be speaking out of turn, so I keep my thoughts to myself.

'Will you keep me posted?'

'Yes, of course,' I promise.

BACK IN THE CAR, I dial the mobile number Sophie has sent me. Unsurprisingly, it rings out. I need to find Alice, but it's unlikely she will pick up a call from a number she doesn't recognise. I debate hanging around to see if Bill Jones returns, but then decide to call Sophie back.

'Can you send Alice a text and find out where she is? If you get an answer, let me know as soon as possible.'

Sophie agrees, and I sit in the car for a few minutes, stroking Mungo. I notice Ethel Smith peeking out from behind her net curtain and frowning as she sees me still sitting in my car.

'Come on, Mungo. We need to go.'

I start up the car, turn it around and head out of West Chiltington towards Storrington. As I potter along the country roads, my windscreen wipers working quickly to clear the rain, I spot a green Defender parked up on the side of the road just as we're entering into Storrington. There are two people seated in the vehicle. I don't know what Bill Jones looks like, but I could swear that the man with his back to me is Karl Edstol. I brake hard, and the female driver in the Porsche Cayenne behind me puts her hand on her horn. I catch a glimpse of her exasperated hand actions in my rear mirror. I can't stop and there's nowhere to pull over, so, exasperatingly, I have to drive to the bottom of the hill and then do an about turn around the mini roundabout to go back the way I came. Just as I arrive, the tail lights of the Defender disappear over the brow of the hill and Karl Edstol— if indeed it was him—is nowhere to be seen.

27

There is a lot of blood. More than ever before. Alice feels faint and she slides down onto the grubby lino floor, clutching the side of the avocado-coloured bath. If she had realised the knife was quite so sharp, she wouldn't have cut that deeply. The knife she'd used after her dad left hadn't done much damage. In fact, it had been thoroughly unsatisfying. This one is the opposite. Nevertheless, it brings her some relief and at least she can channel some of the fury she is experiencing towards her mother. What right does she have to control Alice's life, to decide what Alice will or won't do, and then to keep her captive?

'What are you doing up there?' Martha yells. 'I said a five-minute break, not fifteen!'

When the dizziness has passed and the bleeding has stemmed a little, Alice gets up and rinses the bloodied towel in the bath. It is still stained a brownish-red. Alice uses the last plaster in her washbag. She rummages in Martha's washbag to see if her mother has any, but to her dismay there are none. What will she do without plasters?

Alice squirrelled her mobile phone into the bathroom in

the hopes there might be some reception upstairs. She's worried about the last text she sent to Sophie. It made her sound desperate. When the plaster is in place, she puts her clothes back on and perches on the side of the bath. It toggles between one bar and no reception. She pulls up Sophie's number and starts writing her a text.

Don't worry about me, I'm with

And then Martha knocks on the door. Alice jumps and presses send by mistake. She shoves the phone inside the waistband of her jeans.

'Just coming. Got a heavy period,' Alice says.

Martha peers at her when she comes out of the bathroom.

Alice holds her breath and, with a tensed back, slithers past. 'Just getting a tissue,' she says, as she slips into her miniscule bedroom. She's not sure if Martha is watching her, so she slips the phone into her suitcase as she reaches into it, ostensibly to get a tissue.

'Forty-five minutes practice now, and then a brisk walk to take in some fresh air. It will do you good.'

Alice breathes a sigh of relief that her mother didn't see her phone. She follows Martha downstairs and picks up her violin and bow. She plays the Paganini *Caprice No. 9*. It is a violin solo full of double stops—where two notes are sounded at the same time to make chords. It's not difficult for Alice to play ordinarily, but today she is angry with the world and particularly with her violin. The octaves aren't clear and the crisp little bounces sound muffled.

Martha is sitting on the sofa reading a book. Alice wishes she would go away and leave her alone to practice.

'Ricochet!' Martha says, letting the book slide to the floor.

'What?'

'Ricochet! You're bouncing the bow too near the tip. Use your little finger on the bow to manage the weight on your down bow!'

Alice turns away from her mother. How dare Martha tell her how to play the violin! Martha is a pianist, not a violinist. How the hell does she know what the correct bowing technique is anyway?

'You haven't got the clarity or the crispness! Concentrate, Alice!'

Alice throws the bow onto the floor. 'I can't! I'm not in the mood and it's a waste of bloody time.'

Martha stands up, her hands on her hips. 'How dare you talk like that! Your father and I have dedicated the past sixteen years of our lives to supporting you in making your dreams come true. That bow costs as much as a small car. And now, when the opportunities are ready for the taking, what do you do? You throw a childish hissy fit! Go outside and get some fresh air and think about how lucky you are! This is your time to shine, whilst poor Cat is missing, and shine you will. Get your coat and come back in thirty minutes for lunch.'

Alice hesitates.

'Get a move on!'

Alice picks up the bow from the carpet and places it and her violin back in the case. Then she hurries upstairs, all the while listening hard to ensure Martha isn't following her. She rummages in her suitcase, finds her mobile phone and her wallet, and stuffs them deep into the pockets of her anorak. Slowly she walks back downstairs.

'Have you got your watch on?' Martha asks.

Alice nods.

'Be back here for 10.30 a.m. precisely. If you're late, you will be punished.'

Alice wonders what Martha can do to punish her any more.

~

IT IS FREEZING cold outside and lightly drizzling. Alice has no idea where she is. She walks along the road in the direction she saw her dad drive off in. The cottage is totally in the middle of nowhere. There are no houses, no cars; just sheep huddled together in corners of fields, long lines of broken dry-stone walls and the occasional clump of short trees.

Alice lets the tears flow. My own mother is keeping me captive, she thinks, her shoulders sagging. When she can no longer see the little cottage where they are staying, she sits down on a jagged pile of rocks, gets out her mobile phone and switches it on. She still has ten per cent battery left, so she needs to conserve it carefully. Alice can see that the half-written text went to Sophie, but now there is no reception again. She knows Sophie thinks she's a useless little squirt, but Sophie is the only person Alice can trust. Then Alice opens her wallet. She only has a handful of coins. She gets up and carries on walking. The road will have to lead somewhere.

Alice loses track of time. After a while the air doesn't feel quite so damp and cold anymore. She regains sensation in her fingers and loses herself in the rhythm of walking. For the first time in a long time, Alice's mind is empty. When a small white car drives up from behind her, she literally jumps. She hadn't heard it. Alice steps back onto the verge of short grass to let it pass, but the car stops alongside her.

'Hello, young lady. What are you doing out here on the moors?' The woman has ruddy cheeks and grey frizzy hair, and is wearing a mud-stained green jacket. A Jack Russell sitting on the passenger seat gives a single bark, then turns away from Alice.

'Actually, I'm lost. Would it be possible for you to give me a lift to the nearest town?' Alice's heart is hammering. She's never done anything like this before. Martha's words of warning about the dangers of hitchhiking thump in her ears.

'You're in luck, young lady. I happen to be on my way to Macc. Hop in. Buster, back seat!'

The dog gets up slowly and, eyeing Alice with what looks like an expression of disdain, climbs into the back of the car.

'So what brings you up these parts?' the woman asks. 'You staying in Pete's cottage?'

'Um, no. I'm doing the Duke of Edinburgh scheme and I got lost.'

The woman frowns. 'Strange time of year for doing that. Are you just doing a recce?'

Alice nods. She remembers hearing all about the Duke of Edinburgh scheme on the radio a few months ago. She had thought how exciting it must be, going off exploring the countryside with a backpack and a couple of friends. She'd mentioned it to Martha, who had laughed in that mean, high-pitched cough-like laugh she has when someone says something she thinks is ridiculous. 'Don't be such an idiot. You'd hate it, getting muddy in the countryside. It's for children from posh families.'

The car bounces over cattle grids and passes through low-hanging swirls of mist.

'You don't sound like you're from these parts,' the woman says.

'No.'

'Shall I drop you at the station?'

'Yes please. That would be very kind.'

Alice is startled by her mobile phone ringing in her pocket. She's annoyed. She thought she had switched it off to conserve the battery.

'Aren't you going to answer it, then?' the woman asks.

'Um, no. It's no one important.' Alice takes the phone out of her pocket. She doesn't recognise the number.

They drive down a steep hill towards some houses. Dark grey, thick stone houses, constructed to keep out the inclement weather. Alice reckons she would like to live in one of those, all cocooned up. Much nicer that the flimsy house they live in in Sussex.

'How old are you?'

'Um, seventeen.'

'You look young for your age. Oh well, what do I know. Got no kids of my own. The station is just up there on the left. I'll drop you on the corner. Good luck with getting your award.'

'Thank you,' Alice says as she slips out of the car. 'It was very kind of you to give me a lift.'

'You'd be disqualified, you know, if anyone knew I'd given you a lift mid-challenge!' The woman's eyes crease in the corners. 'But I won't tell if you won't!' She guffaws, holds up a hand in a wave, leans over to pull the passenger door closed, and drives off.

Alice stands for a long minute on the side of the road, bereft. She hadn't realised that there are genuine, kind people around, people who don't want anything in return. She wonders if they're different up here, wherever here is. She turns and walks up the hill towards the entrance of the train station.

She stands patiently in the queue for the ticket desk. And then it is her turn.

'I would like a ticket to Horsham, please.'

'To where, love?'

'Horsham.'

The clerk punches something into the computer keyboard.

'You'll need to get the train to London Euston, cross London via the tube to London Victoria, and take the train south from there.'

'How long will that take?'

'Three hours and thirty-one minutes.'

'And how much will that cost?'

'One hundred and one pounds and seventy pence one way, unless you've got a student railcard, in which case it'll be sixty-seven pounds and fifteen pence.'

Alice takes out her wallet. She counts out her notes and change. Eleven pounds and twenty-seven pence, saved up from the measly allowance Martha gives her.

'Is that all you've got?' the clerk asks. There is a snigger from behind Alice. Her cheeks flush.

'Right, love. Step to one side please. There's a long queue behind you.'

28

I give chase. It's not easy trying to catch up with a car when exiting a small town, and it's even harder following someone along narrow country lanes when the roads are slippery and full of tight bends. I can see the Defender two cars ahead of me, but the vehicle in front is driving painfully slowly. Its speed would drive me insane even if I wasn't in a hurry.

'Come on, come on!' I screech, pulling my car into the middle of the road to try and overtake. But I can't. It's too dangerous. And then the Defender is gone. I pull over into a cul-de-sac to turn the car around. Mungo gives me a look which I interpret as disdain.

And then my phone rings. I grab it and accept the call without looking at the incoming number.

'Yes,' I say, abruptly.

'You left me a message.' Her voice is faint.

'Is this Alice?'

'How do you know my name?'

'I've been given your number by Sophie Buck. She is worried about you. My name's Pippa. Where are you, Alice?'

There is a long silence.

'Alice?' I ask again.

'How do I know I can trust you?'

'I'm a friend of Sophie's and am involved in trying to find Cat. Are you safe, Alice?'

'I don't want to talk to the police or Karl or Venetia. I just want to go home to Dad, but he's not answering his phone and Granddad isn't either and I've got no money to get home.'

'And your mother? Is she with you?'

'No,' Alice whispers.

'Tell me where you are and I'll come and rescue you.'

'I'm in Macclesfield.'

I gasp. 'But that's over two hundred miles away! What are you doing there?'

'I ran away. I haven't got enough money for a train ticket.'

I think for a moment. There is no way I can drive all the way to Macclesfield to rescue Alice. It would take four to five hours to get there, but then I think of Flo. If someone had offered my daughter a safe haven, might she be safe and well today? I've got to save Alice and I've got to find Martha. First, I need to take Alice somewhere safe, and then I need to lure her mother and find out what the hell she is doing abducting her own child and, quite probably, keeping Cat locked away somewhere too. My brain is racing.

'I'll pay your ticket and meet you in London. I'll make sure you're safe. How does that sound?'

'Okay,' Alice says, sniffing.

'I'll book you a train ticket online and call you back with the reference number. Where are you at the moment?'

'In the waiting room at Macclesfield Station.'

I ring off. With fumbling fingers, I go to NationalRail.com and buy Alice a single ticket to London. Then I call her back with the reference number.

'Stay on the phone whilst you collect the ticket,' I instruct.

It takes forever, but eventually she says, 'I can't buy it. I need your credit card number.'

I curse. 'Let me talk to the ticket salesperson,' I instruct.

It takes several long minutes before he is prepared to release the ticket to Alice.

'What train will you be on?' I ask.

'I've just missed one. The next is at 10.26. It gets into London at 12.21.'

'I will be there to meet you, Alice, and if for any reason I'm late, just wait near the top of the ramp where you come up onto the concourse.'

'How do I know what you look like?'

'Don't worry. I will recognise you.' I don't want to tell her that I was in the audience when she bolted from the stage.

I HURRY HOME. There is an envelope lying on the door mat. I pick it up and toss it into my handbag, give Mungo his supper two hours early, then race out of the house. I decide to drive to Gatwick Airport, leave my car in the short-term carpark and take the fast train up to London. There is no way I could cross London by car in time to meet Alice off her train. It's ridiculous that it takes me as long to get to London Euston from Storrington, a distance of 60 miles, as it does to get from Macclesfield, at a distance of 188 miles. I am the most single-minded I recall being in ages. I have a purpose. I am going to save a girl: at least one, and possibly two. And it feels good.

We have just pulled out of Three Bridges Station when I reach into my bag to grab a tissue and find the envelope I shoved into my bag. I open it carelessly and pull out two sheets of a paper, unfolding the newspaper cutting first. As the image sears my brain, I gasp. My hand flies to my mouth and my eyes smart with tears. I know this photo well. It is the one issued to the media when Flo went missing. This is a photocopy of the headline in The Daily Mail. *Where did Flo Go? British girl Florence Durrant, aged 18, disappears in Cape Town on Gap Year.* My hand is shaking as I unfold the second piece of paper. It is typewritten in bold capital letters. *STAY AWAY FROM THE MISSING MUSICIANS OTHERWISE CAT KINGSLEY WILL END UP LIKE FLO. DEAD. GONE FOREVER.*

I drop both pieces of paper. They flutter towards the filthy train carriage floor. The young man sitting opposite me reaches down to pick them up. I make a lunge. I don't want anyone else to read them.

'Are you all right?' he asks.

I nod, unable to speak.

'Bad news?'

I nod again.

'Sorry,' he mumbles as he turns his head away and stares out of the window.

My brain feels scrambled. I know I should ring Joe and tell him about this, but then I'll have to admit where I am and what I'm about to do. I can't let Alice down. That would be unforgiveable. We had plenty of cruel false hoax leads in the months after Flo disappeared, and my gut is telling me that this is one of those. Perhaps it has been sent to me by Cat's abductor? It has to be someone connected to the Academy, someone who knows of my involvement with the case. But, for now, I need to forget about myself and concentrate on Alice. It's a horrible note, but I don't really think I'm in danger.

The train pulls into Victoria Station on time and I dart through the crowds, dodging groups of lingering tourists and pre-Christmas Saturday afternoon shoppers laden with brightly coloured plastic and paper bags bulging with gifts that most probably will be discarded by Boxing Day. I run down the steps towards the underground, glad that most people are going in the opposite direction, and hop onto a tube train just before the doors close.

Less than ten minutes later, I am racing up the escalators at Euston Station and standing in front of the Arrivals Board, peering to see which platform the train from Manchester and Macclesfield is expected to arrive into. And then I am there, just in time to see people pouring out of the train and hurrying up the slope from the platform towards the main concourse. I keep my eyes peeled for Alice. At one point I think I spot her; a young girl with her hair tied back and a rucksack on her back, but as she gets nearer I realise she looks nothing like Alice. So I wait. And I wait. And eventually the last stragglers leave the train and amble towards me and carry on into the body of the station. The only people left are the train staff, loading rubbish onto trolleys and lifting crates of drinks and food back onto the train.

'Shit,' I murmur under my breath. It never crossed my mind that Alice might do a runner, might get off the train somewhere other than London, or perhaps she never got on it at all. Have I been hopelessly naive? And then it strikes me. Perhaps Martha found Alice and she's taken her away. What should I do now?

My phone rings and I grab it quickly. My heart sinks. It's not Alice, but Joe. How ironic that only a day ago I would have been delighted to speak to Joe, but not now. He will have to wait. Besides, I know he won't approve of what I'm doing. I don't answer the call, and instead try Alice's number. It goes straight to voicemail. Either it's switched off or she's ignoring my calls. How can I rescue someone who doesn't want to be rescued?

I turn around. I need a coffee or, ideally, something much stronger. I must save Alice. I cannot let another girl disappear. With sagging shoulders, I walk slowly towards the nearest coffee shop. I order a double espresso and sink into an uncomfortable metal chair. What a waste of a Saturday. What a waste of money that I don't have to spare.

I drink the coffee too quickly and burn the roof of my mouth. It'll be ulcerated by tomorrow. It always is when I drink something too hot. A momentary lapse of concentration that results in several days of pain.

And then I catch sight of a young woman with long, golden hair and an oblong box slung over her shoulder.

'Oh my God!' I say out aloud, my hand rushing to my mouth. A man in a suit sitting in the adjacent table glances up from his laptop and, with his rubbery face and slit eyes, sneers at me. I jump up and run, pushing my way between lingering travellers, shouting, 'Out the way, please! Out of the way!'

I feel many pairs of eyes on my back and sense my cheeks flushing. I am just a few feet from her now as she steps onto the escalator, holding onto the rail on the right-hand side. There are too many people in front of me so I can't push forwards, but I can shout her name.

'Cat!' I yell. 'Cat!'

A few people turn to stare at me.

'Catherine Kingsley!' I shout, but the woman with the violin case over her shoulder doesn't turn around. As she steps off the escalator, she walks steadily towards the ticket machines. I push my way through and then I am right next to her. I place a hand on her shoulder.

'Cat?'

She turns around. This woman is at least twenty years older than Cat. She has a lined face and pale grey eyes, and wears an expression of disdain that I suspect is etched on her face permanently rather than specifically directed at me. She looks absolutely nothing like the photograph the police have been circulating.

'I'm so sorry,' I say. 'I thought you were someone else.'

I hurry away.

I almost don't hear it, so drowned I am in my own misery

and embarrassment, but I manage to grab my phone just in time.

'Pippa?'

'Speaking.'

'I'm here. Where are you?'

29

I hurry back to the exit from Platform 2 and there she is, her arms tightly wound around her torso, her face ghostly pale.

'I thought you'd missed the train!' I say, trying to sound light-hearted.

'I got off at Milton Keynes. I shouldn't have done.'

'No worries. You're here now, safe and sound. Let's get you home, shall we?'

I start walking but Alice stays rooted to the spot.

'Home?'

'Well, not your home. Not unless we can track down your dad. I was thinking about my home. I've got a nice spare room and a Labrador who will love you and be your very best friend.' I know I'm twittering, but I want her to feel safe and come with me so that I can protect her. 'Don't you have a bag?'

She shakes her head. 'I started walking and then I didn't stop, and then I got a lift to the station and, well—'

'And your violin? Where's that?'

Tears well in Alice's eyes. She looks away.

'No problem,' I say, putting my hand on her arm. 'Come on. Let's head over to Gatwick. That's where my car is.'

She follows me then, and when the crowds get denser, I put my arm through hers and hold on to her tightly. I don't want to lose Alice, and I don't rate her chances of surviving a night alone in December in London. It's standing room only on the train from Victoria to Gatwick, so there's no the chance to talk. She follows me out of the station to the short-term parking lot, and waits patiently whilst I pay the extortionate parking charge. When I click open the doors to my car, she hesitates.

'How do I know you are who you say you are?'

I smile, my head tilted to one side, my palms facing upwards. 'I was in the audience when you bolted off the stage at The Cadogan Hall. Afterwards, I spoke to Sophie. Then, when Cat was reported missing, I went with DS Swain to meet Venetia and Karl Edstol. I've also spoken to Christophe and Vadim and met little Lisl. I'm a psychologist and I look after people. I've even been to your house and I met your grandad. He's been very worried about you.'

'I don't want to go back to the Academy.'

'Why don't you hop in the car and we can chat about it on our way home?'

She does as I suggest and settles into the passenger seat.

Once we're on the M23 southwards, she speaks again. 'I mean it. I don't want to go back to Edstols. I don't want to be a violinist.'

'I won't be taking you there. I promise. All I want to do is keep you safe.' I know now isn't the time or the place to be asking such a question, but I can't help myself. 'Are you scared of your mother?'

I sense Alice shifting towards the window, away from me, but I can't take my eyes off the busy road. She doesn't say anything. In fact, she doesn't speak another word until we're home, and when I park up in front of my small cottage, I realise she's fast asleep, her face relaxed and her mouth slightly open.

'Alice,' I say softly. 'Alice, you need to wake up now. We're home!'

She awakes with a start and immediately bursts into tears.

'It's all right, darling. You're safe. Let's get you inside and have something to eat.'

I have a surge of inappropriate maternal love.

30

Scott and Daughter's Auction House is situated in a large warehouse in open countryside, neighboured by a working cattle farm and a minor B-road. The nearest town is Petworth, a rather lovely market town which, together with the 17th-century Petworth House and Park—now run by the National Trust—has become a mecca for up-market antique shops and luxury independent boutiques. Although Scott and Daughter's was historically an agricultural auction house, it now receives a mishmash of items to sell. Few of great value, though.

Milo Sneddon receives daily alerts from all the European auction houses. Every morning between 10 and 11 a.m.—he is a late riser—he drinks his milky white coffee whilst studying the upcoming catalogues. In the days when his brother Jonno and sister-in-law Marissa had money, he would use their funds to bid for instruments. These days, with no cash in the bank, he has to hope he will spot something the other experts miss. Of course, official auction catalogues aren't Milo's only source of information. His evening brandy is drunk whilst perusing the Dark Web, seeking out the spoils of crime and occasionally placing an order for something that catches his eye. Since Jonno's Guarneri has gone missing, Milo has been spending more time on the Dark Web. But it is luck, and only luck, that brings him to Scott and Daughter's auction this dreary December afternoon.

Unlike his brother Jonno, who is short and compact in stature with a symmetrical face and a natural ability to charm the ladies, Milo was born with one leg shorter than the other and a face kindly described as similar to a bashed-in pug's. At fifty-three years, he has never had a relationship that didn't require him to buy sex.

The party the previous night was like any other, but included a clutch of up-market Russian prostitutes and was held near Midhurst, in a grand and very nouveau country estate owned by a collector acquaintance of Milo's. The evening had not gone well, and Milo left the following morning. It just so happens that he finds himself passing Scott and Daughter's Auction House at the moment a young member of staff is hanging a sign that reads, 'Auction Today!' Milo pulls his leased Mercedes into the parking lot and waddles into the sale room.

'Got any musical instruments?' he barks.

'I think we have a couple of violins, an accordion and a piano from some house clearances,' the young woman at the reception desk says, smiling. 'They'll be in the second room on the left. We're just about to collect all the lots for the auction this afternoon.'

Milo nods and makes his way through. The excess of alcohol and drugs from the night before has turned his head into a cauldron of bright lights, pounding drums and intense pressure, so it is nothing short of a miracle that he even recognises the second violin he picks up.

'Holy fuck!' he says, grabbing onto a mahogany armoire to stop himself from sinking to the ground. When the dizziness abates, he glances all around him to make sure no one is watching, and lifts the violin up. He peruses it carefully, looking inside the f holes into the body of the instrument, feeling the carving of the wooden scrolls on the neck, running his podgy fingers over the back of the instrument to be sure that it is still crack-free and in one beautiful piece. The tailpiece has shifted and one of the strings is broken, but Milo would recognise this little lovely anywhere. He has spent enough time studying it. Placing it gently back onto the table, he mutters under his breath.

Another young woman wearing a white blouse and black trousers strides past.

'Excuse me! What's the reserve on these two instruments?'

'The one in the case I think has a reserve of £100. The other one was a late entry, and I think it's got an estimate of between thirty and fifty pounds. I can check on the system for you.'

'When's the sale?'

'This afternoon, 3.30 p.m.'

Super alert now, Milo picks up the crappy violin with the £100 reserve. 'I'm really interested in this little beauty.'

The woman nods and hurries away.

Milo debates stealing the violin, but he's spotted the little blinking security cameras in the corner of the room. He hasn't even got time to get one of his contacts to raid the place later. Instead, he decides to risk it. He'll return at 3.30 p.m.

AFTER A LOUSY PUB LUNCH, Milo is seated in the third row of the auction house. There is a poor showing, maybe twenty or so people and, to his immense relief, no one Milo recognises. He knows most of the instrument dealers in the UK. He debated calling Jonno, but didn't want to get his hopes up. Besides, Jonno might do something stupid. To avoid raising suspicions, Milo bids on a few other things and becomes the unhappy owner of a twee cut-glass angel for £15 and the piano accordion for £25. He decides he has to bid for the other violin, but there is no one bidding against him, so when it gets to £90, he shakes his head. As it hasn't reached its reserve, the violin remains unsold. And then, three lots later, Milo raises his hand again. He is trembling. The auctioneer starts off at £20, but to Milo's dismay he realises there's someone bidding against him: a person seated behind him.

To begin with, Milo keeps his eyes firmly on the auctioneer, but as the bidding increases rapidly to £120, he turns around and sees that the other bidder is an elderly woman. A music teacher no doubt, he decides. The tension builds as the auctioneer raises the price in £20 increases, but Milo will pay any price, and he almost laughs out aloud at the thought that the auctioneer should be using £10,000 increments, not £20 ones. At £220, the violin is his, and Milo feels dizzy with relief. He collapses into his chair, his back sticky with sweat, his breathing loud and heavy. As they say in the trade, Milo has picked up a sleeper, something of value that no one else has spotted. And what a sleeper it is!

His next problem will be Jonno.

After a few further lots, Milo gets up and walks out of the auction room, trying very hard to control his grin. Back at the reception desk, he takes out his wallet. 'I'm here to collect lot number 187, a violin, lot 55, an accordion and lot 123, a glass angel.'

After signing a form, the woman works out the total owed, including twenty per cent commission and VAT on the commission. Milo grimaces as he hands over the cash, but inside he's dancing with joy. He waits impatiently for a boy to bring out the items.

'Can I help you carry them to your car?' the young lad asks.

'Give me the violin and you can take the rest.'

He hands over the violin, which is in an old battered case

Milo doesn't recognise. He opens the case just to double-check, and bites the side of his cheek to stop a grin from bursting across his face.

Ten minutes later, he's speeding through the country lanes on his way to Jonno's.

⌇

'YOU'RE GOING to fucking owe me on this one,' Milo says as he places the violin case carefully on Jonno's kitchen table. He leans over to his brother. 'Is that maid of yours around?' he asks in a whisper.

'No. She's out shopping and Marissa is asleep. Why?'

'Because I've got some bloody good news for you! And it's news that you and me are going to keep between us. Capiche?'

Jonno shifts uneasily.

'But first we're gonna do a deal. Fifty per cent to you, fifty per cent to me.'

'What do you mean?'

'When the insurance money comes in, you're going to give me half. Got that, big bro?' Milo has always liked to tease Jonno that although he's the eldest, he's the smallest of the two.

Jonno squirms. 'The police are investigating.'

'Yup, but they've got no evidence.'

'How do you know?'

Milo stands up and opens the case. 'Ta da!' he exclaims, waiting for his brother's face to light up with joy.

But it doesn't.

'Is that my violin?'

'Yup. The Guarneri currently valued at £3.2 million, worth a little under half of that.'

'Where did you find it?'

'At Scott and Daughter's Auction House. At least one of us is on the ball. Picked it up for £500 cash—money which you owe me, by the way.'

'But we need the cash, the insurance payout!' Jonno says, shaking his head.

'And we'll get it, because now we have our hands on this lovely jubbly instrument. We can destroy it and prove that it's a gonner. And you can get your hands on the dosh and try to save Marissa, and I can buy a bloody house. Think I'll move to Thailand and pick myself up a young bride.'

'We can't destroy an instrument of such worth, with a heritage like this!' Jonno says, an expression of horror on his face. 'I know you fly close to the wind, but this is too far.'

Milo stands up. He's not getting the reaction he'd expected from Jonno and it's making him feel nervous. When Milo feels nervous, he gets aggressive; particularly in relation to his smaller, but older, brother.

'No fucking around on this one, Jonno.' He leans towards him, menacingly. 'Don't lecture me about flying too close to the wind! You've been alongside me every step of the way, particularly when it comes to valuing the instruments in your collection. We need the money and pronto. I've put myself on the line for you time and time again. You are going to destroy this violin. You owe me.'

Jonno bunches up his eyes and rubs his fingers over his brows.

Milo carries on. 'You don't do what I say, and I'll drop a few hints to the police. Not sure what you get for insurance claim frauds these days, but I'm sure it'll be a year or two in jail at least. Just long enough for your lovely wife to die without you.'

'Bastard!' Jonno yells. 'You'd do that to your own brother?'

'Needs must, bro,' Milo says, a slow smile creating four double chins. 'I'll let myself out, shall I?'

He ambles away, not waiting for an answer.

31

J onno stares at the violin. He had hoped Milo was wrong, that this wasn't his Guarneri, but there's no doubting it. It has that slight asymmetrical quality; f holes that are just ever so slightly crudely cut and not exactly identical; and a pale, gold-amber hue to the wood. He turns the violin over and studies the back, with its flame-like markings that run up and outwards from the centre, where the two perfectly-matched pieces of spruce align. It's exquisite. The grain is straight, with just the one tiny imperfection where a crack was restored in a bygone era. Jonno lets out a groan as he places the violin back on the table. It's his. For once, Milo is right about something. But now what?

What choice does he have? He needs the money. He has to have the money. Marissa's life depends upon it. For one moment, he considers selling the Guarneri legally. What might it fetch? A million, perhaps? But not more. It's not one of Guarneri's best instruments, and the provenance is just a little dubious. But then it will come to light that he has over-insured it, and what if it doesn't sell quickly? They'd be back to square

one. The rate Marissa is declining at terrifies Jonno. He needs
the money now; not next month or next year.

If he is to do what Milo suggests, he needs to medicate first,
dull the senses with a bottle of whiskey. He walks over to the
drinks cabinet, an antique globe—finely painted with a world
map—that lifts up to reveal a belly housing bottles. Jonno
calculates there's enough left in the bottle to numb the pain,
but not sufficient to make him unwieldly with the hammer. He
puts a cut-glass tumbler on the table alongside the bottle of
Lagavulin 16. Then he walks out of his study, down the hall and
—braving the foul weather—hurries out to the right-hand side
of the courtyard, where there are garages and a workshop. Once
upon a time they housed a Bentley and an E-type Jaguar; now
they are chock full of worthless clutter. He wrenches open the
door to the workshop, which used to be the home of their full-
time grounds-man come maintenance manager, and switches
on the light. Three work benches are covered in dust and
debris, and the tools hanging up on the wall are laced with
cobwebs.

Jonno looks at the hammers and wrenches. He selects one
of each, wipes them down on his rust-coloured corduroys,
turns the light off and slams the door shut behind him. He
supposes he should keep it locked, but right now he can't be
bothered to find the key.

It's so quiet back inside the house. That's what he misses
the most: the sound of Marissa practicing, the repeated trills
and scales and melodies that at the time drove him close to
insanity as she played them over and over and over again.
Every day, the house gets quieter. She's even playing her record-
ings less and less frequently now. It's as if snow has fallen inside
and muffled everything.

He sees Kaya slip into the kitchen. It would be better if Kaya
wasn't in the house, but he hasn't got the luxury of time. The
police could pop up again unannounced, or Karl could start

asking more questions. He grabs one of the old mohair throws from the sofa in the living room—not the pale blue and white angora throw, shot through with threads of pale pink, because that one is Marissa's favourite. Instead he chooses an old one in shades of taupe and mushroom; a throw that, as far as he is aware, has no significance. Hurrying back to his study, he shuts the door behind him. He wishes the door had a lock, but none of the downstairs rooms are lockable. Wrapping the violin in the throw, he places it on his desk. Then he pours himself a full glass of whiskey and drinks it in one go, his throat burning in a satisfying, masochistic way. He pours another full glass and tips that one back too, then sits down on his swivel chair and waits for the alcohol to numb his body.

The old pipes start clanging, indicating that Kaya is helping Marissa wash. He needs to hurry. Swallowing down whiskey-flavoured bile, he stands up and walks around the leather-topped desk, his back to the door. He lifts the hammer high up into the air, and closes his eyes just as it makes contact with the delicate instrument. Despite the muffling provided by the layer of mohair, he hears the wood splinter, the pinging of a string, the shattering of dreams. Jonno offers up a silent prayer to the gods of antiquities. Emboldened now, he lifts the hammer again and throws his whole weight behind it, again and again. Trembling, he places the hammer to one side and gently opens up the throw. The violin is now a pile of splintered wood, more broken and fractured than his beloved wife.

'What are you doing?'

Jonno swivels around with a start. 'Marissa, what are you doing here?'

She wheels her chair towards the desk. Jonno leaps to stand between her and the table, blocking her way.

'What's that on the table?'

As she's in a wheelchair, she's at a lower height than the table and doesn't have a clear view. Jonno leaps back, folds the throw into the centre and then wraps it around and around into a small parcel, packaging the broken wood in the middle. But a few splinters come loose and stick to the furry fronds of the mohair.

'What's inside the rug?' Marissa wheels herself nearer.

Jonno freezes.

'Come on, darling. No secrets.' The once-beautifully clear enunciation of her consonants is fading so it sounds as if her mouth is full of marbles.

'I'm sorry,' Jonno whispers.

'What have you done?'

'I'm sorry, darling. I did it for you, so we can make you better.'

'Did what for me?'

'The insurance money. We will be able to afford for you to take the new immunotherapy drug. We can go to America and can continue supporting the clinical trials. I'm going to make you better.'

'Jonno, what's in there?' Anyone other than Jonno might struggle to decipher what Marissa is saying.

'I did it for you,' Jonno says quietly, bending down and taking his wife's hands in his own. 'The Guarneri. It's broken.'

Marissa struggles to remove her hands from Jonno's grasp, but her howl startles Jonno and he steps backwards.

'What have you done? Please, not the Guarneri! It's priceless!'

'Darling, I've done it for you. For our future.'

'But where did you get it? Please tell me you haven't had anything to do with the girl! You haven't, have you?' Marissa is shaking now, her head trembling backwards and forwards as if her neck is a delicate flower stem trying in vain to hold up a heavy stone.

'What sort of person do you think I am!' Jonno shouts. 'I have no idea where she is.'

'Of course I'd like you to have someone else when I am gone, to line someone up...' Her fragile voice peters out.

'I'm not interested in twenty-year-old girls!' Jonno paces around the room. 'And don't talk about when you're gone! You're not going anywhere!' He can't look at his wife.

'Oh my God, oh Jonno!' Marissa's voice is rasping. 'You have destroyed an antique, something priceless! Please tell me it's not true!'

'But it's only a bit of wood! It might save your life!' Jonno runs his fingers through his hair.

The tears pour down Marissa's cheeks. 'I am dying. What you are doing is madness. Accept it, Jonno. Accept it.'

There is a knock on the door and Kaya pokes her head around. 'Is everything all right?'

'Yes!' Jonno snaps.

Marissa tries to turn her wheelchair around, but her hand slips on the lever. Her cries sound like a distressed animal caught in the clutches of a predator.

'Madam!' Kaya rushes forwards and kneels down in front of Marissa. 'Don't cry, please don't cry!'

Kaya stands up and stares at Jonno, but he turns his back to the room, his eyes fixed on the window, unseeing. What has he done?

32

By 9 p.m. Alice is tucked up in my spare bedroom, the room that I secretly allocated to Flo for her homecoming. It has the same white curtains with yellow daisies that Flo had in her room at our family home, before she went missing, before Trevor and I divorced, before George morphed from our hard-working, sweet-natured boy into an angry stranger. It has Flo's red and white mohair blanket on the bed and her favourite childhood teddy bear placed on my old rocking chair, sitting, waiting, patiently waiting for her to return. But the rest of Flo's belongings are in boxes, a few in my loft and the rest in Trevor's in his new home that he shares with the most recent young Mrs Durrant.

I pour myself a large glass of wine and collapse onto the sofa. I think about the private investigator in Cape Town. His requests for more money to pursue leads come two or three times a year. I pay up and then nothing further happens. I wonder if the time has come to find a new private investigator.

My phone rings, cutting through my thoughts. It's Joe. Once again, I don't want to answer it. I don't want to have to tell Joe that I have Alice, all safe and sound. I don't want to hear about the fun he is having with his daughter, Holly. And I don't want to tell him that I spotted Bill Jones and Karl Edstol, heads bent low towards each other.

But I do wonder if I'm doing the right thing. Sophie thinks she's in danger. Is she really? Should I be telling Joe and getting him to protect her? And what about the note pushed through my letterbox, warning me to stay away? But by the time I have thought this through and dithered, the ringing stops. A few seconds later, I listen to his message.

'Hi Pippa. I'm very sorry about the night before last. I wasn't expecting Holly home so soon. Would you mind if we take a raincheck on meeting up for a couple of days? I'll be in touch regarding the case as soon as we know any more. Could you analyse the writing of the kidnapper for us?'

There are no words of endearment, none of the flirtatious messages he normally leaves. I chuck the phone onto the sofa and take a large swig of wine.

I am watching the news on television when Mungo barks. He walks towards the back door, the fur on the nape of his neck standing on end. He growls.

'What is it boy?' I ask quietly, worried about waking Alice. I follow my dog as he prowls through to the kitchen and into the utility room, ears pricked, fur still raised. I don't switch the light on. I stand still, letting my eyes adjust to the darkness, trying to spot any movement outside.

Mungo growls again. My heart starts thudding. I need to feel safe in my own home. And then through the window of my back door, I see the silhouette of a person moving swiftly across the back of my house. Mungo barks ferociously. Terror clenches my gut; not just for Mungo and me, but for the girl asleep upstairs.

Mungo is scratching the back door, desperate to get out, but I don't want to put him in any danger despite his deep bark and bared teeth, I doubt he would actually attack a burglar. He is a gentle Labrador through and through.

Now the figure is just four feet away, a dark, featureless outline. Just as I'm about to unlock the door, something is hurled through the kitchen window, the splintering clatter of glass making me gasp.

'Help!' I scream. Mungo's barking is frantic. I race back into the kitchen. Glass is scattered across the kitchen sink, the counter tops and onto the floor. A brick has been thrown through my kitchen window. I am terrified that something will be thrown through Alice's window.

'Stay back, Mungo!' I instruct. I need to make sure he doesn't cut his paws. I grab the telephone and race to the back door, unlocking it and swinging it open. Mungo rushes out, but immediately stops barking.

There is no one there. I shine the beam of my torch onto the flower beds and the small lawn. I walk gingerly around the side of the house. Then I stand on tiptoes and point the torch towards my neighbour's garden. After a few long moments, I walk back into the house, locking and bolting the door behind me. Just as I am about to pick up the phone to call the police, I am startled by a voice.

'What's going on?' Alice is standing at the bottom of the stairs, pale and shivering in the oversized T-shirt I loaned her.

'It's nothing to worry about. He's gone now. Why don't you go back to bed whilst I call the police?'

If she heard the breaking glass, she doesn't say anything. She just nods and returns back up the stairs.

I ring Joe. It goes straight to voicemail. I am surprised as, when we spent nights together, he kept it switched on. But perhaps he is fully off-duty and spending precious time with his daughter. Besides, it is late. I leave a message anyway.

'Someone is threatening me, Joe. They threw a brick through my kitchen window just now, and want me to stay away from the missing girls. I'll call 999 just because. Actually, don't worry. Let's talk in the morning.'

I ring 999 and am put through to a central call-handling station. The man doesn't know anything about Cat Kingsley's kidnapping.

'Are you in imminent danger?' he asks.

'No,' I admit. I am positive there is no one here anymore. Mungo is calm now.

'We will send someone around in the morning,' he says. He gives me a crime number and ends the call.

Unsurprisingly, after clearing up the glass and taping a black bin liner across the broken window and drinking a large brandy, I feel brutally awake. What if he comes back and climbs into the house through the hole in the window? Should Alice and I decamp somewhere safer, to my brother Rob's house, perhaps? But what will that do to her fragile state of mind? Shortly after midnight, it occurs to me that there might be such a service as a 24-hour glazier. I go online and find one in Worthing and another in Horsham.

'Hello.' His voice languid with sleep.

I apologise for waking him and ask if he could come out and board up my window. The price he quotes is exorbitant, but I have no choice. Shortly after midnight, the doorbell rings.

'Could you do this as quietly as possible, please?' I ask.

He raises his eyebrows but doesn't say anything. No doubt he has seen his fair share of unspeakable situations in his long professional career.

But I still toss and turn all night long, getting up at 3 a.m. to double check all the doors are bolted, and again shortly before 5 a.m. when I think I hear the slamming of a car door.

The phone rings at 9 a.m.

'What's happened, Pippa?' Joe asks. 'I'm sorry I had my phone switched off.'

I tell him about the newspaper cutting and the threatening

note, and the brick through the kitchen window. For some reason, I don't tell him about Alice. I know it's wrong, but I want to protect her for a few more hours. I know Joe will be livid, but I have to put Alice's emotional wellbeing first, and I am the best person to assess that. Joe offers to come over, but I tell him that I have already been allocated a case number and the local police will be stopping by later. I promise myself that I will tell Joe the truth by the end of the day. I just need a few hours with Alice, a few hours to assess whether her parents are abusing her.

By 10.30 a.m. on Sunday morning, there is still no sign of life from my spare bedroom and I haven't had a visit from the police. My first thought is that Alice might have run away, and then I launch into the dreadful 'what if' scenarios that I try to help my clients avoid. Has she cut herself and bled to death on my spare bed? Has she taken an overdose? I have all the strategies at my fingertips to avoid the traps of neurotic think-ing, and try to use them. *How likely is that, really? Last night, did I evaluate her as being a danger to herself or others. No, I didn't.*

At 10.35 a.m. I knock gently on the door and then softly open it.

'Alice, are you awake?'

The curtains are closed and the mound under the duvet shifts. She opens her eyes and blinks at me.

'Did you have a good sleep? It's gone 10.30 a.m. so I thought you might like some breakfast.'

She rubs her knuckles into her eyes and yawns. Then she sits up in bed, the navy and white-striped oversized T-shirt I gave her to wear crumpled around her.

'Have you spoken to Dad?'

'No. I don't have his number. Why don't you get up and then we can try and call him.'

She nods. I leave the room and go back downstairs.

I am frying some bacon when the phone rings, so I don't even glance at it as I answer.

'Pippa, there's been a further development in the case. Alice's parents have surfaced, but have reported her missing,' Joe says. 'I want to interview Bill Jones, Alice's father, and I'd really value your input. Any chance you could join me?'

'It's not her father you need to be investigating. It's the mother. She's the—'

At that moment, Alice appears in the doorway.

'Sorry but I've got to dash. I'll call you later.' Hurriedly, I hang up. The phone rings again, but I ignore it and let it go to voicemail. I know it's fundamentally wrong not to tell Joe that I have Alice, but it's just for a few hours. It's the only way to keep the girl safe.

ALICE EATS her breakfast in silence and I feel awkward, unsure of what to say, and start muttering about the weather and making inane comments about how much I admire musicians. Eventually she asks what happened to the window.

'Someone threw a brick through it last night,' I say. 'There's a gang of youths terrorising the area.' The statement is quite ridiculous. This is sleepy, gentle, rural Storrington, as far removed from a London sink estate as one could imagine.

But Alice doesn't question any further. She just continues munching her breakfast.

'What would you like to do today?' I ask as my small talk runs out.

'Find Daddy. Can you take me home?'

'Will you mum be there?'

Alice shrugs.

'Why don't you try calling him first?'

'The battery on my phone has died.'

I reach across the table for my phone and hand it to her. She dials and holds it up to her ear. After a few moments, she puts it back on the table, her eyes watery.

'There's no answer.'

'Do you want to let your mum know that you're safe?'

She shakes her head.

'Have you any idea as to what has happened to Cat?' I ask.

I study her face and her body language, but the only expression I see is bewilderment; bewilderment that morphs into fear.

'Am I safe?' she whispers.

'I will make sure that you are,' I say, praying that I have not made her a false promise, and wondering whether I have put her in even greater danger than she was in before.

I DRIVE Alice to her house, but the Defender isn't parked at the front and Alice explains that she doesn't have a key, so there's no way that we can get inside.

'Would you like to visit your grandparents?' I suggest.

Again, she shakes her head, so instead I drive to the Downs and we take Mungo for a brisk walk. We stop for a late lunch at a pub just outside Pulborough and, although Alice is quiet, I relish the fact that her cheeks have some colour and that her shoulders are no longer clenched high up towards her ears.

Even Mungo is yawning by the time we turn into my road, darkness settling early as we approach the shortest day of the year. I let out a short squeak when I see the police car parked up outside my house.

'What are they doing here?' Alice is blinking furiously.

'I expect they're here to investigate the breaking of the window,' I say brightly.

As I park the car, a shadow falls over my window. I look up and my heart sinks. It's Joe. He raps on the window.

'I'm coming!' I say, turning off the ignition and opening the door.

'Get out!' he spits. This is not my Joe.

I climb out and shut the driver's door behind me. I don't look at Alice.

'What the hell are you doing with Alice Jones?' It's as if his eyes are sparking.

'I rescued her,' I say quietly. 'She ran away from her mother. She's obviously scared. I think Martha has something to do with Cat's kidnapping.'

'Martha Jones is accusing you of abducting her daughter.'

'What?' I exclaim. 'How did she even know she was here?'

'An app called FindFriends. It's on Alice's phone, so Martha was able to pinpoint exactly where her daughter is. She filed a MisPer last night and today notified us of your address. What the hell are you playing at?'

'I'm not playing at anything!' I walk away from the car and Joe follows closely on my heels. He then reaches out for me and tries to turn me to face him.

'Don't touch me!' I say.

He is startled. He opens his mouth as if to say something, then closes it. He turns his back to me, paces a few steps away and then returns. 'What's going on, Pippa? Between us?'

'I don't know. Nothing. Actually, I think we should cool things a bit.'

His face crumples, as if I have stabbed him. I try to soften the blow. 'I'm sorry Joe. This case has got in the way. Besides, you will be spending Christmas with your lovely daughter and it's probably sensible to cool things before either of us gets hurt.'

I am appalled at how easily I spurt such tripe, such platitudes. And it's not even as if I mean them. I have no idea why I'm pushing him away.

His back stiffens. 'Right. I'll ask a colleague to interview you. We need to investigate the threats to you, and Martha Jones intends to press charges. In the meantime, I'll take Alice back to her parents, where she belongs.'

'Any news of Cat?' I ask.

'Under the circumstances, you are no longer involved in the case. You are now personally involved as both an offender and a possible victim of crime. I am sure you understand.' Joe is tense, his voice curt and cold.

I want to run up to him, throw my arms around his rigid body, beg for forgiveness, feel his lips on mine. But instead I nod, let Mungo out of my car and walk down the path to my front door.

33

'I've received an envelope containing fragments of wood. I think someone destroyed the violin and sent it to me,' Jonno says.

'And how would they know you are the owner?' Joe asks. He wishes he was in the same room as the Viscount Sneddon, with Pippa at his side so she could assess the veracity of his statements. Instead, they are having this conversation on the phone.

'It's common knowledge. Just look at any of Cat's recital programmes and it says the artist is playing on a Guarneri violin kindly loaned by Viscount Sneddon.'

'Did it come with any note or information on the whereabouts of Catherine Kingsley?'

'Nope.'

'I'll send an officer around to collect the envelope and contents. We'll need it for forensic testing.'

'But my insurance broker will also need it.'

'We'll release it when this case is solved. Until then, it is evidence. And we'll need to take your fingerprints too.'

〜

JOE IS IN A FOUL MOOD. The progress on the case is painfully slow and his bosses are demanding answers. But most of all, he cannot understand why Pippa has pushed him away and he is livid about her intervention. He recalls the words of his deceased father: Never mix business and pleasure.

Mia stands in front of Joe's desk. 'Martha Jones has arrived home, sir. Shall I take Alice back there now?'

'I'll come with you. I want to interview both parents. How did you get on with talking to Alice?'

'She told me she ran away, that she no longer wants to be a musician and that she hates her mother. Apparently she contacted Sophie Buck, who put her in touch with Dr Durrant. It does corroborate with what Dr Durrant said. I don't think there are any grounds for abduction. Alice is sixteen years old. She can do what she likes.'

WHEN THEY KNOCK on the front door of the Jones's house, Martha rushes out and flings her arms around Alice, who stands rigid as a door post, pale as milk.

'Darling, I was so worried about you! I thought something terrible had happened. Well, it had, hadn't it? You were abducted! Are you all right, my little chicken?'

Mia catches Joe's eye.

'Can we come in and have a word, please?' Joe asks.

'Of course.' Martha reddens, lets go of Alice and stands to one side.

'Is your husband here?'

'Um, no. He's gone away on a business trip for a couple of days.'

Alice frowns. 'Dad never goes away,' she says quietly.

'Yes, he does!' Martha says, all gung ho. 'Silly you! Don't you remember he went to Blackpool for a few days back in March, and last year he had a conference in Manchester.'

Alice gives her mother a strange look. Once again, Joe wishes Pippa was here to translate the expressions.

The house feels cold and damp, unloved and unlived in. They follow Martha into the small kitchen and, at her encouragement, sit at the round pine table. There are no cooking implements on the work surfaces, no pictures on the walls, no homely knickknacks. Alice disappears upstairs. Martha doesn't offer them a cup of tea.

'Where have you been the last few days?' Joe asks.

'In the Peak District. We rented a cottage for a few days for a little holiday. We felt Alice needed a break after the concert in London. She's been very upset about Cat's disappearance.'

'Why didn't you tell anyone where you were going?'

Martha flushes. 'We don't normally give notice. Why can't we go away for a few days?'

'Your husband didn't turn up at work, Alice didn't go to school, and your in-laws were extremely concerned.'

'They're elderly with dementia. They get worried about the slightest change. And we did notify the school. Karl and Bill spoke at length. Alice has been expelled, so she has no school to go to.'

'Has she indeed?' Joe asks.

THERE ARE lights blazing from every window of the Academy, unlike during their previous visits when the place seemed dark and foreboding. Joe rings on the doorbell whilst Mia scans the driveway and adjacent bushes for any signs of unusual activity.

Venetia opens the door. Her face is flushed and her eyes are red.

They follow Venetia into the small room with the pink and green chintz curtains. She closes the door behind her.

'Have a seat.' She gesticulates to the chairs.

'Is your husband joining us?' Joe asks.

Venetia turns away, answering with her back towards Joe and Mia. 'No. Karl is out today.'

'Where?'

She hesitates for a moment. 'Visiting his mother. She is in a nursing home in Worthing.'

'I would like to interview the two young men who perform with Cat and Sophie.' Joe laces his fingers together and glances at Mia.

When Venetia is out of the room, Mia stands up and starts looking around the room. 'There's something suspicious going on here. I wonder where Karl Edstol is, really.'

'My thoughts exactly,' Joe says. 'I'm going to call him into the station tomorrow.'

They just have time to have a look through the bookshelves when Venetia returns with Vadim.

'Where is Christophe?' Joe asks.

'Locked himself in his room,' Venetia says, sighing loudly. 'He does that sometimes.'

'I trust you have told him that the police want to talk to him?'

'I have tried, but short of knocking the door down, I can't get him to answer. He is playing music very loudly.'

'And smoking pot,' Vadim says under his breath.

Joe gestures for him to sit down.

Vadim ignores the request and leans towards Joe, his dark eyes shining. 'Do you have information on Cat?'

'No, sorry.'

Vadim's shoulders sink. 'You need do something. You not doing enough!' His Russian accent is heavy and his voice sounds low and guttural. 'Cat, she could be dead! Have you paid money?'

'We never give in to kidnappers' demands,' Joe says.

Vadim throws his hands up in the air. 'But you must! How else will we get her back? You have money, no?'

'That is not how the police operate in this country,' Joe says.

'So you pay!' Vadim points his finger at Venetia.

'We don't have that sort of money!' she exclaims.

'This is not how we negotiate. Vadim, please sit down.'

'No!' His voice is loud and he is pacing around and around the small room, as if, by walking faster and faster, he can arrive at a solution. 'No! This not good enough! I have contacts in Russia. I speak to them.'

'Absolutely not!' Joe says, his voice low and commanding. 'If you don't pull yourself together, I will take you to the police station.'

'This is how you do things in your civilised country, yes? Threaten, bully. You're just as bad as the kidnappers. I speak to my father.'

'Vadim, where have you been during the last twenty-four hours?'

'So now you question me! I be here, practising violin all day yesterday, all day today. Last night I sleep in my bed. I go nowhere! You find Cat!'

'Vadim, love, please calm down.' Venetia tries to placate him.

'No!' He strides to the door, flings it open and slams it shut behind him.

After a few awkward moments, Venetia says, 'I'm sorry. He is acting very out of character.'

'Could you go and get Christophe, please?' Joe says. 'I assume you have a key to his room?'

Venetia nods.

When she has left the room, Mia asks Joe, 'Do you think Vadim is a suspect?'

He shakes his head. 'No. I think he's a love-sick twenty-year-old who could be dangerous if he starts employing the rough-justice tactics of the Russians.'

Again, Venetia returns quickly. 'I'm sorry but Christophe won't come. He says he is sick. Does he have to talk to you?' Venetia looks terrified.

'No, but if we have reason to think he is withholding evidence or is a suspect, then we will arrest him and bring him to the police station.'

'He's an emotional young man, is Christophe. Much like Vadim. Our musicians are all highly sensitive. It goes with the territory, I'm afraid.

'Are you a musician, Mrs Edstol? Are you highly sensitive?' Joe asks.

Venetia blushes deeply.

～

AFTER MIA HAS TAKEN a statement from Venetia, she and Joe return to the car.

'Are you going to bring Dr Durrant in to interview the young people?' Mia asks.

Joe sighs. 'I don't know. I don't know.'

34

She was pathetically grateful for the cheap violin and bow. I bought them off eBay for fifty quid. They're not of the quality she's used to playing on, but beggars can't be choosers. She cried when I gave them to her. More bloody tears.

I was worried she might not be able to play with her hand being all bandaged up but, amazingly, it doesn't stop her. She's umbilically attached to the instrument day and night. And she's playing the same bloody tune over and over and over again. It's driving me insane! It's a simple melody that becomes increasingly complicated, but the damn refrain is there all the time. It sounds a bit like Bach mixed with a lullaby in places. And it's giving me the earworm from hell.

I'm upstairs in the kitchen, having a drink and trying to think. I slam my hand on the table, then get up and stride down the stairs to the basement.

'Shut up!' I shout, banging on the locked door.

The music stops. I wait a few moments, then climb back upstairs. Less than five minutes later, she starts again.

'Shut the fuck up!' I scream. I race back down the stairs. After sliding the bolts undone on the top and bottom of the door, I insert the key and unlock it. She is cowering in the corner of the room, the offending instrument lying on the mattress.

'Play something else,' I growl.

She nods but doesn't meet my gaze.

'I said play something else.'

And still she doesn't move.

'Do you want me to chop off another finger?'

She glances up at me then and I smile at the terror in her eyes. Respect. That's what she has for me now. She shuffles towards the bed, keeping as much distance as possible between us. I know this is normal. I've done my research.

First there was anger and fury. I loved the fire in her belly, the way her cheeks blossomed with redness, how her pupils dilated and how she planted her legs far apart. When she realised that there was nothing she could do, for a while the fury gave way to disbelief. Then came acceptance. When she knew she had to relinquish all control to me, the fire fizzled out and in came apathy and fear. The apathy is unattractive and I need it to pass, quickly.

The fear is good.

Very good.

35

I am watching one of David Attenborough's wonderful wildlife programmes on television. Mungo has his head resting on my knee and I am absent-mindedly stroking his chin. After the fiasco with Alice, I am exhausted. The glazier has returned and fitted a new pane of glass, and I have double-checked all the locks around the house. I am trying to work out who might be threatening me, and decide that if Joe has taken me off the case, then quite probably I don't have anything to worry about. I ponder the wording on the note. Whoever wrote it knows all about me. This person has latched on to my personal tragedy. This has nothing to do with Flo and everything to do with Cat Kingsley. On the up side, it also means that Cat must still be alive.

At 8.30 p.m. the phone rings. It's a withheld number. I am startled, and for a moment hesitate to answer. Just before my answer machine kicks in, I pick up the receiver.

'Dr Durrant, this is Venetia Edstol. We need your help. Vadim is manic. Quite out of control. I would like to get the school doctor to sedate him, but he is speaking in Russian and the only words that make sense are *call Dr Durrant*. Obviously I

want as little fuss as possible, and it would be terrible for
Vadim's medical records to include any mental health issues; it
may even result in the withdrawal of his visa, so I was
wondering whether you might see him on a private basis?
Ideally tonight.'

'I'm sorry, Venetia, but I'm no longer involved in the case.'

'But this is nothing to do with the case. I need you to see
Vadim in a professional capacity as a psychologist. Please. It's
really important. Surely it's your legal duty to care for him?'

I sigh. It's certainly my moral duty. 'I'll be with you in thirty
minutes.'

Joe will be furious with me. Again.

THIS IS the first time that I have been into the living quarters of
Edstol's Music Academy. Venetia leads me past a staircase,
opens a fire door, and I follow her down a long corridor with
doors on either side. The floor is utilitarian lino in dark blue,
and the white walls look as if they last had a lick of paint a
decade or two ago. There is a cacophony of sound.

'This is the boys' corridor. As one of the eldest here, Vadim
has a larger room at the end.'

'Do the students practice in their rooms?' I ask.

'On the whole, yes. Unless they're pianists, in which case
they can practice on the music corridor. This is a small school.
The larger music schools have dedicated practice rooms with
soundproofing. Unfortunately, our finances and facilities do
not extend to that. We have a strict "no playing after 10 p.m."
rule.'

She stops outside the last room on the left and raps hard on
the door. 'Vadim, Doctor Durrant is here.'

The door opposite is flung open and a teenage boy pokes
his head out. 'Mrs Edstol, is Vadim ill?'

'Go back into your room, Dom,' she says sharply. He does as he is told.

Venetia knocks again and then opens the door. She stands back to let me pass. The room is dark, with just a blue light flashing on what I assume is a laptop. I can make out a mound on the bed. I glance at Venetia.

'I'll leave you to it,' Venetia says, stepping back into the corridor and letting the door close behind her. I am plunged into darkness.

'Vadim, switch on a light,' I say.

I feel a deep unease, as if out of my depth, though I know that all my training and credentials and experience are quite sufficient for me to support a young man. I suppose that the commanding tone of my voice propels him into action. He sits up, fumbles around and switches on his bedside light.

I am shocked by his appearance. His hair is standing on end, he is ghostly pale, and his eyes are swollen and red.

'I've done something terrible,' he cries, his hands covering his face.

My heart gallops. I stare at him, knowing I must concentrate.

'It's my fault. It's all my fault.' He starts sobbing again, incoherent, body-shaking sobs so violent it's as if he is vibrating the whole room. I wonder if Venetia should call a doctor. Perhaps he does need sedation.

I perch on the end of his bed. 'What is your fault, Vadim?' I wonder if he is going to admit to throwing the brick through my window.

'Cat. It's my fault. She is having our baby. It was never meant to be like this. We were going to run away together. I had it all worked out. But now they've cut off her finger and they're demanding so much money and I don't have any money, so they'll kill her and our baby, won't they?'

'She's pregnant!' I exclaim. I wonder if Joe knows. Whilst this might explain her disappearance, it makes the situation all the more alarming. It doesn't fit with the ransom demand and the chopped finger. And then Sophie's words come back to me; her fear that Vadim was involved. I have been so engrossed in rescuing Alice, I never told Joe about Sophie's worries. Have I failed to follow up on a lead? 'Why is it your fault she was taken?'

'I talk to...' He shakes his head and slams the palm of his right hand against the wall. 'They think I have money, but I don't!'

He edges closer to me. I stand up and take two steps so that I am on the other side of the room, standing in front of his desk.

'Do you understand, we need money. Now! I find a way to get money.' He mutters something else in Russian, incomprehensible mumblings. My heart is pumping hard now. I wonder if he is psychotic. There is something terrifying about him, something I hadn't noticed before. I look at his eyes, trying to see if they are unusually dilated, but the light is dim and he is looking away from me.

'Money is not the solution. One must never negotiate with kidnappers or terrorists.'

'What do you know about kidnapping? You, who live in this little safe country with its rules and money and moaning people! The police are bloody useless. All talk, no action. And what do you know? I do this my way!'

He jabs a finger into the centre of his chest and then propels himself off the bed and stands in front of me.

'Has Cat been kidnapped because of you?' I ask quietly, trying to keep my trembling from showing up in my voice. 'Do you have Cat?'

'Why do you say that?'

He steps towards me, a look of menace in his bloodshot eyes. I try to focus on his face, looking for those micro-expressions that suggest he's lying, listening hard to his phraseology.

He isn't giving direct answers and is deflecting the question. He knows something.

'Vadim, it would be best if you speak to the police; tell them everything you know. They will be able to help.'

'No police! You said before that our conversations are confidential. Do you change your mind?' He is standing so close to me now I can feel his breath on my face. I step backwards and, in doing so, knock a pile of papers off his desk.

'You would tell DS Swain if you are involved in something illegal, wouldn't you?' I ask as I bend down to pick up the papers, all the time keeping my eyes on him. But as I place them back on the desk, I glance at them. They are letters, all written in small, jagged script on lined paper. The one on top says, *My darling Cat.* Lying next to Vadim's laptop is a small pink book with the word *Diary* written on it. In that instant I realise he has Cat's diary and the letters he has written to her. The breath catches in the back of my throat.

'Why have you got letters you wrote to Cat and her diary?' I ask in a small voice.

He rubs his eyes. 'I took them from her room. I want everything that we had so she is close to me.' He rams his fist against his heart.

'How did you get them?'

'I have key to her room.'

'Did you take Cat?' I ask.

'No!' Vadim yells. 'Why don't you believe me?' His eyes are sparking.

'I do believe you,' I reassure him, although I don't. 'You need to give the letters and diary to DS Swain so he can investigate them and make sure there is nothing in them that might help with the investigation.'

I edge away from the desk and around the room so I am next to the door.

'*Nyet*! *Nyet*!' And, in that instant, he has me pinned up with my back against the door, his fingers curling around my neck.

'No!' I shout, but my voice is strangled and the pressure from those strong musician's fingers is increasing. All I can think about is my son George and how I may never see him again, and will he carry on the search for Flo when I am dead?

36

The door swings open and I tumble backwards, almost squashing Venetia. Vadim lets go of my neck and pushes past me.

'What's happened?' Venetia squeals.

I pant, trying to catch my breath. I rub my fingers around my neck and collapse onto the floor in relief. I will see George again. I may even see Flo. I shut my eyes, and when I open them, Venetia is crouched on the floor next to me. Music is still playing, a strident cacophony that bashes any coherent thoughts from my brain. Did I imagine that? Did Vadim really put his fingers around my neck and try to strangle me?

'Vadim?' I ask, but I sound croaky. I shut my eyes again, and as I open them, I catch sight of a figure running towards the end of the corridor. The fire door swings open and slams shut behind him.

'Vadim!' I point towards him, trying to get Venetia to understand. 'He tried to strangle me!' I stroke my neck again. It feels bruised. I try to control my breathing.

'What?' Venetia's expression is one of bemusement.

'You need to go after Vadim,' I say. 'Get someone to follow him.'

'Oh my goodness!' she says as she stands up and smooths down her mottled brown tweed skirt. Then she turns and hurries off in the direction that Vadim fled. But Venetia is slow and restrained, and follows her rule of no running in the corridors. Vadim will be long gone.

I stay seated on the ground, back against the wall as I let my heart slow and my breath return to normal. I touch my neck again and it feels sore; probably not visibly bruised, but definitely sore. I wonder if I have finger marks. The memories of eight years ago, when I was nearly strangled to death whilst helping the police in another case, come soaring back. I promised myself back then that I wouldn't expose myself to danger again, and here I am in exactly the same position.

Eventually Venetia returns. 'Why don't we get you a nice cup of tea and then you'll feel better. Come along. You can sit in my study and we can call the police.'

I get up carefully and nod. I walk back into Vadim's room and collect my handbag, the pile of letters and the diary.

I follow Venetia out of the boys' corridor and along the corridor towards the front entrance. There is no one to be seen. We go into a small study, a room I haven't been in before. It is dwarfed by a grand piano, shining black. There is just enough space for a small desk and chair. Venetia gestures for me to sit on the chair. She picks up the phone.

'DS Swain. We need you at the Academy. Vadim assaulted Dr Durrant and he has run away.'

After a short exchange of words, she puts the phone down.

'Did you know that Cat is pregnant?' I ask Venetia. My neck feels sore, but my voice sounds normal. He obviously didn't strangle me as hard as I thought.

I watch Venetia's face carefully. I note her raised inner and outer brow, the raised upper eyelid and the open mouth. She is surprised, dismayed even. She grips the side of the piano.

'Vadim is the father,' I say.

And now the lower outer edges of her eyebrows tilt outwards, her head tips slightly backwards and there is a brief glimmer of a smile across her lips. I wonder why the revelation that Vadim is the father makes Venetia feel relieved.

She exhales loudly. 'So Vadim is the kidnapper?'

'We don't know that, but I suppose it's possible.'

'It's a crime of passion. What a waste. Oh good heavens!' Her hand rushes to her throat. 'Maybe he'll kill her now. Do you think that might happen?'

'I don't know,' I admit. 'Is Karl here?'

'Is Karl here? No, he is out. He is visiting his mother.'

But her expression changes, and I spot the tell-tale admissions of a lie, the tugging of her ear, the repeating of the question. What is it she is hiding? Why do I get the sense that everyone in this music school has secrets?

We are both silent as we wait for the police to arrive. I stare at the painting on the wall behind the desk. It is a portrait of a young woman, painted in delicate watercolours. There is something familiar about her.

'Is that you?'

'My sister. She was very beautiful. I'll get you a cup of tea.'

As she leaves, I stand up. I wonder if I should go, run to my car, bolt my doors and wait until Joe arrives. Will Vadim return? Will he try to finish me off properly or will he be contrite and beg forgiveness. Is he the kidnapper, holding Cat because she has decided to get rid of the baby? Or is he just delirious with grief and worry? And what is it that Karl and Venetia are hiding? My mind is in turmoil. I stare at the portrait. She has Venetia's high cheekbones, and the tumbling curls pinned on top of her head remind me of Cat's. The family resemblance is all too obvious now.

And then Joe and Mia arrive.

'Mrs Edstol, please go with PC Brevant, who will take your statement.' Mia looks at him with a strange expression. He stands with his back to me, waiting for them to leave. When the door closes, he rushes over towards me, bends down into his knees and grabs my hands. 'Are you all right, Pippa?' His face is etched with concern.

I tug my hands away. 'Yes, I'm fine.' I try to remain detached, not showing the longing in my heart. I cross my arms.

'Please don't be like this,' Joe says, his eyes wide and imploring, as he stands up again.

'Do you need to take my statement, Joe?'

I can see the dismay and incomprehension, but I am resolved. I must keep Joe at a distance. I refuse to get hurt any more.

Joe removes his notebook from his jacket pocket. His face is now an unreadable mask, although a flickering nerve gives away the tension in his jawline.

'Kindly explain to me exactly what happened.'

37

Joe and Mia are back at the police station. It is late on Sunday evening and neither of them want to be there. Mia has a new boyfriend, a graphic designer who holds down a normal job and doesn't understand her willingness to be on call day and night. Reluctantly, she's accepting the relationship is unlikely to survive. Joe wants to be at home with Holly, although when Holly realised that he wouldn't be around to cook for her and do her washing, she flaunted off to her mother's house. He's angry. He promised himself he would be a good father and put Holly first. And he's even more upset and angry that Pippa has rejected him. He has no idea why, and he's missing her.

'Right. Let's pull together all the strands and go through the forensics again. Then we'll create a checklist and an action plan to share in tomorrow's early morning briefing.'

Mia nods. She wonders if she'll have as much energy as Joe when she's his age. Her dad is two years younger than Joe and all he does at a weekend is lounge around on the sofa, drinking beer and watching the football.

'What forensics have we got back from the severed finger?'
Joe asks.

'We've matched the DNA to items removed from Cat's room
and it's been confirmed that it is her finger. There were
numerous fingerprints on the envelope the finger came in, but
the only prints on the box itself were Karl and Venetia Edstol's,
and the young pupil who retrieved it from the doorstep. As we
know they received the box, we would expect to see those. The
box must have been wiped clean before it was sent. We've got
the writing on the envelope and on the note. Has Dr Durrant
analysed them yet?'

'No, but even so, the analysis isn't going to be much use
unless we've got something to compare it to. So we've got
nothing of interest back from forensics?' Joe lets out a puff
of air.

'Actually, we do.' Mia grins as she picks up a printed report.
'There were some interesting things found on the finger, in
particular under her nail. There was a yellowish white powder,
but that turns out to be resin. It's a solid form of resin obtained
from conifers, and string players use it to make the hair on their
bows grip the strings of the violin better. So it's not surprising
that Cat would have traces of this on her fingers. But they also
found what looks like miniscule bits of soil and chalk. The
report identifies it as coming from an area with shallow, lime-
rich soils over chalk or limestone.'

'And that would be found where?'

'Along the high areas of most of the South Downs.'

'So she has—at some time in the recent past—been either
on the ground or has picked up a piece of chalk or stone from
the whole of this area?' Joe points at the detailed map fixed to
the far wall that shows the whole of the south-east of England.
'Anywhere from Eastbourne along the Downs, westwards all
the way towards Bournemouth, and north from there.'

'It's a big area,' Mia agrees, 'but at least it gives us some pointers. What's even more interesting is that forensics have found some traces of ash under her fingernail.'

'What sort of ash?'

'They think it's cigar ash, but they need to do further analyses to be sure.'

'Does Vadim smoke?'

'I don't know, but I doubt a young man would smoke cigars.'

'We know for sure that Viscount Sneddon smokes cigars, and I wonder if Karl Edstol does too,' Joe muses. 'Get forensics to confirm what brand it is.'

'Will do.' She writes some notes down on the pad on the desk.

'What about Cat's mobile phone?' Joe asks.

'It's been switched off ever since she went missing. Forensics have also found a trace of fibre under her nail. It's blue and synthetic, and wasn't obvious under her pale blue nail varnish, which incidentally was chipped. According to Venetia Edstol, Cat only wore black, so the fibre could be from her kidnapper or from some textiles in the location where she's currently being held. Forensics are carrying out further tests and are also checking the cotton-wool the finger was lying on. It'll take a few days to get more results.'

'A few days we may not have.' Joe sighs. 'Venetia and Pippa think this is a crime of passion. Vadim is distraught that Cat wants to abort the baby and or end their relationship. He kidnaps Cat and cuts off her finger. Why would he do that? And why would he be asking for so much money as a ransom demand? It doesn't make sense to me. If he is guilty, then time is running out. He may be killing Cat as we speak, or has already done it. We need to know what those letters say. Can you have a quick read through the letters and diary that Pippa gave us.'

'Will do,' Mia says. She picks up the pile and takes them to her desk, a couple of paces away.

'We have a list of suspects as long as my arm.' Joe takes a black marker pen and starts writing names on the whiteboard.

'Names, motives, opportunity,' he mutters.

'Jonno, Viscount Sneddon. Motive: needs money for his wife's treatment. Plenty of opportunity. Cat would have trusted him and gone with him willingly. But I can't see how it would benefit him to kidnap Cat. Why would he be requesting ransom money from the Edstols, who he knows are hard-up and wouldn't be able to get hold of funds like that.

'Then there's Karl Edstol. Motive: money. The school is run down and, frankly, I'm surprised Ofsted allows them to continue. He's got form. He's beaten up a parent before.'

'But he and Venetia seem to genuinely love Cat.' Mia glances up from the diary she is reading.

'There are things going on there. Call it intuition or having been a policeman for thirty years, but mark my words: Karl is far from innocent. Do we believe Venetia when she hesitantly told us that her husband was visiting his elderly mother? Can you double-check that please?'

'Will do.' Once again, Mia scribbles on her notepad.

'Then there's the Jones family, who are odd in the extreme.'

Joe's phone rings. It's the police enquiry officer who logs the cases and mans the front desk. 'Sarge, there's someone here who wants to talk to you. Something to do with a missing violin.'

Joe takes the man into an interview room. He is wearing scruffy jeans and a sweatshirt with the logo of a local building firm. Joe reckons he must be in his late twenties.

'First of all, I'm really sorry,' the man says, gesticulating with his tattooed hands. 'I shouldn't have done it.'

'Done what?' Joe pulls out a chair for him to sit down.

'Taken the violin. I heard about it on the news that you was looking for the girl and the expensive violin. I dunno if it's the one you was looking for, but I found it.'

'Let's slow down,' Joe says. 'Start at the beginning.'

'I was driving to work and I saw this box thing lying on the side of the road by the bus stop. I stopped the van and picked it up. It was a violin, so I was a bit disappointed, to be honest. I flung it in the back and forgot about it. There's been a load going on. My girlfriend had to go to hospital. Thought she'd gone into early labour, and they asked me to do some extra shifts at work. Anyway, I was driving past Scott and Daughter's Auction House on my way back from Petworth and saw there was a sale going on. So I stopped by and offloaded the violin. We need every penny you see, for the baby that's coming. I shouldn't have done it. Am I going to get done?'

Joe smiles. 'You should have handed the violin into the police station, but I think we'll be lenient on you this once.'

The man leans back into the chair and briefly closes his eyes.

'Do you know what happened to the violin?'

'Yeah. It got sold. I got a couple of hundred quid or so. Do you want me to give the money back?'

'I'm sure that won't be necessary. It's more important that we track the instrument down. The chances are that it isn't related to the case of the missing girl, because that instrument has been destroyed. We are waiting on the forensic report for fragments of wood that were purportedly from the valuable instrument.'

Joe takes a statement from the man and ushers him out of the police station.

JOE AND MIA are at Scott and Daughter's Auction House at 8 a.m. on Monday morning. The auction house is quiet, and theirs is the only car in the visitors' car park. A young woman is sitting at the reception desk.

Joe and Mia show their police identification cards and the woman pales.

'We are interested in a violin that was sold at the auction that took place last weekend. Could you please let us know who bought it?'

She hesitates. 'Data protection,' she murmurs.

'This is for a police investigation. We can get a warrant, but we would appreciate your cooperation.'

'Yes, sir,' she says. She brings up some pictures on her computer screen. 'There were two violins in the sale. One didn't meet its reserve price, so it wasn't sold. I believe we still have it. The other one was sold for £220. It was a late entry into the sale.'

'That'll be the one we're interested in. Can you tell us who bought it?'

She clicks through a few more screens.

'It was sold to a Mr John Smith of 187 Jones Street, Midhurst. He paid in cash so we don't have any further details.'

Joe and Mia look at each other. He sighs. She rolls her eyes.

'And the lot number for the violin was...?' Joe asks.

The young woman scrolls back through her screens. 'Lot number 187.'

'Rather a coincidence that his house number was the same as the lot number,' Joe says sarcastically.

'Oh.'

Mia types something into her mobile phone. 'It's a fake name and a fake address,' she says.

'Can you get us the violin that didn't sell, please,' Joe says, pacing backwards and forwards.

The young woman dashes away and returns with two violin cases. 'This is the violin that didn't sell, and this is the case from the violin that did sell. He didn't want the case.'

'Is it unusual not to take the case?'

The woman shrugs. Mia takes the empty case and starts rummaging in the long pocket on the front.

'Was there anything taken out of the pocket before the sale?' she asks.

'I'm sorry, I wouldn't know.'

'Here we go!' Mia says, extracting a small scrap of paper the size of a postage stamp. 'I recognize that writing. And look.' Mia points at the small heart drawn with an arrow across it and a C on one end with a V on the other. In the centre of the heart, the word LOVE has been written in small letters. 'Vadim's writing.'

'We need to take this violin case away for testing, as part of our ongoing investigation.'

38

The very last place Alice wants to be is in her own home, alone with her mother. But this is where she is, lying in her own bed, unable to sleep.

Unsurprisingly, Martha was apoplectic with rage after the police left. She grabbed Alice's shoulders and shook her.

'What the hell were you thinking?' she screamed, so loudly Alice wanted to put her hands over her ears. But Martha was enraged and didn't pause to allow Alice any time to speak. 'You ran away! That's what ten-year-old immature children do! Run away! Is that what you are? And you hook up with a total stranger! How did you know that woman wouldn't do something terrible to you? I thought I'd brought you up properly. Ingrained some common sense into your peanut brain! I simply can't believe you behaved so irresponsibly, so selfishly! I had to involve the police! Didn't you think for one moment? Clearly not.'

She paced around the room, waving her hands in the air, and then jabbed her index finger at Alice. 'You are grounded indefinitely. No meeting with friends, no going out. You will practice all morning and then you will do your school work in the afternoons and practice again in the evenings. Do you understand?'

Alice felt herself shrinking inside. The schedule Martha described was almost identical to the one she had been following anyway. And who are Alice's supposed friends? Sometimes she wonders if the person she is bears any resemblance to the person her mother thinks she is.

'Go to your room now and we will discuss things again in the morning.'

THERE IS a banging on Alice's door. Alice turns over in bed and glances at her clock. She's shocked to see that it's nearly 9 a.m. Her alarm didn't go off.

'Get up,' Martha says, standing in the doorway with her hands on her hips. 'You are very lucky that I let you sleep in, under the circumstances. Breakfast is on the table. Be downstairs in five minutes.'

It's normally Bill who wakes Alice up in the mornings.

'Where's Dad?'

Martha groans. 'As I told you before, your father has gone away on a business trip for a few days. Someone has to earn the money in this household to pay for you.'

But Alice doesn't believe Martha. And the expression on Alice's face sends Martha into a rage. Spittle foams at the corners of her mouth and her face turns red and shiny.

'Get up!' Martha shouts.

Sighing, Alice slips out of bed and walks towards the door, intending to slip past her mother to go to the bathroom.

'You have brought shame and embarrassment on our entire family!' Martha gives Alice a little push and she stumbles slightly, stubbing the big toe on her left foot on the door frame. Her eyes smart and she grits her teeth to stop her face from expressing the pain.

'Why are you being so horrible, Mum?' Alice asks.

Martha's posture softens. 'I'm sorry, love, but you have caused us untold problems. I just don't know what you were thinking when you ran off the stage like that. You may well have ruined your future.'

'Will I be going back to school?' Alice asks quietly, her eyes on her toe, wondering if it will swell up.

'I haven't decided yet. If necessary, I will home-educate you.'

Alice shivers. The thought of being home-educated by Martha is a thousand times worse than staying at Edstol's or going to another music school. She walks towards the bathroom and stands in the open doorway.

'Can I go to a normal school?'

Martha's face becomes engorged with redness and the lines around her eyes become more pronounced as she narrows her lips, exposing her crooked front teeth. 'After everything we have sacrificed to allow you to become a musician, you have the audacity to ask if you can go to the local school? Have you no ambition? No guts? No staying power? You'll grow up into a nobody!'

'Like you!' Alice whispers so quietly that, for a split second, she wonders if she actually said it out loud. And when Martha slaps her, slamming the palm of her hand onto Alice's left cheek, Alice knows that she did articulate it.

'How dare you! You can practice in your bedroom today and no breakfast for you!' Martha screams.

With her cheek burning and her toe throbbing and her heart crushed, Alice returns to her bedroom and slams the door behind her. She drags her bedside table in front of the door so Martha can't get in, she switches the light off, then collapses onto the floor on the far side of her bed and lets the tears flow. All she wants is for the blackness to swallow her up. The house is quiet. The window in her room faces the front. She opens the curtains a little. It is still almost dark outside.

Her bedroom is lit by the street lamp, painting what used to be a comforting orange glow across the room. Now she wishes she was in Pippa's house, which was so cosy, in a room where the curtains blocked out all the light, in a bed with a mattress as soft as feathers. She peers out of the window, desperately hoping that the Defender will be parked outside, signalling that her dad is back home. But it's not.

Alice can't stop the tears from flowing, but she doesn't need clear vision. Bending down under her small desk, she lifts up the carpet in the corner of the room, and when her fingers feel the cool, smooth handle of the serrated kitchen knife, she lets out a deep sigh. Maybe she'll go a bit harder this time. Maybe she'll let the blood out of her wrists instead of her thigh. Maybe that will allow her to vent her fury and maybe bring her the oblivion she's craving.

It is harder to press the blade down on her wrists. Her hands have been her everything and the scars on her wrists will be visible for all to see. For a split second, she hesitates, as she imagines the audience peering at the snaking white lines at the base of her hands, but then she remembers. She isn't going to be a violinist anymore. No one will see. No one will care. In fact, no one cares about her at all. She's just a means to an end.

So Alice presses down, fast and hard, slicing, and the blood flows and then it pumps, spilling out onto her duvet, her mattress. Alice's last coherent thought is that Martha will be livid. How will she get that much blood out from a perfectly good duvet?

'ALICE, open up! Alice! I've decided to bring you breakfast after all. Eggs on toast, although you don't deserve a decent meal after all you've put us through. For God's sake, Alice, open the bloody door!'

Alice can hear the words, but they sound as if they're coming through a thick blanket of fog. And then there is a heaving, scratching noise as Martha pushes the door open with all her might, pushing the bedside table out of the way sufficiently for her to edge through the opening. She switches the bedroom light on, and when she sees her daughter and the blood, all of that blood, Martha drops the small plate she's carrying. The toast bounces across the floor and the egg, softly poached although Alice only likes her eggs well done, breaks up as it hits the ground, its yolk and milky whiteness curdling in the pool of blood seeping onto the floor.

39

It's Monday morning and I am reading through my notes for the various clients booked in to see me today. I slept last night, but only because I took a sleeping pill and drank two large glasses of wine. Not good tactics for a psychologist, but needs must. The shock of having Vadim's fingers around my neck was much greater than the pain.

My office phone rings. 'Dr Durrant, I have DS Swain on the phone for you.' I recognize Mia's voice. So Joe can't even call me himself now? Or perhaps it's because he knows that I won't take his call.

'I am sorry to disturb you,' Joe says, his voice tight and contrite, as if speaking to a stranger. 'Please can you head over to Worthing Hospital? Mia will meet you there.'

'Why, what's happened?'

'Alice tried to take her own life.'

'Oh God! Is she all right?'

'I don't know. She was barely conscious when the ambulance arrived, and the only word they could make out was Durrant. It seems like she was asking for you.'

'That's terrible. The poor girl. She's going to need to more care than I can give her.'

'Indeed. But for now, I think you might be able to bring her some comfort. Assuming she's all right, that is. How soon might you be able to go there?'

'I have clients this morning. I should be able to go around lunchtime.'

'Thank you. Much appreciated.' He hangs up. His tone of voice is so formal, so distant. Of course he is angry with me, but I suspect the anger is more because I have cooled our relationship rather than the fact that I was potentially impeding the inquiry. I am torn. Am I even doing the right thing by pushing Joe away?

It is busy at Worthing Hospital. I park the car, grabbing the last space in the carpark, collect my ticket and pace towards the reception area. I wonder for a moment if they will let me see Alice, as I'm not family. The receptionist is busy helping out a family with three young children, so I hover behind them. A female voice calls out my name. I swivel around and am relieved to see Mia.

'Let's go and find her, shall we? Don't look so surprised,' Mia laughs. 'Sarge said you'd be here at 1 p.m.'

I nod and smile.

Although she is young, there is something reassuring about Mia. She has a calmness and maturity well beyond her age. She walks briskly back out of the reception area and across the carpark towards another entrance.

'I assume you've been here before?' I ask.

'Unfortunately I know the place like the back of my hand. We're heading over to Accident and Emergency. They're expecting us.'

'Do you know what happened?'

Mia shakes her head. 'Martha found her. I feel terrible. We knew that Alice was cutting herself but we didn't do anything about it.'

I wonder if I should have done more. Could I have helped Alice? But the timescales have been so short. Other than sectioning her, which would have been totally inappropriate, there was nothing more I or any of the authorities could have done. At sixteen, Alice is deemed an adult.

Mia flashes her police badge when we enter A&E and is greeted by a nurse of a similar age to Mia.

'She's stable. We're finding a room for her.'

'Is she able to talk to us?'

The nurse shakes her head. 'The doctor is with her at the moment. You should be able to see her within thirty minutes or so. Can you take a seat in the waiting room? As soon as we've settled her into a room, I'll give you a shout.'

We do as we're told, and perch on uncomfortable chairs in a waiting room that is packed with the walking wounded. After a couple of moments, Mia's phone buzzes.

'Just going to take this outside,' she says.

Mia is gone for what seems a long time. And then the nurse appears.

'You can come through now, Dr Durrant,' she smiles. I wonder how she knows my name.

'I need to go and find Mia,' I say.

'Don't worry. I'll bring her in as soon as she's back.'

Alice is in a small room, her wrists bandaged up, arms atop a pale blue cotton blanket. A tube from an IV bag on a stand is attached to the inside of her right elbow. Her eyes are closed and her face has a grey tinge. She looks so young, so very vulnerable. I want to scoop her up in my arms, give her an enormous hug and tell her that everything will be all right. Instead, I perch on the grey plastic chair at the side of her bed.

A couple of minutes later, the door swings open. I expect it to be Mia or a nurse. It's not.

'Who are you?' she asks, her eyes narrowing.

I realise who she is immediately and my heart sinks. Have I been naive coming here? Has Joe set me up? Am I about to be beaten up for the second time in twenty-four hours? I stand up and walk towards her.

'How dare you come here!' Martha Jones ignores my outstretched hand. 'This is all your fault. I nearly lost my daughter because of your meddling and inappropriate behaviour. Rest assured, I will be reporting you to whatever official body you're a member of. You'll never work as a psychologist again.'

I can see why Alice is scared of her mother. There is something hard about the woman, as if she has lived a harsh life and harbours bitterness. She is scrawny thin, with narrow shoulders and narrow lips that do little to hide smoker's teeth. Her mouse-brown hair is scraped back into a tight ponytail, but her eyes, which are currently fixed on mine, are beautiful. Almost violet in colour. And whilst I assume her face suggests she's older than she is, her hands could belong to a model. With long fingers and perfectly manicured short nails, her hands look as if they should be attached to another person's body. I remember that she is a pianist. Evidently all her self-care goes into her hands.

'I am sorry that you see it that way. I simply did what Alice asked me to do, to look after her, make sure she was safe and had a bed for the night. I accept that I should have insisted she call you, but she's sixteen years of age now and no longer a minor.'

'It's pretty bloody obvious you don't have a teenager!'

I shiver and feel myself bristle. Little does she know it, but she has hit a raw nerve. Martha Jones is right. I failed to look after my own daughter, so what right does it give me to try to care for hers? Taking a step backwards, I inhale deeply.

'Your daughter reached out to me in a professional capacity. She admitted she had been cutting herself.' Of course this isn't strictly true. It was Sophie who told me Alice was cutting. 'She is crying out for help.'

Martha's voice becomes quieter, menacing. 'Stay out of our affairs. I will decide who cares for my daughter. It is nothing to do with you.'

'Fair enough.' I try to keep my voice light. 'In any case, she will be looked after by CAMHS, the Child and Adolescent Mental Health Services here in Sussex. She will be cared for by a psychiatrist and a psychologist.'

'There is nothing wrong with my daughter's mental health!' Martha screeches.

I am staggered. Her daughter has tried to kill herself. She has slashed her wrists. She is lying attached to tubes in a hospital bed right next to us, and Martha is in complete denial.

'If you don't stay away from us, I'll make sure you get what you deserve.' Martha glowers.

'What are you threatening me with, Mrs Jones?'

40

I had often wondered if I could be a killer, and even before I became one, I knew I had what it takes. But you don't really know until you do it; you don't know how much strength you have until you test yourself. What I hadn't expected was the elation, the sense of achievement, the free path to taking what is rightfully mine. And it is so easy.

Perhaps it wouldn't be so easy without the element of surprise, but he plays straight into my hands. He is acting like a bloody madman. All out of control and screaming and shouting and arms waving around. But no one accuses me and gets away with it.

'Let's go for a walk and calm down a bit, shall we?' I ask. 'We can talk it through rationally.' But I can see that he is spitting blood. There is no way he can be rational. 'I know a lovely walk down by the river. I often go there to sort out my head.'

He nods.

'Do you know something you're not telling me?' he asks after a while.

I turn my head away from him and smirk. Not so bloody clever, then. 'Why don't we think things through logically?'

I can be his friend and confidante.

He tells me what he almost did to the doctor. I laugh. 'But you didn't really do anything, did you? It was just self-defense.'

His shoulders relax and his pace begins to match mine. His breathing slows. We come to the end of the track and turn left, into the field. It's a bit muddy here, and I wonder if he will suggest we turn around and go back. Fortunately, he doesn't. The footpath is right next to the river here. And then we arrive. There is a little stone bridge that crosses the river at its deepest point. Some of the wall has collapsed into the river, and an idiot from the council has put red and white tape across it, as if that would stop anyone from tumbling in.

'I often wonder what fish swim in this river,' I say. I stop and walk over to the wall, leaning my hands on the section adjacent to the crumbled bit. He doesn't take the bait. I stay there, silent for a while.

'Think I might go back,' he mumbles.

'God! Is that what I think it is?' I lean as far forwards as I can over the wall, peering into the murky brown waters below.

'What?' he asks.

'Come and look!' I say.

And then it happens so quickly. One little shove as he leans over the tape. His legs and arms scramble at the air as he tumbles into the river. It's hilarious. I would like to roar with laughter, but the river is neither deep nor fast flowing and it's all too possible that he might be able to crawl out having suffered just a few broken bones. I rush around to the side, where there is a pile of rocks and a few sizeable stones.

I pick up a medium-sized stone, grey and angular. It's heavy, but not too unwieldly. I needn't have worried. He's lying in the water, face down, not moving. But I can't risk it, so I bring the stone down heavily on the back of his head. The sound is one I will never forget. Such a satisfying crunch and splash. The ripples cascade outwards in satisfying circles. The motion pushes his body slightly and the current drags him under the bridge. He doesn't emerge on the other side. I wait. I had thought I might have to drag him out and hide him in the undergrowth, but I don't have to do a thing. He is caught directly under my feet. I wonder how long it will take for some unsuspecting punter to discover the bloated body. Weeks, I hope. Months even. He'll be eaten by the fish by then.

Good riddance.

And still I wait. I wonder if the water will become tinged with crimson, but it stays that murky brown, the colour of shit. When I hear voices, I straighten up. I see a couple ambling towards me, arm in arm, walking their dog—a stupid little fluffy thing.

'Good afternoon,' I say, politely.

They nod back. I watch as they cross the bridge and disappear around the corner, the dog walking on ahead, its tail swinging from side to side. And then I leave and stride back the way I came, a broad smile on my face.

41

As I walk back through my front door upon returning from the hospital, my phone rings. It's Sophie.

'I want to leave Edstol's Academy and was wondering if you could help me get out?'

'That's not really my role.'

'I've got no one else to help me. If I tell you something, will you promise not to breathe a word to anyone else?'

'If it's legal, then you have my word. I take an oath of confidentiality as part of being a psychologist.

I feel myself tensing, wondering if she's about to reveal anything else pertinent to the case.

'I had an audition at The Royal Academy of Music in London, and they've offered me a place. I didn't tell you that when we met the other day because I only got the letter yesterday. They gave me a full scholarship, so I can start there next September. But I need the Edstols to let me go, and I know they won't. They'll put out rumours about me or bump me off. Remember I told you about Sarah Bellingham? She was the one who's body was found washed up on the beach. I expect it'll be Cat next. And if I try and leave, it'll be me.'

'You do realise what you're saying Sophie, don't you? You're accusing the Edstols of murder.'

'Yeh. I dunno. Perhaps they did, perhaps they didn't. Anyway, I asked you before and I need to ask you again. Please, will you help me?'

I don't know what to do. Of course I want to help Sophie, but none of these girls are my daughters. It's rare that I feel conflicted, but now I do.

'Can you give me some time to think about this, Sophie? I would like to help you as your friend, but you must understand that I'm involved with both the Edstols and the police in a professional capacity.'

'Ok. But please don't leave it too long. I'll need to accept the offer soon.'

FELICITY SMITHERS-WRAY IS one of my favourite clients. Yes, I know a professional psychologist should not have favourite clients, but I can't help but admire Felicity. A professional artist, her eyesight is deteriorating at an alarming speed and yet she still manages to remain positive. In some of her early sessions with me, she shed an occasional tear, but these days she only visits me once a month. I sense she views me as her friend and, despite her conviviality, I wonder how many people fully understand the terror she is suffering as, day by day, the vibrancy of her world fades.

I have my consulting room phone turned to silent, but it flashes when a call comes in. The flashes occur twice in quick succession. And then the doorbell to my consulting room sounds. I ignore it the first time, but when it rings again, I apologise to Felicity. This happened once before in a consultation with Felicity, and she was incredibly gracious when Joe butted in.

'I will ignore it,' I say.

'But dear, you don't know who is in real need. I couldn't live with myself if you ignored a client and something happened to them. Give me a top-up of water and go to the door.'

I sit closer to Felicity than I normally do with other clients, so she can see some of the expressions on my face. I hope she can see my smile as I get up.

Just from the tall silhouette visible through the opaque pane in the top of my consulting room door, I know it's Joe.

'Why are you disturbing me?' I hiss. Joe seems to think that his work is of far greater importance than mine. In some ways it is, but if more resources went into prevention and emotional support, then less crime would happen.

'It's urgent. Can you come with me to the station now?'

'No. I'm with a client.'

'Can't you shift clients?'

'For heaven's sake, Joe. Don't disturb me.' I speak too loudly and immediately regret it. As her eyesight has deteriorated, Felicity's hearing has become more acute.

'Oh, it's the lovely gentleman who visited you last time.' She appears behind me and shuffles forwards so she is practically in Joe's personal space. 'As I said last time, his needs must surely be much greater than mine. Pippa dear, just give me a few extra minutes next month.'

Joe bites the side of his lip to stifle his grin. I don't find it amusing.

'Let me get your coat, Felicity,' I say as I return to my consulting room and remove her coat from the hook on the back of the door.

'Will you be all right? What time is your taxi due?' I ask as I help her pull the sheepskin over her slender frame.

'I haven't got a taxi today. My friend and neighbour, Paul, has given me a lift. He's in the red Toyota reading a newspaper.' She peers towards the road, but I can easily see the red Toyota. I accompany her across the road and smile at Paul, who jumps out of the car and takes Felicity's arm. I am glad she has a new friend. I then run back across the road, shivering as I enter my consulting room and shut the door behind me.

'I hope you've got a bloody good reason for interrupting,' I say, scowling at Joe.

'Vadim is dead.'

42

'How did he die?'

We are standing in my consulting room. I wrap my arms around my torso and, despite the warm cowl-neck jumper I am wearing, shiver. I am deeply shocked. Whatever Vadim did or didn't do, his death is a tragedy. If his death was suicide, then I am culpable. Did I push him over the edge? I try to recall what I said to him, but all I can think of are his strong hands around my neck, his hot breath on my face. If it was suicide, I will have to report myself to the Health Care Professions Council. Again. I wonder if I will be struck off. I feel sick at the thought.

Joe takes a step forwards as if to hug me, but restrains himself. The atmosphere between us is awkward. 'He drowned in the river. His body was found by a man walking his dog near Broadbridge Heath.'

I shiver. I have walked Mungo along that stretch of public footpath many times. It's beautiful, with rolling hills to one side and the river meandering through woodland. In late spring, the ground turns into a mauve carpet with a mass of indigenous bluebells. Wild garlic lines the side of the riverbanks with a cloud of white flowers accompanied by a surprisingly pungent smell.

'The river isn't even deep there. How could he have drowned? Did he slip and hit his head?'

'Initial thoughts are that his death is suspicious.'

'You mean he was murdered?'

Joe nods, his lips pressed tightly together. 'At my last count, our suspects include Karl and Venetia Edstol, Viscount Sneddon, Christophe and Sophie.'

'And Martha and Bill Jones,' I add.

'Possibly, but I fail to work out what their motive might be.'

'And I struggle to see why Christophe and Sophie might want to harm either Cat or Vadim. They both want to get out of the Edstols' clutches. Sophie rang me last night requesting my help. If anything, I wonder if they're in danger too, especially if they try to run away from the Academy.'

'In which case we need to interview Karl and Venetia at the station. I would really appreciate your assistance. I'll get them taken there and we can interview them later. In the meantime, I want to search Vadim's room. He was very eager to find the money to pay Cat's ransom. Perhaps he even knew who the kidnappers are.'

'So you think that his murder and Cat's kidnapping are connected?'

'For sure. Would you accompany me to Edstol's, and then sit in on all the interviews? I want to speak to Sophie and Christophe first, then we'll interview Viscount Sneddon, followed by the Edstols. We have too many suspects right now. It's essential we work out who has what motive.'

'I thought I was off the case?' I say.

'I'm sorry Pippa, it's just—'

'It's all right,' I interrupt. 'I'll help you.'

He bends down, as if to kiss me, but I dart out of the way. 'I'll just get my coat and bag.'

When I come out of the house with Joe, I see Mia getting out of the front passenger seat and sliding into the rear of the car. We greet each other, strap ourselves in, and Joe drives us away.

On the way to Edstol's, Joe brings me up-to-date on the investigation. He tells me about the forensics report on Cat's finger, about the violin that was sold at auction, and his suspicions of Jonno.

'But we've got to prioritise resources,' he sighs. 'Vadim's death must be fully investigated first, with Cat's kidnap alongside. The missing violin is of secondary importance.'

'We should get the forensics results through by the end of the day,' Mia says.

When we arrive at Edstol's Music Academy, Karl is standing on the steps. Mia is out of the car first and walks around to the boot to remove a bag. As I reach down to pick up my handbag from the footwell, Joe's hand accidentally brushes against my arm. An involuntary shiver runs through me and Joe freezes. I must ignore him. I do not want to get hurt any more.

Karl watches us get out of Joe's car with an inscrutable expression, but when we get closer, I can see that he is struggling to repress fury.

'You lot are grossly inefficient.' He wags an index finger at us. 'You have failed to find Cat, and now one of our students has been murdered. It will destroy our Academy.'

'I assure you that we are doing all we can,' Joe says brusquely.

'Perhaps you could explain what you are doing here?' Karl says.

'We would like to interview Sophie and Christophe, and examine Vadim's room.'

Karl visibly grits his teeth, but nods and we follow him in. I am the closest to him and I get whiff of a scent. Cigar smoke. It must hit Mia at the same time, because she sidles up to Joe. Karl strides well ahead of us.

'Karl smokes cigars,' she whispers.

'Find out what brand he smokes,' Joe instructs.

Mia nods.

I WANT to scoop both of them up in my arms. Christophe is slumped in his chair, shoulders rounded, chin on his chest. His foot is bouncing up and down. He looks as if he hasn't slept in days. Sophie jumps up when she sees me, and promptly bursts into tears.

'What's happening?' she sobs.

'No one knows, but we're doing our best to find out,' Joe says. He gestures for them to sit down again, then pulls out chairs for Mia and me. The five of us sit in a circle.

'Where were you last night, Sophie?'

She blushes and bites her lip, sniffing away her tears. 'I've got a new boyfriend. He's called Matt Fleeting. I was with him.'

'And where does he live?'

'In Southwater. He's got his own flat. He's normal. Not like us musicians.'

Christophe shifts in his chair and throws a glance at Sophie. 'Speak for yourself,' he mutters under his breath.

'Where did you meet him?' I ask.

'At the pub. All four of us went to The Hare and Hound the weekend before The Cadogan Hall concert. Me, Cat, Vadim and Christophe. We hooked up with a few other people.'

'Can you give me his telephone number please,' Mia asks.

Sophie nods, takes her mobile phone out of her pocket and hands it to Mia.

She starts sobbing again. 'I can't believe Vadim is dead. It's horrible!'

I get up and kneel down in front of Sophie, holding her hands to try to comfort her.

'And Christophe. Where were you last night?' Joe asks.

'Here, practicing.'

'I assume plenty of people can vouch for that?'

'I expect so,' Christophe says. 'I stayed in my room all evening, just had supper in the dining room.'

Sophie wipes her eyes and I get up and sit back in my seat.

'Does Vadim have any enemies?' Joe asks them both.

Sophie replies no at exactly the same time that Christophe says yes.

'Who might want to hurt Vadim?' Joe asks Christophe.

'Loads of people. He's a jerk.' Christophe keeps his eyes to the floor and his hair flops over his forehead, making it difficult for me to study his face.

'What do you mean by that?' Joe asks.

'He'd meet up with these dodgy Russian guys after dark. Couldn't understand a word of what they were saying.'

'Where did he meet them?'

'He used to sneak out. Get into people's cars. I don't know where they went.'

'Do you think he might have had something to do with Cat's kidnapping?' Joe says.

'Of course he did. Just dunno why you've taken so long to put two and two together.' He kicks the leg of his chair. His mannerisms are those of a sulking teenager, and I think of my son George and how he transformed into a monosyllabic, angry young man after Flo disappeared. Christophe stands up and shuffles towards the door. When he has his back to us, he says, 'Are you going to pay the bloody ransom money now, or will one of us have to die too? Should I ask my dad to pay? He's loaded.'

'Wait,' Mia says as Christophe opens the door.

Joe shakes his head at her. 'Let him go,' he says softly.

Sophie is convulsed in tears again. 'I don't want to stay here anymore,' she says, rubbing her eyes with the sleeve of her grey sweatshirt. 'Can I go and stay with Matt? I'm scared.'

'Of course you are scared. It's totally natural in this situation. Can she stay with her boyfriend?' I ask Joe.

'I don't see why not. We will need to speak to him and see where you will be living.'

A phone buzzes. Mia stands up. 'Excuse me, I need to take this call.' She slips out of the room.

Joe turns to Sophie. 'Do you own your viola?'

She looks at Joe with surprise. 'Of course not. I can't afford to go out for a cup of coffee let alone buy a viola and bow worth thousands of pounds.'

'Who loaned it to you?'

'Venetia and Karl.'

'Do all the students play on loaned instruments?'

'No. Christophe owns his cello because his dad is rich, and Vadim, I think he plays...played...on his own violin, but I never asked. Why?'

'Do you know who Viscount Sneddon is?'

'Of course I do. He's here all the time, and he is Cat's benefactor. None of us are allowed to forget that.' She rolls her eyes. 'Actually, he was here this morning.'

'Who was here?' Joe frowns momentarily.

'Viscount Sneddon. He's got a gorgeous British racing green E-type Jaguar. He was pulling out of the drive about eight o'clock this morning, just as Matt dropped me off.'

'Was he indeed?' Joe shakes his head very slowly, a grin briefly tugging at the edge of his lips.

'Can I go and get some of my things from my room?' Sophie asks.

'Yes, of course,' Joe replies.

Mia returns a moment after Sophie leaves the room. 'Sarge, I've just heard from forensics. They've established the brand of cigar ash found under Cat's fingernail. It comes from a cigar called Nostrano del Brenta Il Clandestino.'

'Search Karl's office and, if necessary, the Edstols' apartment and find out what brand he smokes.'

'I've already done that. He had a packet lying on his desk. He smokes a cheaper brand called Davidoff Demi Tasse.'

'Good work,' Joe says. 'I wonder what brand Jonno, Viscount Sneddon smokes? Mia, I'd like you to stay here and keep an eye on everybody. I'll get a squad car to you and you can bring Venetia and Karl into the station. Pippa, are you free to join me in paying the Viscount a visit?'

43

'He's not here,' the woman says.

'Can we speak to the Viscountess?'

'She's sick.'

'We know that, but it's very important.'

The woman seems torn. It is clear that her loyalty lies with Marissa and she wants to protect her boss.

'It's regarding a murder investigation. We will get a warrant if necessary and request Marissa Sneddon's presence at the police station. I am sure you will all wish to avoid that.'

I know Joe is only doing his job, but I don't like this hard side of him.

'Follow me,' she says.

Marissa is sitting in her wheelchair in front of an electric fire, eyes closed as she listens to classical music.

'Madam, the police are here to talk to you.'

She opens her eyes and stares at us. They are the colour of dark chocolate, clear and unwavering. But her face is sunken, her skin has a waxy paleness to it, and her hair is fine and thinning.

She whispers something that sounds garbled.

'Did you come about Jonno?' Kaya asks.

'Yes,' Joe says.

Kaya sits next to her, stroking Marissa's hand and translating for us.

'Madam says, he took a hammer to the violin and now is claiming for the insurance money. He thinks he can save me, but he can't. I don't want saving, not anymore.'

It is immensely distressing, watching and listening to Marissa. The emotional turmoil that she is in compounds her difficulty in speaking.

'Are you saying that the violin wasn't stolen? That your husband had it all along?' Joe questions.

'No. Milo found it at auction and brought it to Jonno, who smashed it.'

'Has your husband got anything to do with the missing girl?' Joe asks.

'No, of course not!' Her eyes widen.

'Viscountess Sneddon, do we have your permission to search your house?'

Both women start shaking; Marissa violently. Kaya is just trembling.

'There's no one here!' Kaya says. 'I'm sure I would know!'

'Go,' Marissa whispers.

Jonno's study is the adjacent room. It is dark and wood-panelled, and there is an overwhelming stench of stale cigar smoke. I would like to fling open the window. On the large leather-topped desk is a silver box.

'Please don't touch anything, Pippa,' Joe instructs.

I nod.

He pulls on some rubber gloves and lifts the lid of the box.

'Cigars. Nostrano del Brenta Il Clandestino Cigars. The ash that was found under Cat's fingernail.'

I gasp. 'Do you think he abducted Cat and made it look like she stole the violin?'

Joe picks up the waste paper bin under the desk.

'And here are our fragments of wood from the violin. He hasn't done a very good job of concealing it. I would have thought he'd have burned the thing. I'll get these bagged up and will ask forensics to check them against the wood that he purports came in the post to him.'

I pace around the room, looking at the books on the shelves; books on music, mainly, and piles and piles of old auction catalogues.

Joe is flicking through papers on the desk.

'Now this is interesting!' He holds up a handwritten letter.

Dear Jonno,

I am desperate to find my dearest Cat. I know you have done so much for us already, but could you find it in your heart to pay up the ransom demand? I will do everything I can to pay it back to you over the next few years.

Yours,

Venetia

PS – please don't tell Karl I've written to you

'Why would Venetia ask Jonno to pay the ransom money if Jonno is as broke as he says he is?' Joe tilts his head to the right.

'Unless he's not broke really, or perhaps Venetia doesn't know he's broke. Or perhaps Venetia is hoping that he will use the insurance money from the violin to pay off Cat's kidnapper?'

'Good point,' Joe says. 'It makes sense she would hope Jonno would pay the ransom demand from the insurance money, but it also suggests Venetia doesn't suspect Jonno of kidnapping Cat. Excellent reasoning, Pippa.'

'Don't you think it's strange that the letter is from Venetia only? Why does she say *I* am desperate to find Cat, rather than *we* are desperate to find Cat? It suggests that Karl doesn't have the same concerns.'

Joe nods in agreement. 'We need to put out an alert for Jonno, and I'll request his mobile phone records. In the meantime, I want Venetia and Karl brought into the station. I want to interview them both.'

'Do you think the Academy will be forced to shut down?' I ask Joe. He is driving fast, but to my disappointment hasn't got the blue lights flashing.

'I can't imagine many parents would be keen for their children to study at an establishment where one pupil has been murdered and another kidnapped,' he says.

'And don't forget poor Alice, who tried to take her own life. Do you know how she is?'

'Mia checked in with the hospital. She's doing as well as can be expected. They hope she'll be released in a couple of days.'

'That's quick. I hope she gets the proper care she needs.' I shake my head to try to dispel the memory of Martha's threatening words.

Once we're at Crawley police station, Joe leads me to the interview suites, a part of the station I am by now familiar with. The small rooms, the vinyl floor, the nose-twitching smell of disinfectant combined with sweat and fear, almost pass me by. Almost. It's late and I'm tired, but I know I need to be mentally alert.

Venetia is already seated in the small room with Mia opposite her, writing notes on a pad of paper. Mia stands up as we enter the room. Venetia doesn't.

'Mrs Edstol, you are here as a voluntary attender under the provisions in section 10 of the Police and Criminal Evidence Act Code C. You are not under arrest and may leave at any time. If you decide to remain here, you may obtain free and independent legal advice by phone.' Joe passes her a piece of paper. 'This sets out your rights as a voluntary attender. Please let us know if you need refreshments or need to use the facilities.'

'I just want Cat brought home,' she says, pursing her lips.

'Please can you tell us more about how you select students for your school?'

'Academy,' she says. 'On the whole, they come to us. We are an elite establishment, offering musical tuition for young people from the age of twelve to twenty-five. Unlike other music schools or conservatoires, we are also an agency and represent our students so they get sponsorship deals, opportunities to perform in the best venues. We are like the old-fashioned impresarios, nurturing our students and helping them launch their careers. Students audition and we offer places to the very best of the best. Occasionally Karl is an adjudicator at international competitions. That's how we picked up Vadim. He was performing in a small town some five hundred miles from Moscow. And now—' Venetia's eyes well up and she takes a sip from a glass of water. Her hand is shaking.

'I understand that students are contractually signed to Edstol's Music Academy and are unable to earn money elsewhere for five years after they leave. Is that correct?'

I am watching Venetia carefully. As we think at least ten times faster than we speak, I need to look out for any deceptive behaviour within the first five seconds of the question. I'm good at this now, but I still need to concentrate hard.

'Good heavens, no! Where did you get that information from?' Venetia carries on talking, and I'm glad she poses it as a rhetorical question, as I wouldn't want Joe telling her we received that information from Sophie and Christophe. 'We take twenty per cent of the student's earnings and of course they can leave whenever they wish. Termly fees are paid in advance, but all of our students are on full bursaries supported both by a government scheme and wealthy benefactors. If students leave mid-term, then they forfeit the fees. We're not a prison!'

Venetia is sitting quite still as she speaks, her hands on her lap. Her inner and outer brows are raised symmetrically with surprise, and I don't see any suggestions of lying. She isn't deflecting her answer or posing questions; she hasn't asked for clarification, and there is no verbal and non-verbal disconnect, for instance when someone nods yes when they're saying no. Venetia is telling the truth. And that means that her students are either under a misapprehension that they are bound to Edstol's, or Sophie and Christophe were lying. But I would have spotted if they were lying, not so?

'Do you know who might wish to harm Vadim?' Joe asks.

'No. He has only been with us two years and he was doing so well. I knew that Cat liked him but I didn't know they were sleeping together. The stupid child!' She blinks tears away.

'You told us that your husband was visiting his mother in a nursing home yesterday morning. Where was he yesterday afternoon when Vadim ran away?'

'That's a good question. He spent the whole day with her. He does that from time to time, but of course the poor woman has such a terrible memory, she can't remember what was is said from one minute to the next. That's what dementia does to you.'

Venetia is lying. The lengthy explanation was unnecessary, and the tapping of her fingers on her thigh, as if practicing scales, is a giveaway of her unease. I wonder why she is covering up for Karl. Joe is one step ahead of me.

'The nursing home will have records of when visitors arrive and leave, and undoubtedly they also have CCTV, so perhaps you would like to reconsider your answer?'

Venetia's eyes are wide. The muscles in her jaw contract and her lips flatten. 'I don't know where my husband was, but I am sure he has an innocent explanation.'

But she shakes her head almost imperceptibly as she says that. She knows all too well that Karl will not have an innocent explanation.

'We have a copy of a letter written by you to Viscount Sneddon. asking him to pay the ransom money. Why did you write that note?'

She squirms in her chair. 'Because I thought he could pay, would want to pay. It turns out he doesn't. He says he can't afford it.'

'Why did Viscount Sneddon come to visit you, and why did he leave at 8 a.m. this morning?'

'What? It's n...not unusual for him to be here early in the morning,' she stammers.

'What was he discussing with you?'

'It wasn't with me, it was with Karl. I'm not sure. Probably about how to raise money to rescue Cat. There was some talk about crowdfunding.' She jerks her head backwards, her eyelids stretch outwards and tighten, and she bunches her hands up in her lap. Venetia is scared. No. I change my mind. Venetia is terrified. And she's lying.

'I've said everything I wish to say.' Venetia bunches her hands into fists. There are red spots high on her cheekbones.

Joe sighs, but brings the interview to a close. Mia escorts Venetia out of the interview room.

Joe swivels his chair around to face me. 'Venetia was lying,' I say. 'And she's scared.'

'I agree that she's hiding something from us. We will have to dig further.'

And then Mia returns with a broad smile on her elfin face. 'Jonno Sneddon's phone records have come back. He received a text from Cat Kingsley the day she disappeared. It reads, "*It's all done.*"'

'What the hell?' Joe exclaims. 'He must have been in cahoots with Cat. Are we now thinking he set up Cat to steal the violin?'

'Isn't it more likely that whoever kidnapped her was instructed by Viscount Sneddon, and the person used Cat's phone to send him a message? After all, we know for certain that she had her finger chopped off,' I suggest.

'Yes, Pippa. You are right. Mia, get an arrest warrant out for Viscount Jonno Sneddon.'

'Karl Edstol asked if he could be formally interviewed tomorrow. They don't like to leave the school together. Something to do with staff rostas. I agreed. I hope that's ok?' Mia says.

'Yes. Bring him in for 9 a.m. tomorrow morning. Jonno Sneddon is our primary suspect.'

44

'You are not bloody listening to me!' Martha is screaming. Her face is puce. She chucks the small diary across the room, but her aim is off and it slams into the half-full mug of tea next to the kitchen sink, knocking the mug off the vinyl work surface to smash on the stone floor. Milky tea drips down the counter into a puddle. Bits of bright blue broken crockery are scattered across the room. It was Bill's favourite mug, the one Alice had given him for his birthday a few years back with the words, *The World's Best Dad*.

'Now look what you've made me do!' she yells.

'This isn't about you, Martha. It's about Alice.' Bill speaks softly. He's learned the hard way. In the early days he used to match Martha's tone and pitch; that was, until he spotted little Alice, maybe three or four years old, cowering in her nightdress at the top of the stairs, big fat tears dripping down her face. He had rushed up to her, scooped her up in his arms and carried her back to bed.

'What have I done?' she had asked.

'Nothing, Pudding. You've done nothing.'

'But why are you and Mummy shouting?'

'Sometimes mummies and daddies shout at each other. It doesn't mean we don't love each other.'

'Are you sure?' Alice had asked.

Bill had kissed Alice on the forehead, pulled the duvet up under her chin and tucked in bunny next to her. As he walked down the stairs, he wasn't sure. Thirteen years it has taken him. But now he is sure.

'Alice is ill and the reason she is ill is because we have pushed her too hard.'

'Well of course *I* have pushed her!' Martha shouts. 'Someone has to, because you're just a lazy lay-about with zero ambition or ability. I didn't want her growing up to be like you!'

'What has happened to you, Martha?' Bill shakes his head. 'You're not the woman I married.'

'And you're not the man I married. If you had achieved all the things you promised me, I might not be on anti-depressants, desperate to leave all of this behind!'

'But this isn't about us. It's about Alice and what's best for her.'

'And what's best for her is to get her back into the Academy. Have you done what we discussed?'

'No,' Bill says, lowering himself into a kitchen chair.

Martha's voice rises another octave. 'Then I'm going to do it!' She makes a lunge for the phone. 'Alice has told us Karl is a paedophile! All we need to do is threaten to tell the papers and he'll accept Alice back into the school, won't he?'

'Stop it, Martha. Why would you want to send Alice back into the lion's den? If Karl is such a monster, I don't want our daughter anywhere near him.'

'Don't be such an ass!' Martha says, although her tone has lowered a bit. 'Of course, Karl isn't a paedo. He wouldn't be allowed to teach if he was. It's just Alice and her histrionics. Did you even speak to him?'

Bill sighs and stares at the puddle of tea. 'Yes, I did. And I asked him about Sarah Bellingham. He denies it. He won't take Alice back and that's that.'

'No it bloody well isn't. Our daughter can be the best violinist in the world!'

'She doesn't even want to be a violinist,' Bill says, his face turned away from Martha.

And then Martha loses it. Again. She jams her fist into Bill's face, the ring on the middle finger of her right hand catching his eyebrow, her knuckles slamming into his eye.

Bill is up and out of the chair. He roars as he lunges towards Martha, who slips and crashes to the floor as her right foot slides in the puddle of tea. But he doesn't bring his fist down into her face. He just stands over her, as she trembles, wondering what has turned his wife into such a heartless bitch. As she lifts the palm of her hand to examine the cut where she has slammed her hand onto a jagged piece of broken mug, Bill shakes his head in disgust and turns away. When he reaches the doorway, he turns. 'I'm filing for divorce, Martha. And I'm going to get custody of Alice. I've had enough.'

'No!' She's up off the ground now, but Bill is faster and has the back door open. Martha picks up a plate and hurls it towards him. It shatters the pane of glass to the side of the back door.

'Come back!' she screams.

Bill slams the door behind him before Martha can reach it. He knows she won't follow him. She would never scream and shout in the garden in case the neighbours might hear. Sometimes Bill wonders if Martha is so delusional that she's forgotten she lives in a run-down semi rather than the grand detached house she aspires to. The walls are thin on both sides, and he knows perfectly well their arguments fuel the gossip of the street.

It's raining outside and he pauses for a moment, turning his face up towards the leaden sky, welcoming the cool splatter of rain on his throbbing, bleeding face.

'Is everything all right?' Ethel Smith peers over the fence. She's just a couple of feet from Bill, short sleeved as normal, unperturbed by the weather.

'Crikey,' she says, as her hand rushes up to her mouth. 'What has happened to you?' Her eyes are wide as she stares at Bill's face. But before he can answer, she hurries back inside her house, slamming the door behind her. He can hear as she pull the bolts across her door.

Bill hesitates for a moment. But then he wipes his face with his sleeve and, as he puts his hand in his pocket, his fingers curl around four sets of car keys. Two sets for the Defender and two sets for his little Astra. Martha won't be going anywhere soon.

Now it's time for him to go.

He walks around through the side gate to the front of the house and climbs into the old Defender. As he turns the key, he prays it will start first time. He gets lucky. It coughs and splutters, then he puts his foot on the accelerator. When he turns out of the cul-de-sac, he glances in his rear-view mirror. Martha is peering out of the living room window, waving her arms around, her face wild.

Goodbye, he thinks. *Good riddance.*

45

By Tuesday morning, Jonno has still not surfaced, but Karl is at the police station for questioning. Yet again, I have had to rearrange two clients, and I am worried about the effects this police investigation is having on my private practice. Even so, I know I need to be here for Cat Kingsley and Alice Jones, if for no one else.

'Do I need a solicitor?' Karl is leaning back in his chair, legs wide apart, affecting nonchalance. But I can read him. Karl Edstol is anything but nonchalant. Whilst his wife, Venetia, found it impossible to disguise her fear, he is clearly trying a different tactic and attempting to brazen it out.

Joe explains to Karl that he is not under arrest and is at the police station voluntarily. Karl places his hands on the table and shifts his chair back as if to stand up.

'In which case, I'm going.'

'And I will arrest you on suspicion of murder,' Joe says slowly. Mia sits up a little straighter. I wonder how much Joe is pushing the boundaries of the law. Karl sits back down again.

'You are entitled to a solicitor. Would you like one?' Joe asks.

Karl shakes his head.

'Please explain what you were doing on Sunday?'

'I went to see my mother. She has advanced dementia.'

'And before that, what time did you meet Bill Jones?' He pauses for a moment, as if waiting for Karl's expression of dismay. As it duly flickers across his face, Joe continues. 'Bill Jones, your pupil Alice Jones's father?'

I am pleased Joe believed me when I told him I thought I saw the two men together in Storrington.

'I don't know what you're talking about,' Karl says.

'You were seen in Storrington chatting to Mr Jones. We have an independent witness.'

'Well, I might have done. I don't remember. It wasn't important. We just happened to run into each other and I was enquiring about young Alice, as she hasn't been at school all week.'

'I trust you understand that I will be corroborating your statements with Mr Jones's, and if I find that they don't match, then I may have to charge one or the other of you with withholding information pertinent to our investigation.'

Karl doesn't say anything, but tugs the collar of his button-down shirt away from his neck.

'Did you attack Bill Jones, Mr Edstol?'

'Is that what he told you?' Karl places his hands on the table and leans forwards aggressively.

Joe leans back in his chair. 'Calm down, please. I am asking you the question. Did you attack Bill Jones?'

'I don't know how the bastard got a black eye!'

'So you confirm you met him, you talked to him and you noticed that he had a black eye?'

'Yes,' Karl says, scowling.

'And what did you talk about?'

'I've already told you. I asked when Alice was coming back to school.'

'And Mr Jones said what?'

'He didn't know.'

'We have been led to believe that you expelled Alice from the school. Is that correct?'

'No.'

'Are you aware that Alice tried to take her own life?'

Karl's eyes widen and he tugs at his shirt again, more aggressively this time. I note that this has come as a shock to Karl. I wonder if he is concerned for Alice, or for the implications it has on the school.

'Do you have any idea as to why Alice might have attempted to kill herself?'

'Probably because she has the pushiest mother I have ever met, and believe me I have come across many pushy mothers in my time. It's endemic in the music world. All those women, unfulfilled in their own lives and trying to fulfil themselves through their offspring. Tragic. After Alice running off stage and screwing up the performance at The Cadogan Hall, I assume her mother was livid.'

'A pushy mother that you nevertheless employed as a piano accompanist.'

'Used to employ. After she dropped the piano lid on Cat's fingers, I fired her. It wouldn't surprise me one iota if she has kidnapped Cat. Have you fully investigated her?'

'Did you accuse Bill Jones of being complicit in Cat's kidnapping?'

'I might have done.' He glances around the room, looking everywhere except at us.

'Who threw the first punch?'

Karl draws back his shoulders and looks Joe straight in the eyes. He is a big man with arms the size of my thighs. I wonder if it's muscle or fat inside those sleeves. I also wonder how on earth such a well-built man can play as delicate an instrument as a violin.

'Not me.'

Karl is telling the truth. I want Joe to ask the next question: did you beat up Bill Jones? Frustratingly he doesn't, and as he specifically requested that I didn't intervene in the interviews, I can't pose it myself. I stifle my groan. Instead, he asks a question that takes even me by surprise.

'Why did you kill Vadim Maximovich?'

'For God's sake, I didn't bloody kill him! Next you'll be telling me I kidnapped Cat! Why are you pointing fingers at Venetia and me? You should be out there finding the real killer!' Karl is roaring now and jabbing his index finger at Joe.

'Please calm down, Mr Edstol,' Mia says.

'Perhaps you could explain what Viscount Jonno Sneddon was doing at Edstol's Music Academy at 8 a.m. yesterday morning?'

This is a clever tactic of Joe's, asking a question he knows will rile Karl, and then firing off the question to which he really wants the answer. But it does get me thinking. I have never really considered Karl as a suspect in relation to Cat's kidnapping, but he isn't her blood relation; he is just her guardian. Could he be involved? Does he have a thing for Cat? Has he hurt her? As I'm pondering this, I almost miss Karl's reaction to Joe's question. The scratching of his head with his right hand, then crossing his arms across his broad chest; the eyebrows drawing up and together, increasing the depth of the broad lines he has across his forehead; the lower eyelids tensing and his mouth very briefly flattening out, as if the corners of his lips are being pulled towards his ears. It all happens in a millisecond and it makes me realise I must concentrate. If I am to play a role in helping these young people, I need to know when the suspects are lying. And the expression that flies across Karl's face is fear. Karl Edstol does not want the police to know that Viscount Sneddon visited yesterday morning.

'He wasn't—'

'Before you indict yourself again, we have yet another independent witness, and your wife has confirmed it, so I suggest you tell the truth.'

Karl narrows his eyes at Joe. I can understand how the children might be fearful of the man. His face becomes thuggish and intimidating. 'To be honest, I was going to say that he wasn't visiting us specifically. He was in the area, so dropped off an instrument he is loaning us for a new pupil.'

'What were you arguing about?'

'We weren't arguing.'

'Thank you, Mr Edstol. You've been very helpful.'

I am surprised that Joe is bringing the interview to such an abrupt close. Has he really got all the information out of Karl that he needs? And why end things when we know Karl has just told a lie? It isn't until Joe leans back in his chair that I see the phone Mia has placed in front of him. Both Joe and Mia stand up quickly.

'You are free to go, Mr Edstol, but we will need to talk to you again, I suspect, in the very near future. Make sure that you are available at all times.'

Mia accompanies Karl out of the room.

'What's happened?' I ask Joe.

'There's been another ransom demand. It's been increased to a million pounds, along with the threat that Cat will be killed if the cash isn't delivered within three days. And another digit has been received. According to Mia, Venetia thinks it's a toe. She's having hysteria.'

'Was the ransom letter sent to her like last time?'

'No. It was sent to Sophie.'

I look at Joe in horror.

46

'Sophie will only talk to you!' Mia says as she strides towards Joe and me. We are in the open-plan office standing in front of Joe's desk, which looks remarkably tidy; probably because Joe hasn't actually been at his desk for several days. He explained once that the police have a clean-desk policy, so he has to clear all his paperwork away before leaving for the night. From the grimace he made when he told me that, I assume he finds it very difficult. Joe isn't a messy person per se, or at least his house isn't, but I would hardly call him a neat freak either.

'She's distraught,' Mia says quietly as we huddle together.

'I'm happy to go over to the school,' I say, glancing at Joe.

'You won't have to do that. She's here. One of our constables is comforting her. They're in an interview room downstairs.'

'How did she get here?' I ask, surprised.

'Her boyfriend brought her. A young man called Matt Fleeting.'

Joe claps his hands together. 'Makes our lives easier. Let's go and talk to her.'

Sophie is pacing around the small interview room. Her face

is red, blotchy and tear-stained. She looks young and vulnerable, and for a moment I feel an overwhelming urge to sweep her into my arms and ask her if she'd like to be my foster daughter. But Joe's matter-of-fact manner sweeps the thought away, and as we sit down around the table, she throws me a weak smile.

'Sophie, can you tell us exactly what happened?' Joe asks.

'I didn't take much with me yesterday, so after my lesson this morning, I went back to my room and packed a few more things to take to Matt's. I saw Venetia. I thought she would be livid about me leaving the Academy and staying at Matt's, but she wasn't. She was really understanding. Christophe told me that I was a lucky cow to be able to leave, and we had a quick chat about him leaving too. I explained that I was only moving out temporarily, and that I would stay on at the Academy until the end of the year. When Matt arrived, I put my case in the back of his car and then went to say goodbye to Venetia. I was in her office when one of the younger kids knocked on her door and delivered a parcel addressed to me. I opened it.' She shudders.

Mia puts a small box and a letter, both secured inside clear evidence bags, on the table in front of Joe.

Joe picks up the note and reads it out aloud. '*Dear Sophie, Bring me £1 million in cash. Get it from your rich music friends. If you don't, then you and Christophe will be kidnapped next. You will receive instructions where to leave the money. If you tell the police or if anyone stalks us out, Catkin will die. If you don't do this, you'll be kidnapped next and we'll get Christophe too. We are following you.*'

Joe places the note back on the table and picks up the bag with the small box in it.

'Please don't open it, not here!' Sophie says, putting her fingers over her eyes.

'It's a toe,' Mia says. 'I'll get forensics to match it up.'

'Why do you think anyone would want to harm you, Cat and Christophe?' Joe asks.

Sophie shakes her head. 'I don't know.'

'Professional jealousy?' I ask, thinking of Martha.

'We're not that good,' Sophie says. 'And it's not like we've even won any competitions. We were only runners up in X Factor.'

'I think we need to get you and Christophe to a safe house.'

'But you said I could stay with my boyfriend!'

'It's for your own protection. Who knows about the existence of Matt, your boyfriend?'

'Only Venetia, I think.'

'Why can't you just pay the kidnappers? Viscount Sneddon's got the money, hasn't he?' Sophie asks.

Joe and Mia glance at each other.

'It doesn't work like that,' Joe says. 'As a matter of principle, we never negotiate with kidnappers or extortionists.'

'But then they'll kill me and they'll kill Cat! I knew I shouldn't have gone back to the Academy! Matt told me to skip classes for a while, but I ignored him.' Sophie gets up and starts pacing around the small room, tugging at the pockets of her jeans, chewing the side of her mouth.

'We will keep you safe, Sophie,' Joe says.

'And what about Cat? And Christophe? And Vadim, who is already dead? Why are they coming after us?'

'Mia, would you accompany Sophie back to Matt's place and do a risk assessment, please.'

'I've got to go back to school first. I left my viola there in the rush.' She rubs the back of her hand across her nose. 'Can Dr Durrant come with me too?'

'Pippa?' Joe asks.

'Of course,' I say, not that I have any desire to go back to the school.

·   ·   ·

MIA AND SOPHIE walk ahead of us along the corridor.

'Are you all right?' Joe says, touching me tenderly on the elbow.

I nod.

'Now we've received a toe, I'm discounting any claim for hand insurance. I think that was a red herring.'

'It's horrible. We have a quartet of music students. One is dead, one has been kidnapped and the other two are clearly in danger. And the substitute violinist is in hospital having tried to take her own life.'

'Forensics have confirmed that Vadim was hit on the back of his head with a rock. He drowned.'

'That's awful.'

'We've also had a report from Miss Ethel Smith, the Jones's neighbour. She has reported suspected domestic violence.'

'Has Martha beaten Bill up?'

Joe stops still and stares at me. 'How did you know? Most people would assume it was the man beating up the woman!'

'You've forgotten that I'm a psychologist and I can read people!' I smirk at Joe. The awkwardness between us has dissipated somewhat. 'I told you Martha was suspicious. It still wouldn't surprise me if she had something to do with the kidnap and murder.'

'I hear you,' Joe says. 'I've sent a couple of officers to pay the Joneses a visit. They'll be reporting back soon.'

I feel the tension release from my shoulders. If Joe had discounted my professional opinion again, I was ready to walk away from the case. And walking away from the case would have meant walking away from Joe for ever. I bite the inside of my mouth to stop myself from smiling.

47

As we're getting out of Mia's marked police car at Edstol's Music Academy, I place my hand on Sophie's arm. It is clear she doesn't want to be here. Her shoulders are bunched up and her pale complexion is almost white.

On a hunch, I turn to Mia. 'Would it be appropriate for me to have a look in Vadim's room?'

'I don't see why not,' she says. 'The police have searched his room and we've got the letters he and Cat wrote to each other, along with some other bits and pieces taken away for evidence and analyses. I'll take Sophie to her room to collect her viola.'

There is a distinct air of *froideur* about Venetia as she lets us into the school. She holds herself stiffly, and I get the sense she has aged several years during the past few days.

'Please can you accompany Dr Durrant to Vadim's room?' Mia says.

Venetia narrows her eyes at me and purses her lips. I follow her straight back, clad in a charcoal grey polo-necked jumper, along the boy's corridor. It's strangely quiet. I suppose the students are in lessons. She turns the key in the lock and opens the door for me.

'What are you looking for?' she asks.

'I'm not sure. I'll need about five minutes.'

'His uncle is coming to collect Vadim's belongings at the end of the week.'

I nod, my heart full of pity for a talented life lost so young.

She huffs as she hesitates in the doorway. I turn my back to her and let my eyes trail over the room. I glance over my shoulder as the door closes with a gentle thud. Venetia has gone. Even though I'm alone in the room, my heart skips a beat as I recall the last time I was in here. Taking a deep breath, I look at Vadim's desk. The papers and books have been tidied up into neat piles.

I flick through the exercise books, where he has written out pages and pages in his small, angular script. There are textbooks on the shelf above the desk, and to the right of the desk is a pile of manuscript paper. As my music-reading skills are elementary at best, all I can do is scour the words written on the pages. Most of them are Etudes. Near the bottom of the pile is a sheet of music penned in a different hand. The notes are more carefully drawn and sit rounded on the staves. I turn over the sheet and see that I have been reading the back. The title is written in pencil. *A lullaby for our unborn baby.* I let out a gasp.

This must be a piece of music composed by Cat that she gave to Vadim. My legs feel wobbly. I stagger to the other side of the small room and collapse onto the bed. It has been stripped free of linen. Vadim is dead, and Cat could be anywhere. Is she still pregnant, or perhaps the baby has been born? She could even be dead. It is a tragic scenario, whatever.

There is a knock on the door.

'Are you done in here?' Mia asks as she pops her head around the doorframe. 'You ok?' she asks, frowning as she sees me perched on the edge of the bed.

'Yes, I just found something.' I stand up and follow her out of the room and back down the corridor, the sheet of music in my hand.

'Do we need to bag that up?' Mia asks, eyeing the piece of paper.

'In a moment.'

We exit the building. Sophie is leaning against the police car, her viola case at her feet.

'Could you sing this for me?' I ask, holding the sheet of music out to her.

'I haven't got a great voice but can probably give it a go.'

Sophie sings the melody. It is hauntingly beautiful, sweet but simple, with a melancholic catchy tune.

'What is this?' Sophie asks as she hands the manuscript back to me.

'I think Cat wrote it for her unborn child. I found the music in Vadim's room.'

Tears spring to Sophie's eyes. 'Sorry,' she says as she wipes her face too vigorously.

I place it on the back seat of the car. Sophie climbs in next to it.

'Hold on a moment,' Mia says.

I glance up and see Christophe strolling up to the front door of the academy, a beanie pulled low over his head and the white wires of headphones hanging from his ears.

'What's up?' he asks, eyeing me and Sophie in the back of the police car. 'What's she done?' He tilts his head towards Sophie.

'We're concerned about your and Sophie's safety. There have been credible threats made towards you both. DS Swain thinks it would be sensible if you are moved to a safe house.'

'What!' he exclaims. 'You're taking the piss?'

'No.' Mia crosses her arms.

'What do you mean by "credible threats"?'

'Another ransom note has been received.'

'Okay,' he says, drawling out the word. 'I think I'm able to look after myself.'

'Vadim wasn't,' Mia says, narrowing her eyes.

'Don't compare me to him! I've got a judo black belt.'

'You seem to taking this rather lightly,' Mia says. 'Why aren't you scared?'

Christophe shivers melodramatically. 'Of course I'm bloody scared. I'm just not going to let it get in the way of my everyday life. Thanks for the offer, but I'll pass.'

He shoves the earbuds back into his ears and saunters in through the front door to the school.

48

Mia offers to drop me off at home, despite it being out of her way. But a couple of minutes after we have deposited Sophie at her boyfriend's apartment, Mia's phone rings.

'Viscount Sneddon has walked into the police station as a voluntary attender. I would appreciate having you both there when I carry out the interview,' Joe says, his voice sounding tinny on Mia's speaker phone.

'Of course, Sarge. We'll be back at the station in twenty minutes. That okay with you, Dr Durrant?'

I nod.

JONNO CAN'T SIT STILL. He shifts backwards and forwards in the chair, tugging at his earring, putting his hands underneath his tan-coloured corduroy-clad thighs and then removing them again, playing with the signet ring on the little finger of his right hand. Seated next to him is his obese solicitor, this time wearing just a shirt and tie, the white tinged with yellow in wide stains under his arms.

'Why do you want to interview me?' he asks as soon as we enter the room.

'Hold fire,' the solicitor says.

When we have taken our seats—Mia next to Joe, facing Jonno and his solicitor, and myself in a chair against the wall behind Joe and Mia—Joe starts speaking. He switches on the recording device and states the date and time, and introduces himself. He then asks everyone else in the room to introduce themselves so their voices are identifiable on the recording. All the while, the haunting melody Sophie sang to me plays over and over in my head.

'You do not have to say anything. But it may harm your defence if you do not mention when questioned something which you later rely on in court. Anything you do say may be given in evidence. You are not under arrest or obliged to remain here for this interview.'

Jonno starts to stand up. His solicitor grasps Jonno's forearm and leans over and whispers something in his ear. Jonno sits back down again, but his face is stony.

'Could you please explain how your cigar ash came to be found under the nail of Cat Kingsley's severed finger?' Joe asks.

The blood drains from Jonno's face.

'What?' he whispers.

'You smoke—' Joe glances down at the notes in front of him. '—Nostrano del Brenta Il Clandestino cigars, do you not?'

'Yes,' Jonno says.

'Forensics have found that ash under Cat's fingers.'

'It's not possible,' Jonno says, shaking his head so hard it looks as if he is trying to dislodge something inside. 'I haven't seen Catkin in weeks. Someone else must be smoking those cigars.' A small man to begin with, Jonno looks as if he has shrunk further, shrivelling up into the plastic chair.

My heart skips a beat when I hear Jonno call Cat 'Catkin'. Although I can only see the back of his head, I can tell that Joe has clocked it too. He sits up straighter and throws a glance at Mia. He scribbles something on his notepad.

'Why were you at Edstol's at 8 a.m. on Sunday morning?'

'I was telling them to get their bloody house in order.'

'So you were not lending them another violin?'

'I don't have any more violins to lend.' He crosses his arms.

'What have you done with Cat Kingsley?'

'I don't bloody well know where Catkin is!'

'Have you lined Cat up as your next wife?' Joe asks.

I am shocked by the question. Jonno is enraged. He stands up, letting his chair topple backwards. He leans towards Joe, eyes narrowed into slits.

'How fucking dare you!' He jabs an index finger towards Joe. 'I love my wife and I am doing everything in my power to find a cure for her and save her life. I am not interested in little girls or any other women. If you want to find a paedophile, look at Karl Edstol! He's the one you should be investigating, not me. He smokes bloody cigars too!'

'Sit down, sir,' his solicitor says. His voice is surprisingly soft and high-pitched for such a big man. Jonno does as he is told.

'Yes, he does smoke cigars, but typically not your favoured brand.' Joe pauses for a moment and then leans back in his chair. 'If you were concerned about Karl Edstol's proclivities towards girls, why haven't you reported him?'

'Because he's a clever bastard and covers his tracks. Besides, he was trying to blackmail me.' Jonno is now slumped in his chair, anger gone, with the expression of a man who knows his time is up.

'How was he trying to blackmail you?'

'If I give him fifty per cent of the insurance money, he won't report me for insurance fraud.'

'Are you confirming that the violin was over-insured?'

'Sir!' His solicitor is more energised this time. 'You don't need to say anything that—'

'I know I don't need to say anything. I know how this bloody well works, but I want to say something. I did not have a thing to do with the kidnap of Catkin or the murder of Vadim, but I did over-insure the violin. On the say-so of Milo, my brother. I smashed the bloody thing up as well, because Milo threatened me. Go after my brother if you must, but investigate Karl Edstol first. There was that suspicious death of a student, what's her name?'

'Sarah Bellingham,' I interrupt.

'Yeah, her. Karl had something to do with that. Everyone said so but the coroner ruled it was suicide. Don't know how Karl got away with it. He's a nasty piece of work. And to be honest, I've always thought he was a bit too keen on Catkin. It was "Cat this" and "Cat that", and she wasn't his real daughter. It was a bit pervy, but you know I couldn't prove a thing, so I had to let it go. Besides, I hoped that Venetia would stop anything.'

'Why would Karl kidnap Cat and send a ransom note to himself?'

'Suppose he was hoping I'd pay up. I don't know.'

'We have investigated your financial affairs and you have three hundred and forty-one pounds in the bank. What other investments or assets do you have?' Joe asks.

'None. That's it. All gone. I'll have to sell the castle next, and that'll break Marissa's heart. We're living in the never-never land. The insurance dosh was meant to save us.' He rubs his knuckles into his eyes.

Joe rummages in a folder in front of him and removes a large photograph. 'For the purposes of this interview, I am showing Viscount Jonno Sneddon a photo taken of a text message received on his phone. You received a message from Cat Kingsley's phone on the day of her disappearance, saying, *It's all done.* What was all done?'

'No, I didn't! I don't know what you're talking about!' Jonno is agitated again, eyes darting around the room.

'The time and the date are here. This is when it was received on your phone.' Joe points to the date and time on the photograph. 'Are you denying you received this?'

'You don't need to answer...' his solicitor tries again.

'I did receive it, but it came from an unknown number. I haven't got a clue what Cat's mobile number is! I only ever spoke to her through the Edstols or after a concert. I didn't know what it meant, and assumed it had been sent in error. I deleted the message!'

'Yes, we can see that you deleted the message.'

'Why would Cat send you that message?'

'I've just said! It was a mistake. Or someone must be trying to set me up! Karl fucking Edstol, I suppose. He knows what cigars I smoke! He knows what both our mobile numbers are! And I've refused to give him the insurance money because I won't get any now. It must be him, the bastard!'

'Is it not more likely that you were looking to get the money through kidnapping Cat? You knew you were on the edge of bankruptcy, that you needed to get hold of money quickly for your wife. Anyone with any business sense will know that it takes some time to get an insurance payout for a stolen instrument. We, the police, take our time investigating, and insurance claims experts need to do their due diligence. How much faster it would be to demand ransom money. No one would suspect you of doing that, because you are perceived to be the rich guy. You were hoping that the Edstols, who clearly love Cat Kingsley very much, would have other means of raising the money. The perfect crime, surely?'

Jonno is quivering. He opens and closes his mouth, but no words come out. He looks as if he is going to pass out.

Eventually, when he speaks, his voice cracks. 'I didn't do that. I would never do something like that.'

'For the purpose of this interview, I am showing Viscount Sneddon a copy of the ransom note sent to Sophie Buck. You will see that the ransom note calls Cat "Catkin". You are the only person who calls her by the nickname Catkin. Please explain.'

'I'm being set up! Can't you see that? That bastard Karl Edstol has set me up!' Jonno is shaking. His eyes are bloodshot, and his face has assumed a greenish tinge.

'What proof do you have that my client has done what you accuse?' his solicitor asks.

'Shall we take a break, sir?' Mia asks.

I am glad she suggests this, because I was just debating saying the same. Jonno looks as if he is going to throw up.

When he, his solicitor and Mia have left the room, Joe swivels around in his chair to face me.

'So, what do you think?'

'He's telling the truth.'

'What!' Joe says. He stands up. I can tell from his expression that he is disappointed but perhaps not surprised. He lets out a puff of air. 'I agree with you,' he says eventually.

'I think you need to back off Viscount Sneddon and concentrate on investigating Karl Edstol. He has the means and the motive.'

'I would be a foolish man not to listen to your professional opinion. The previous times I dismissed your evaluations, I was mistaken. I am sorry, Pippa.' His smile is wry.

I throw him a brief grin and hope that my cheeks don't show the warming flush coursing through my body. 'What now?' I ask.

'We tell Jonno to go home and we talk to Karl again. The trouble is, we don't have enough evidence. It's all circumstantial and based on other people's assumptions. We'll need to go back to the school, re-interview him and see if we can pin down any evidence.'

'And what about the insurance fraud?'

'Jonno has admitted fraudulent behaviour, so it will be further investigated and he will no doubt be arrested for that. But, right now, it's not our priority.'

'Poor Marissa,' I say.

'I'm worried about you, Pippa. So long as we haven't arrested anyone, it's a possibility the scare tactics against you will ramp up. Do you have any concerns?'

'I didn't particularly,' I say, 'but now you put it like that, I don't feel so easy. What do you suggest?'

'Could you go and stay with your brother, perhaps?'

I turn away from Joe. My brother Rob's house used to be my bolthole in times of trouble, but more recently Joe has taken me under his wing. He even took me to his home under the pretext that it was a safe house. The fact he isn't offering this time hurts. It hurts a lot.

49

That sense of foreboding I felt the first time I came to Edstol's Music Academy has never receded. If anything —knowing what has been going on there—it is even worse now. Is Karl really such an evil man? Could he have been abusing the students? Could he be hiding Cat? Joe and I have made the journey in silence, in my car. I need to go home after this, to see some of my own clients. And I also want to make sure all my windows are firmly closed and the doors bolted top and bottom.

We arrive before Mia, who is coming in a marked police car with another officer.

'I'd like to wait for Mia before we go in,' Joe says.

It suits me. I need some fresh air and some head space. 'I'll have a quick wander around the outside.'

Joe nods.

The days are so short now that it seems as if it never gets properly light. I follow a stone path along the side of the red-brick building, past bushes that are bare and prickly. There is a large yew tree set back from the corner, the sort normally found in church yards. It is beautiful and I wonder what knowledge it holds. As I walk under its branches, I glance up at the building and all those darkened windows. Are the students happy here? Are they safe?

And then, as if floating on the whispering wind, I hear a few beautiful notes. I walk closer to the side of the house. There is a window that, despite the cold, damp air, is slightly open. The music is coming from inside. A dark, haunting tune played on a cello. It sounds familiar but I can't place it. I stop and listen. And then, with a jolt, I realise what it is. The lullaby that Cat composed for her unborn child.

The open window is on the first floor, just a few feet up from the ground.

'Hello!' I shout. 'Hello!'

The music stops. A couple of moments later, the window is flung fully open and a head pops out. 'What are you doing here?' Christophe says, his floppy fringe masking his eyes.

'I'm just...' I remind myself that I don't need to explain my actions to him. 'That piece of music you were playing, what is it?'

'Why?'

'Who wrote it?' I feel a chill pass through me and tug my down-filled coat tighter around my torso.

'Do you know much Brahms?'

I shake my head.

'Gustav Brahms was known for writing *Wiegenlied*, the famous lullaby, but he wrote others too, ones that have only surfaced recently. You should listen to them. Anyway, nice to chat and all that, but I've got a class now, so had better get a move on.' He disappears inside and pulls the window closed.

I stand stock still. Too much unnecessary information. Christophe was lying. That piece wasn't written by Brahms.

'Pippa! Pippa!'

Joe is calling me, so I hurry back the way I came.

'You look as if you've seen a ghost!' Joe's eyes crinkle with concern.

'The piece of music that Cat wrote? Christophe was playing it.'

'And?'

'Why would she have shared it with Christophe? She wrote it for her and Vadim's unborn baby. Do you think we've been looking in the wrong place all along?'

'What? You think Christophe has got something to do with it?'

'I don't know,' I say, but I wonder. 'He told me it was Brahms, but it wasn't. Why did he lie to me?'

'Well, let's go ask him,' Joe suggests. He strides ahead of me, and whilst I know his distant behaviour is a result of me cold-shouldering him, I miss his strong embrace, his confidence and his humour. But then I think of Christmas just a few days away and remember that he has a daughter who doesn't want me in their lives and I...well, I have no one.

'Sarge, Karl Edstol is here.' Mia is standing at the open front door to the school.

'Good. Take him into his study and get him to wait for us. Dr Durrant and I will be five minutes.'

Christophe is loping along the corridor with his cello case over his shoulder. He is humming a tune I don't recognise.

'Can we have a quick word?' Joe asks.

Christophe's fringe is hanging low over his forehead. He hesitates. 'I've got a class now. What do you want?'

'Just a quick word. Is there somewhere private we can go?'

He shifts from foot to foot, his eyes darting everywhere except at us. Eventually he says, 'Into a practice room.'. He opens a door into a small room barely large enough for the three of us to stand in. He walks in first, uncaring that it nearly swings back into my face. The room is windowless with the exception of a small glass pane in the door that looks out onto the corridor. Christophe switches on the light, a fluorescent bulb that flickers in the middle of the ceiling. He puts his cello case down on the floor and then leans his shoulders against the wall, crossing his arms.

I know that pose. It suggests ease and insouciance, but is anything but. The tightening of his lips and narrowing of his eyes, along with the crossing of his arms, gives his true feelings away.

'Why were you playing the tune Cat wrote?' Joe asks.

'I wasn't. I was playing Brahms.'

'Did you know that Cat wrote a piece of music for her unborn child?'

'What?' Christophe says. He is feigning surprise. 'What do you mean? Is she pregnant?' And then he starts laughing. 'Stupid girl, getting herself banged up.'

'Why were you playing that piece?' Joe asks again.

'My repertoire is broad. It has to be.' He crosses his arms even more tightly over his chest.

'Right,' Joe says. 'What else can you tell us?'

Christophe shrugs.

'I gather you rejected the idea of going into a safe house,' Joe says.

'Somewhat of an overreaction, I suggest,' Christophe says with an air of pomposity. 'I'm quite capable of looking after myself. Anyway, must get going. I'm already late.' He picks up his cello case and goes out of the room. The door swings closed with a creak.

'He's lying,' I say.

'About what?' Joe asks.

'He was playing Cat's composition. He's acting very suspiciously.'

'Maybe, but first we need to question Karl. We need to concentrate on getting him to talk. Everyone is suggesting that Karl is a murderer, a kidnapper and a paedophile.'

As we walk towards Karl's study, Venetia opens the door to her office, but when she catches sight of us, she steps back inside.

I let Joe stride on ahead and knock on Venetia's door, opening it without waiting for her to answer. She looks at me with surprise. Her eyes are red and raw.

'Can we have a chat?' I ask.

She nods and collapses into her chair. Joe closes the door on us.

'Are you all right?'

'No,' she shakes her head. 'This is all getting to me. I'm so worried about Cat. I really love her as if she were my own child. And Vadim. What could we have done to care for him better?'

I perch on the piano stool. 'I know it's easy for me to say, but you mustn't blame yourself. All you can do is give as much information to the police as you can, even if you think it's irrelevant.'

She nods, but I can't help wondering if some of the worry is a result of guilt. Does she know what her husband is capable of? Has she been complicit in his actions?

'Can you tell me what happened to Sarah Bellingham?'

Venetia's face falls. 'Another child we failed.'

'What do you mean?'

'She took her own life. She walked into the sea. Her body was washed up a week later.'

'Was suicide proven?'

'Yes. The coroner's report was conclusive. She left a note and, sadly, it was hardly a bolt from the blue. Sarah had been having psychological support for three years. She was anorexic and suffered from depression. She wasn't even at our school when it happened. The poor child had been discharged from hospital and was at home with her parents, who live in Eastbourne.'

'There are rumours circulating that Karl had something to

do with her death. Why do you think gossip would suggest he was complicit?'

Venetia shakes her head, as if trying to dislodge a thought. 'People always look for a scapegoat.'

'Forgive me for saying this, but it has been implied that Karl has had inappropriate affairs. Is that true?'

Venetia throws her head back and closes her eyes. She lets out a huge sigh. 'Not that again.' Her voice is plaintive. Then she sits upright and fixes her gaze on me. 'There has been historic sex abuse at music schools around the country. You will have seen that on the news. And as a consequence, people jump on the bandwagon. Yes, Karl can be a bit of a bully—after all, he teaches in the Russian method—and yes, Karl did have an affair many years ago with a young teacher, but no, he would never lay a finger on a girl. My husband is not a bad person.'

'When you say "the Russian method", what do you mean?'

'Historically, the Russian method described a certain way of holding the bow, but more latterly it's a broad-brush description of a teaching method. I suppose it is perceived to be demanding, aggressive, requiring the student to copy the teacher precisely, a focus on technical ability sometimes to the detriment of musicality. Karl has high standards and high expectations of our students, and rightly so. We nurture performers who are brilliant technically and bring passion and soul.'

I admire the aspiration, but I wonder how accurate her description is. The students I have met seem fearful and uptight, and fear causes the senses to shut down. Fear does not allow passion, soul and creativity to shine through.

'How is young Alice? I am so worried about her?' Venetia nibbles the side of her thumbnail.

'I'm not sure, but I can find out.'

She leans forwards. 'You should talk to Alice about Karl.

Ask her what she thinks of him. She will tell you what Karl is like as a teacher.'

'That's a good idea. I will.' I pause. 'I've also been told that your students aren't able to leave due to the onerous contract they sign when joining the school. Is that correct?'

'Who would like to leave?'

'Sophie Buck.' I hope that I am not making things worse for Sophie.

'If she wants to, then, in light of the current events, of course she must leave. We will release her from the management contract, but we will be sorry to see her go. She is a talented violist.'

'I think that under the circumstances, Sophie would like to go to another college. I understand she has been offered a scholarship at The Royal Academy of Music in London.'

'Then she must leave. We will release her with our blessings and give her the reference that she deserves.'

'Thank you,' I say. I think how happy Sophie will be, and feel relieved that I have achieved something positive.

'WE ARE TAKING Karl to the police station to interview him. Can you come with us?' Joe asks me as I leave Venetia's office.

'I'm sorry, but I have clients this afternoon. If you send me the recording of his interview, I'll review it. Can you get someone to speak to Alice about Karl? Venetia suggested it. Perhaps it'll give us an insight into how he interacts with his students.' I tell Joe about the rest of my conversation with Venetia.

'Of course she's going to stick up for her husband,' Joe says.

I can tell from his tone that he thinks he's got his man.

50

I can't sleep. Cat's lullaby is stuck inside my head; the most annoying earworm. A mark, I suppose, of a successful song. I have no doubt that Joe is right and Karl is behind all the evil, but I am concerned about Christophe. He is hiding something, and I'm not sure what it is.

I waited all evening to see if Joe would call or message me. I have no idea of the outcome from his interview with Karl or whether anyone has spoken to Alice to find out how she views Karl as a teacher. My phone never rang.

At 2.30 a.m. I switch my bedside light on. I fire off a text to Joe.

How did the interview go?

Then I pick up my Kindle to read a book in the hope that my over-active brain will calm down and become sleepy. I know listening to a meditation would be better, but I need a more compelling distraction.

Within a minute, my mobile pings.

Had to let him go. Why are you texting in the middle of the night? x

I put my book down on top of the duvet and grin. I wish Joe was here so I could lie in his arms.

Could ask the same question of you?! Why did you let him go?

Lack of evidence. Mia got statement from Alice. Karl trod on her toes and rapped his knuckles on the top of her head but didn't sexually abuse her. The Edstols need the money but everything is circumstantial.

Look into Christophe, I text.

Will do. Also need to get more evidence on Karl. Still think it's him. Sleep tight. Wish you were here x

I run my fingers over that last sentence. Joe still has feelings for me. But how can I reconcile that with his rejection of me when Holly was home, and the fact that our relationship is getting in the way of us working together? It's ridiculous that we're playing games at our age and stage. I turn my phone to silent and switch off the bedside light. At some point I must fall asleep, because when I awake, my Kindle is on the floor and my alarm clock is buzzing.

I have a full morning of back-to-back clients, but I resolve to go back to Edstol's to talk to Christophe again. I hope Joe won't mind and that he won't view it as interference.

Mungo has been hard done by over the past few days, so at lunchtime, after hurriedly eating a sandwich, I walk him around the block.

'In the car,' I say, holding open the rear passenger door. He jumps straight in. 'We'll have a walk after I've spoken to Christophe.' Mungo looks at me with his doleful amber eyes and I hope that I will be able to keep my promise.

When I arrive at Edstol's, I am surprised to see a hive of activity, with students carrying suitcases and instruments, loading them into the back of cars. Venetia is standing on the front step, gesticulating as she talks to a middle-aged couple. The girl, who I assume is their child, is standing behind them, her head hanging low, her hand over her mouth in an expression of embarrassment.

Mungo lets out a couple of barks at all the people.

'You stay,' I say. He collapses onto the seat, one eye open, the other closed. 'I won't be long.'

As I walk closer, I hear the man saying, 'I am sorry, but our decision is made. Our daughter will not be returning next term.' The woman turns around, her face steely, and, grabbing the girl's hand, walks her briskly towards a silver Volvo.

Venetia is curt when she sees me. 'It's not a good time. As you can see, it's the end of term and parents are collecting their offspring. That is the second child who is being pulled from the school because of Cat's kidnapping and Vadim's murder. And they're threatening to sue us if we don't release them from the contract for negligence of our duty of care or something like that. Why the hell the police can't sort out what's going on quickly is beyond me. At this rate, the school will be shut down by next term.'

'I won't disturb you. I just need to talk to Christophe.'

'He's gone.'

'You mean, he's gone home or has he disappeared?'

'Gone home, I assume. To be blunt, I haven't got time to keep an eye on the older students. Christophe is an adult and quite capable of looking after himself.'

As Venetia knows that Christophe and Sophie have been threatened, I am surprised by her words. A knot of worry develops in my stomach.

'Do you have Christophe's home address?'

'Yes, of course.' She turns her body away from me.

'Can you give it to me?'

'I'm not sure that—'

'Venetia, this is a police investigation,' I say, wondering if I can get away with this. I certainly don't have the authority to ask her to hand over confidential information.

'But you're not a police—'

'Call DS Swain, if you wish.' I hold out my mobile phone. I'm acting on a hunch here, but my intuition is telling me that she'd rather deal with me than Joe.

She huffs but turns and walks inside. I follow her.

'What are you and Karl doing over the Christmas break?'

'Staying here. DS Swain has instructed us that we are not allowed to leave the country. Not that we had any plans to anyway, with the state of our finances. And we're hardly going to go away with Cat missing.'

I follow her farther down the corridor. She opens a door that has the sign "Private" on it. Inside is an office with a wall full of filing cabinets and a large computer monitor on a grey metal desk. She takes her set of keys out of her pocket and opens one of the cabinets. After extracting a file, she sits down at the desk and writes out Christophe's address on the back of a used envelope. She hands it to me.

Banyan Farm, Banyan Lane, Bury, Sussex.

'So he doesn't live far from here?' I say with surprise. I assumed that the students who boarded would live hundreds of miles away or abroad.

'His father is a conductor. He travels a lot. Christophe's mother passed away when he was a child. Christophe rarely goes home. Most of the time, he stays with his maternal grandparents who live in London.'

'Thank you, Venetia,' I say. 'I hope that they find Cat soon.'

BURY IS ONLY twenty minutes from the academy, a small attractive village at the foot of the South Downs. Mungo and I have had many delightful walks in the vicinity. I have to hurry, though, because darkness settles quickly at this time of year.

My sat nav sends me down a narrow country lane, so tight it feels as if I could touch the tall hedgerows on either side if I

stuck my hands out of the car windows. I cross my fingers that I
don't meet a vehicle coming in the opposite direction. I am
driving slowly and almost miss the small wooden sign indicating Banyan Farm. I turn right off the lane and onto a track
that is full of potholes and chalky stone. I drive even more
slowly, nervous of getting a puncture out here.

The track winds upwards between spiky hawthorn hedges.
I can't see what is on the other side but assume fields. After half
a mile or so, I begin to get worried. What the hell am I doing
out here in the middle of nowhere? What if Christophe *is* the
kidnapper and the murderer? What sort of danger am I putting
myself in? But there is nowhere to turn the car and I don't fancy
reversing all the way back to the main road. So I carry on, and
shortly the track opens up. In front of me is a stone and flint
farmhouse with a sloping Horsham stone roof in a mid-grey
and brown colour. The house is ramshackle and large, with
windows that look like half-closed eyes, with heavy stone lintels
above giving the impression of eyebrows. I shiver.

The house is in a dip and the light levels are low, shrouding
everything in dark grey. Should I turn the car around and get
out of here? Mungo sits up and nuzzles me. The dog needs a
walk.

'I'm going to have a quick look around and then I'll come
back for you.' I stroke Mungo's velvet-soft ears and give him a
quick kiss on the top of his head.

The house is in darkness. Curtains are pulled across most
of the upstairs windows. I walk up to the front door, trying to
avoid the puddles. The door is made from heavy oak with a
hefty brass knocker and a small peephole. I wonder whether to
knock but decide to creep around the outside first. Someone
has been tending the flower beds around the house because
they are raked over and weed-free.

I peer through the living room window. There is a grand
piano and a couple of comfy-looking sofas. The shelves are

sagging with books. As I walk around the side of the house, I hear something. At first I think it's a radio playing. Perhaps to pretend that someone is home? Or perhaps someone is home? How will I explain myself, creeping around like a burglar?

I turn around, intending to go back to the front door, but then I hear it again. It's a melody I recognise. Faint, the dulcet ringing of a stringed instrument. I turn once more and head down the side of the house, past a large, sloping chimney and around to the back. There are no lights on here, but the sound of music is getting louder. I tiptoe forwards and the notes of the violin are even louder. Still faint, but distinguishable. My heart rams in my chest. It's the lullaby. Cat's lullaby. But what now? Is that a violin or a cello that is being played? The notes sound quite deep, but no, it must be a violin.

Is it Cat?

Have I found her?

I put my hand in my pocket and grasp my mobile phone. I need to reach Joe. Hurriedly I type a message.

Think I've found Cat. At Christophe's house. Please come.

I press send, but nothing happens. Unable to send. There is no reception here. No bloody reception!

51

As I creep farther forwards, towards the music, I see it. A faint light coming up from the ground between bare bushes. It illuminates an area not much larger than my hand. My breath is ragged now, and my gut is screaming at me: *Get out of here!* But I must be brave. I owe it to the young people. They need saving. I tiptoe, trying not to step on any branches, and lean over the bushes. There is a small grill set in stone paving. A basement.

The lullaby is slowing down. I try to peer into the grill, to see what is there, but I'm not tall enough, I mustn't stumble, mustn't make a noise.

And then the music stops.

And in the silence, my phone rings, loud, jangling. What the hell! A moment ago, I didn't have any reception. I fumble for it, but in the gloomy light and the panic, I don't press the answer button in time. It stops ringing.

'Who's there?' A male voice yells.

'Help!' A female voice now, screaming. 'Help!'

'Shut the fuck up!'

There is a crashing sound and more high-pitched screams. It sounds as if someone is being beaten.

'Stop!' I yell, shoving my phone into my pocket as I step backwards onto level ground. But I don't know if they can hear me or, if they do, I'm being ignored. I need to help. I rush back the way I came, to the front door. It's locked. I run around the other side of the house and there is a back door set into a little porch. I grab the door handle and, to my surprise, it opens. Before I can think about what I am doing, I am inside.

I stare at a scene of perfect domesticity.

The kitchen is the epitome of a farmhouse kitchen. There is a dark green Aga set against the back wall with a splashback of tiles depicting countryside animals—sheep, ducks, cows. The kitchen units are made from oak, and Emma Bridgewater crockery sits on top of the work surfaces. A kettle is whistling, gently at first, but quickly becomes more insistent. It is old-fashioned and placed on one of the Aga rings.

'Like a cuppa?' Christophe asks languidly. 'I wasn't expecting you, but it's a nice surprise. It's a bit lonely out here by myself. Dad isn't back until Christmas Eve.' He gets up from the kitchen table, a solid oak table pitted with dents and cup rings, the everyday wear and tear from years of family life. He walks over to a cupboard and takes out two mugs.

'How do you take it? Milk? Sugar?'

'I'm fine,' I say.

'You don't look fine,' Christophe laughs. 'You look as though someone has just walked over your grave!' He busies himself with the kettle and some tea bags, placing one in each of two spotted mugs. 'What are you doing out here, in the middle of nowhere?' he asks, casually, his back still towards me.

'I heard the music. I heard the fight.'

'Sorry?' he says. But his shoulders rise ever so slightly.

'Is Cat here?' I hold my breath and glance around for a knife. A kitchen like this would have a knife block, wouldn't it?

But Christophe swivels around to face me and I grip the back of a spindly oak kitchen chair.

'What did you say?' His nose is shiny and pimples peek out from beneath his greasy fringe. His eyes are dark, almost black.

'Do you have Cat?'

And then he surprises me. He laughs. 'If only!' He pours the hot water from the kettle into the mugs, spilling a little. A drip splatters onto the back of his hand.

'Fuck,' he mutters and brings the back of his hand up to his mouth and licks it.

'You should hold it under running cold water,' I suggest.

'And you should leave,' Christophe says, scowling. He pours the second cup of tea into the sink and carries the full cup to the table. Just seconds on, it's as if the pain from the burning tea has dissipated.

'Off you go, then!' He places the mug on the table and waves his right hand at me. He sits down, but I can't move.

'Did you throw a brick through my window? Did you try to warn me off?' I ask.

His dark eyes seem to get blacker. They narrow and his lips thin out in a scowl.

'Did you kill Vadim?' I ask. My breathing is shallow and quick, and I can hear my heart thumping in my ears.

Christophe roars. He jumps up from the table and smashes his palms onto the oak surface. Tea slurps over the side of the mug. He then kicks his chair, sending it skidding across the room and smashing into a cupboard. I step backwards, but there is nowhere for me to go. He is nearest to the back door. I have no escape route.

'Vadim deserved to die!' Christophe yells. 'The bastard deserved everything he got!'

My phone starts trilling again from my pocket.

'Give it to me!' Christophe demands. I try to press accept call, but my fingers fumble and Christophe is too quick. He grabs the phone. Then he hurls it onto the stone floor and brings his foot down, crushing it with the heel of his boot, grinding the glass and the plastic into the floor again and again.

'Do you like music, Dr Pippa Durrant?' Christophe leers at me.

'Yes,' I whisper.

'Have you heard Cat play?

'No. Only just now and on a recording.'

'Come with me,' he hisses.

I shake my head.

'It's not a request. It's an order. Come. With. Me.'

I step away from the chair and in an instant he is behind me, his knuckles in the small of my back, shoving me forwards.

'But why? I ask. 'Why are you holding Cat and demanding a ransom?'

'You think you're so clever, don't you, Dr Pippa Durrant? But really you're not. I know all about you. The daughter you failed. The murders you think you solved. You think you can read people, but you've failed. Miserably. I love Cat. She is my true love, the woman for me, the only person in the world who understands me and can make me happy.'

'Why did you cut her finger off?' He pushes me in the small of my back and I stumble. 'And her toe?'

'Why should I tell you anything?'

'Because sometimes talking about things help.'

He gives me another shove. I carry on walking.

'You think talking makes things better? You have no idea. I gave her a beautiful diamond ring. My mother's ring. I declared my love for her and put it on her finger. She pulled it straight off and flung it at me. So I cut her finger off.'

I shudder. 'But an engagement ring is normally worn on the left ring finger.'

'You're not a musician. Just ignorant. Her left hand is her special hand, those are the fingers that run up and down the fret board, creating those magical sounds. Her left hand will always stay unadulterated.'

He rams me again and I put one foot in front of the other. We are in a dark hallway now. A wooden staircase rises but he pushes me towards a door underneath the stairs.

'Stand against the wall.'

I must talk to him, get him in conversation, distract him.

'Why did you demand such a high ransom?' I ask.

'Cat deserves a beautiful house to live in, somewhere where we can make music and release it via the internet. A house fit for a princess.' Christophe pulls a key from his jeans pocket and puts it in the lock of the door. I glance around but there is nothing for me to grab, nothing for me hit him with. Just walls hung with still-life oil paintings, dark, uninspiring pictures, and a tall Grandfather clock in dark wood, going tick tock in the corner of the hallway. And I know I won't be strong enough to tackle him with my bare hands.

'Go in front of me,' he says as he flings the door open. He switches on a light at the top of the concrete stairs. The walls are exposed brick, and a bare bulb hangs from the ceiling.

'Why can't you and Cat live here, in this house?' I need to persuade him that his course of action is irrational. I need to hide my raw fear.

'This is my father's house and he'll be home on Christmas Eve. Cat and I will be gone by then.'

He shoves me again, and I have to grab onto the handrail to stop myself from tumbling down the stairs. All I can think is: I'm going to die too. Unless I can do something, distract him or surreptitiously call Joe, I will die this afternoon.

The door in front of us is locked and bolted top and bottom.

'Undo it,' Christophe commands.

I can feel his breath on my neck. I do as he tells me and slide the bolts across.

'Stand against the wall and don't move. If you do, I'll kill you.'

He waves the blade of a large kitchen knife in front of my face. I hadn't realised he was carrying that. I feel faint with terror. He unlocks the door.

The room is small, but the walls are covered with posters of cities—London, Paris, St Petersburg, New York. On the floor is a mattress covered with a duvet and a blanket—the old-fashioned waffle type in a mushy green. There is a bucket at the side of the room and nothing else. The girl is cowering in the corner, sitting on the concrete floor, which is covered with a tatty rug in black and cream. She has her arms around her knees, and a violin is on the floor next to her. A plastic beaker —the type toddlers use—and a banana skin are also on the floor. The room reeks of fear and urine.

'Cat?' I ask.

She looks up. Her left eye is bloodshot and a bruise is beginning to bloom on her cheekbone. Her long blonde hair is straggly and unkempt. There is a faint sheen of sweat across her forehead, and she is shivering. I wonder if she's feverish. She is wearing black leggings and a large, over-sized sweatshirt in a dusty blue. But it is her right hand and left foot that I notice. Her hand is bandaged, although three fingers are untouched. How is she managing to play the violin like that? Her right foot is also bandaged, but blood has seeped through, staining it black. Her other foot is bare.

'Who are you?' she whispers. Tears stain her cheeks.

'I'm Dr Pippa Durrant.'

'Are you here to save me?'

Christophe laughs. 'I have saved you, Cat. Dr Durrant is just getting in the way. Don't worry. I'll dispose of her before we elope.'

Cat turns her head away, letting her hair fall in front of her face.

'If you give yourself up now, Christophe, I am sure they will look upon you lightly. You don't want to be responsible for two murders, do you?' I ask, my heart hammering, my mouth is dry.

'They think Vadim was suicide.' Christophe laughs again. It is a brittle, unpleasant sound.

'Vadim!' Cat looks up at us with large eyes. 'Vadim? Where is he?'

'Oh, little Kit Kat. Vadim is dead! Gone for ever. Now our destiny is clear. You see, Vadim didn't want to be with you. He took the cowardly way out.'

'No!' Cat staggers to her feet. 'No!' she screams. 'Did you kill Vadim?' She grabs her violin bow, and before either I or Christophe can move, she shoves the end of the bow into Christophe's eye. She pulls it back and tries to jab it again but, screaming, Christophe punches hers in the solar plexus and she crashes to the concrete ground. Her skull hits the floor with a thud and she lies there, motionless.

'Cat!' Christophe yells. Blood is dripping from his eye, but his screams are for Cat. He reaches down and shakes her. 'Cat! Wake up!' He slaps her cheek. 'Wake up!' He is crying now, wailing. I wonder if he can even see.

I hesitate. His fingers are still gripped tightly around the handle of the knife. Is he going to kill Cat or is he going to come for me? I don't have time to think. There is nothing in this room to hit him with except the violin. I grab it from the mattress and, with the strings facing him, smash it into his face. The wood splinters and cracks. A wire string snaps and pings across his nose, catching his other eye. Christophe drops the knife, which slides across the floor. His screams are even louder this time. Blood pours from his nose.

'I can't see! You bitch! You've blinded me!' He waves his arms around and scrambles across the floor, but I'm quicker. I grab the knife and run up the stairs, two at a time, and I keep on running out of the back door and hurtle straight into two uniformed policemen.

'Downstairs, in the basement!' I screech.

'Look after Pippa!' Joe shouts.

I hadn't even noticed Joe and Mia behind the uniformed officers.

Mia puts her arms around me. 'You're safe now, Dr Durrant.'

'He's down there. Christophe and Cat. I don't know if she's alive,' I gasp.

52

Venetia is sitting at Cat's beside in a secluded hospital room.

'Can we interview her now?' Joe asks the nurse.

'Yes, but don't tire her out. She's got a concussion and is dehydrated. She's on high dose antibiotics for the injuries. And, I'm sorry to say, she's lost the baby.'

Joe grimaces. 'Poor girl.'

I shudder. As if Cat hasn't been through enough. What a tragedy.

When we enter the room, Cat turns her head towards me. She is connected to a drip, her eyes are deep-set, her features skeletal. Nevertheless, she turns her head to look at me and smiles.

'My saviour,' she whispers.

I pull up a plastic chair to her bedside.

'Venetia, would you mind...' Joe says.

'Yes, of course. I'll wait downstairs in the coffee shop.' She leans over Cat and gives her a kiss on the forehead.

'Tell us everything that happened, Cat,' Joe says.

Her voice is quiet and weak. 'I was waiting for the bus after my yoga class. The bus stop is on a country lane in the middle of nowhere. I was meant to be going back to the Academy to get changed, then meet the others at Horsham Station to go to London for the concert. All I remember is being at the bus stop and then not being there anymore. I woke up in that room. There was nothing in it except a mattress, a bucket, some bottles of water and a packet of biscuits.'

'When did you realise who had captured you?' Joe asks.

'I couldn't keep track of time, but I think it was a couple of days later. Christophe wore a balaclava whenever he delivered my food, and he didn't speak to me—just shoved typed messages under the door on pieces of paper. I worked out that it was him. The way he walks, his build...and he's always had a thing for me.' She turns her face away from us, as if embarrassed.

'And then it was dark outside. He'd taken my phone and my watch, so I didn't know what the time was. He opened the door and in he came with a bunch of flowers and a bottle of champagne with two plastic glasses and a little box all on a tray. He'd dressed up in smart clothes. It was so weird. I asked him what he was doing. I begged him to let me go, but he told me he had it all worked out, that we'd get lots of money and move to a beautiful house. He and I would make music together and upload it onto the internet and become icons and make a fortune. It was so warped. I started crying. I tried to get away, but he grabbed me and twisted my arms behind my back. Then he became all conciliatory and said that if I did what he told me to do, then we would both be happy and I would be free.

'He bent down on one knee and handed me the little box. "Open it," he instructed. It was a beautiful diamond ring. "It was my mother's," he said. "And now I want it to be yours. You will become my wife and we'll be happy ever after. We are soul mates. I knew that from the moment I set eyes on you." He grabbed my hand and tried to put the ring on my right ring finger, but I pulled my hand away and the ring flew across the room and skidded on the floor. He went apoplectic. He called me a bitch and told me I'd get what I deserved. I was terrified. I thought he was going to hit me, but instead he left the room for a few minutes, taking the tray with him. I think he smashed the bottle. And he always bolted the door behind him. Then he came back with a knife and he...'

Tears pour from Cat's eyes.

'I'm sorry, I can't,' she sobs.

After a few moments, Cat wipes her eyes with the back of her hand.

'I told him I was pregnant with Vadim's baby,' she whispers. 'I have never seen anyone so angry, so deranged. He disappeared, then. It must have been for at least two days. I was starving. When he returned, he was much calmer; happy even. But it never crossed my mind he had killed Vadim.' She gulps and lets out another sob. 'He brought me a violin and bow. It was a cheap instrument, nothing like the Guarneri, but at least it was something I could play on. And then he got angry because I played the same tune over and over again.'

'The piece you wrote for your unborn child; the piece of music we found in Vadim's room?' I ask.

Cat nods. 'I told Christophe I was pregnant and that I needed more food and better looking after. He was so angry. He called me a tart, a whore and all sorts of horrid names. He bound me to a chair and then pushed a rag to my face. I must have gone unconscious again because when I woke up, my foot was burning with pain. He had cut my toe off. And did they tell you that I lost the baby?' Her sobs rack her body. I reach for her hand and stroke her forehead.

'You have had the most terrible time, but it's all over now,' I say gently. 'I'm going to get Venetia. You should sleep.'

'That's enough for today,' I tell Joe.

He nods.

.   .   .

WE ARE SITTING in Joe's car in the hospital carpark. Exhaustion settles on me like a leaden blanket.

'We're charging Viscount Sneddon with fraud.'

'And Karl Edstol?' I ask.

'Nope. He admitted giving Bill Jones a black eye when Bill demanded they accept Alice back into the school on the threat that they would go to the media about Karl's involvement in the death of Sarah Bellingham. But, as we know, this was an empty threat as Karl wasn't responsible. Under the circumstances, Bill Jones has agreed to drop charges. Other than being a bully and a generally unpleasant man, Karl Edstol hasn't broken the law. I suspect that the school won't survive this level of scandal, and of course it no longer has the funding from the Sneddons.'

'Poor Venetia,' I murmur. 'And what about Martha Jones?'

'Bill Jones says he will bring charges against his wife Martha for assault if she doesn't agree to divorce and giving him full custody of Alice. Martha gave him his second black eye and apparently has been violent throughout their marriage. Completely unhinged. Hopefully Alice will be fine. She has a loving father and grandparents.'

'And Christophe?'

'He was released from hospital and is in custody on suspicion of murder, kidnap and grievous bodily harm. He has lost sight in one eye. It is a cut-and-dried case and I expect him to get life.'

'But what about the cigar ash found under Cat's fingers? How did that get there?'

'Christophe has admitted to trying to set up Jonno. Apparently he holds a major grudge against him because Viscount Sneddon refused to loan Christophe a Stradivarius cello. As we know, Jonno sold off all his good instruments—assuming he even owned such a cello—but of course Christophe didn't know that. Christophe just saw it as a slight towards him. Jonno loans Cat the Guarneri but gives nothing to Christophe.'

'And as a consequence, Christophe tries to implicate Jonno in Cat's abduction?'

'Yes. Apparently, he collected some ash from Jonno's cigar after the concert at The Cadogan Hall.'

'So premeditated,' I sigh.

'He rented a car, knocked Cat out with some substance, took her back to his father's house and locked her in that room, and then still managed to make it to the station on time to perform in London. Quite extraordinary. He even decorated the basement room with posters of all the places he wanted the two of them to perform in. It really is very sad. He claims Vadim's death was not premeditated, that it was an accident, but I doubt any jury will buy that.'

We sit in silence for a while, but I know that if I don't say it now, I never will. I take a deep breath and turn towards him.

'Joe, I can't do this anymore.'

'I thought you might say that. You've put yourself at too much risk.'

'No, not that. I can't do this keeping you at arm's length anymore. I miss you too much. I nearly died at Christophe's house, and it's made me realise that I have to grab happiness now. I love you, Joe Swain.'

I hold my breath, but I don't need to hold it for long. Joe reaches across the car and takes my face between his hands. 'And I love you too, Pippa Durrant.'

He kisses me then and I melt into him, my heart soaring.

'You know, you saved those young people's lives,' he says, holding onto my hands. 'You are quite extraordinary.'

'But you don't listen to me, Joe. You asked for my professional opinion and then you ignored it.'

'I know. Next time—'

'I'm not sure there will be a next time.'

'You are truly invaluable to me,' Joe says, his voice almost a whisper.

'In a professional or personal capacity?'

'Both.' He runs the fingers of his right hand gently across my cheek. 'There's no need to decide straight away if you want to carry on working with the police. There's something more important we need to do first.'

I look at those dark eyes, my head tilted to one side, unsure what he means.

'I would like to go with you to Cape Town. I am overdue a lot of annual leave. Let's find out what happened to Flo.'

'Thank you,' I whisper, blinking the tears from my eyes.

FROM MIRANDA

Dear Reader,

Thank you very much for reading *Fatal Finale*. This book is dedicated to our musician daughter, Ceskie. For her fifth birthday, she requested a yellow balloon and a violin, and so began our journey into the world of music.

The UK is blessed to have some of the leading music schools in the world, and these schools bear absolutely no resemblance to the imaginary goings-on at The Edstol's Music Academy! They are outstanding educational establishments staffed by passionate and accomplished teachers. Also, pupils do not remain at these schools after the age of eighteen, instead moving on to study at conservatoires or universities.

Although the UK government supports schools that are part of the Music and Dance Scheme, the provision of music education and learning to play an instrument in all in other schools is now woefully poor. I suspect this is echoed around the world. This is a great tragedy. I would like to quote Professor Anne Shih, who is an inspirational world-leading pedagogue and a very dear friend: 'Music education should not be thought of as a career path but as a means of education of humanity; therefore an integral and possibly the most important part of a child's education. It refines and develops one's physical dexterity, means of communication, power and usage of knowledge and intellect, spiritual growth, and innate intuition and perception.'

Special thanks to Becca McCauley, Adriana Galimberti-Rennie and Alistair Scott for answering my non-music related questions. All mistakes are mine alone. And thank you to Emily Tamayo Maher for her support during the last couple of years, and to Brian Lynch and Garret Ryan of Inkubator Books who work their magic on my novels, bringing them to life.

If you could spend a moment writing an honest review, no matter how short, I would be extremely grateful. They really do help other people discover my books.

Leave a Review

With warmest wishes,

Miranda

www.mirandarijks.com

ALSO BY MIRANDA RIJKS

FATAL FORTUNE

(Book 1 in the Dr Pippa Durrant Mystery Series)

FATAL FLOWERS

(Book 2 in the Dr Pippa Durrant Mystery Series)

I WANT YOU GONE

(A Psychological Thriller)

Published by Inkubator Books
www.inkubatorbooks.com

45251885R00174

Printed in Poland
by Amazon Fulfillment
Poland Sp. z o.o., Wrocław